D1464547

Please return / renew by date shown.
You can renew it at:
norlink.norfolk.gov.uk
or by telephone: 0344 800 8006
Please have your library card & PIN ready

2013

(27)

NORFOLK COUNTY LIBRARY
WITHDRAWN FOR SALE

NORFOLK LIBRARY
AND INFORMATION SERVICE

Contents

To Ann and Marie and members of Katapult

One

'Right!' exclaimed Mary. 'This is it! Action stations!' She waved a wallpaper scraper threateningly at the living room wall. 'I'll be glad to see the back of this hideous paper.'

Dave came in carrying two mugs of coffee. 'Time to break for elevenses,' he said, poker-faced.

Mary gave him a withering look. 'It's not even half-nine yet.'

'I know, but...'

Mary took one of the mugs and put it down on the bare floorboards. 'You lazy so-and-so. You can't put it off any longer, you know.'

He sighed miserably and blew on his coffee. 'I know. But all this disruption.'

'It'll be worth it. God knows how you managed to live with this paper all these years.'

'I never used to notice it. Much. And I've never been one for D-I-Y.' He sneaked a look at his watch. 'I've... er... just got to pop out for ten minutes. Soon as I've had this coffee.'

Mary glared at him.

'It's all right: I'm not putting a bet on. Honest. I won't be that long. Then I'll come back and get started on this room.'

'Where are you going then?'

'I've got to photocopy my songs and send them to the musical director in Blackpool.'

Mary dipped a sponge in a bucket of hot, soapy water. Although she had her back to Dave, he could tell by her demeanour that she was far from happy.

'I've got to do these gigs,' he explained. 'The money's not bad and it could lead to more work.'

'And what do we do while you're away? Just as the children are getting used to you.'

'Well, I'm sorry, but it can't be helped. It's what I do for a living. How many more times do I have to explain?'

'But why Blackpool of all places? And for six whole weeks.'

'Because that's where the work happens to be.'

'There's no need to shout.'

'I'm not shouting. It's just that you're so irritating. I've got to do it, and that's that. So I may as well get on with me photocopying. I'll see you in a bit.'

He slammed his mug down and left the room. As he squeezed his way past all the living room furniture stacked in the hall, the letter box rattled and an air mail letter fluttered on to the mat. He picked it up and saw that it was addressed to Mary. Curiosity getting the better of him, he returned to the living room and handed her the letter.

'Who do you know who lives in Florida?' he asked.

Her hands trembled as she took the letter. 'Oh my God! It's from him. My ex-husband. How the hell did he find out where I'm living now?'

He saw very real fear in Mary's eyes.

'Ronnie's a twisted bastard. About as dangerous as you can get. I'm sure he's got a screw loose. A real psycho.'

***

The doorbell chimed and Nicky panicked. 'It's Jason. He's early. And I'm not ready.'

Vanessa laughed unkindly. 'Let him see you as you really are. That'll put him off.'

Nicky looked pleadingly at her sister and asked if she would let him in.

'No chance. I don't even know him.'

'Please, Nessa.'

'Tell you what: you let him in and I'll make the coffee while you get dressed.'

'Yes but...' Nicky began to protest, but seeing the wilful look on her sister's face, she dashed out to answer the door as the doorbell chimed again.

Vanessa smiled to herself, picturing Nicky's discomfort as she greeted her new boyfriend in her dressing gown. Nicky's high-pitched, panicky voice brought the contempt she felt for her sister bubbling to the surface. Nicky was such a baby. So un-cool.

While Vanessa switched on the kettle, Nicky hurriedly showed her new boyfriend into the kitchen. 'This is Jason,' she burbled nervously. 'Jason, this is Vanessa.'

'Hi, pleased to meet you.'

He waved a hand at Vanessa. She acknowledged his greeting with a nod, surprised at how attractive he was, although she had seen them both together in the shopping mall. But close up he looked even dishier. Slim, dark and rather intense looking. He looked like he might be an actor or a model.

'I'll leave you two to get acquainted while I get dressed,' said Nicky. 'My sister'll make you a coffee, Jason. Shan't be long.'

Nicky scurried away, ashamed of the way she looked. Vanessa smiled at Jason, who said, 'Nicky never mentioned she had a sister.'

'Oh?'

'Course, I can understand why now.'

Vanessa raised her eyebrows enquiringly and guessed what was coming.

'It must be because you're so attractive. No wonder she keeps quiet about you.'

Pleased with the compliment, Vanessa tried not to let it show, and got the jar of instant coffee out of the cupboard. She could feel him staring at her, undressing her.

'What do you do for a living?' she asked.

He grinned confidently. 'Central heating engineer. I've got my own business.'

She tried not to show her disappointment either.

'I had a job to finish off this morning. That's why I thought – as I had the rest of the day clear – I'd take Nicky out. But I wish...'

He deliberately left the sentence unfinished, hoping Vanessa would take the bait.

She did.

'What do you wish?'

He moved a little closer to her. 'I wish it was the other way round. I wish it was you I was taking out.'

Vanessa tried to conceal a smile but her eyes said it all.

'I don't think that's a very good idea. Do you?'

'Because of Nicky? We don't have to tell her.'

'Tell her what?'

'About us going out together one night this week.'

Vanessa laughed nervously. 'You've got a nerve.

'I can't help it. I've never been so knocked out by anyone before. So how about it?'

Deeply buried resentment of her older sister being the treasured favourite of their father flashed through Vanessa's mind. She made a snap decision and felt a surge of triumph, coupled with revenge.

'Okay,' she whispered. 'I'm not doing anything on Friday night.'

Two

Tears ran down Mary's face. Her hands shook as she read her ex-husband's letter. 'Oh no!' she pleaded. 'Please, Ronnie! No!'

'What's wrong?' asked Dave, stifled by the inadequacy of his question. But there was no mistaking the genuine concern in his voice and Mary looked up from the letter momentarily, love and gratitude in her expression.

Thoughts of the club bookings in Blackpool and the north west struck him, worried that he might have to make noble sacrifices. A sob caught in Mary's throat and he chased away the selfish thoughts and gently touched her hand. He spoke softly but his voice was uncomfortably resonant in the empty room.

'Are you going to tell me what's up?'

Mary recovered slightly, wiped her eyes, and wet her lips before speaking. 'Listen to this – see what you make of it.'

She read from the letter.

'"My darling Mary, I still think of you as my darling, you see, babe. The fact is I can't get over you. I know it's been a long time and we've both had other partners since we split up but – who knows – we might give it another go. Because this here's the good news. I'm coming home. Things didn't work out with me and Sharleen. Or with her kids. Yankee brats! And blood's thicker than water, as they say.

'"I know I treated you badly, but I never stopped loving you, babe. Until death us do part. And that goes for my kids as well. I'm really looking forward to seeing them again. They'll like it over here. Tell them I'm looking forward to taking them to Disneyland. I've got a great job now, hon, selling hush-hush equipment for an electronics company. So I'm going to be doing a lot of commuting across the pond. My first trip is in October sometime, so here's lookin' at you, kid. Love you, babe. Till death. Ronnie."'

Mary stared at Dave, begging for reassurance, protection. He shrugged helplessly.

'I'm not sure. I... I mean, why are you so upset?'

'Because I thought I'd seen the last of him. That's why.'

'But surely he's got a right to see his children.'

Mary shivered involuntarily. 'The man's dangerous. He lives in a fantasy world.'

'Lots of people do.'

'Not like Ronnie. Believe me, he's dangerous.' She thrust the letter into Dave's hand. 'Take a look at the last line.'

Dave squinted, holding the letter away from him. 'He's underlined "death" with a red pen.' He frowned at Mary. 'Why?'

'Because he's a sick bastard, that's why.'

'Dave put his arm round her, protectively. 'It's baking hot but you're shivering. You're frightened of him, aren't you? I mean, I know he put you in hospital that time, but... has he ever done anything to scare you before?'

'Loads of times. He saw me staring at this good looking black guy in a pub one night. He didn't say anything. Just went quiet and moody. When we got home, he stripped me off, making me think we were going to make love. Instead, he smacked me hard with his open palm, slowly, over and over in the same place, so it hurt but it wouldn't show.'

'I know this is probably a stupid question but – why didn't you fight back?'

'I was too scared. Psychological fear was Ronnie's greatest trick. He'd do unpredictable things. He used to love watching violent videos. Anything American he adored. He bought replica guns.'

'Was this before the kids were born?'

'Before, during and after. He used to spoil them rotten. Then, if one of them misbehaved, he'd go to great lengths to inflict the cruellest punishment.'

Mary's eyes filled with tears as she remembered.

'Simon's favourite toy was his Thomas the Tank Engine. Ronnie took a hammer one day and smashed it to bits in front of him. He was only four at the time.'

Dave exhaled slowly. He felt tense. His shoulders ached. Eventually, he muttered, 'How could anyone do that to a young kid?'

'You don't know Ronnie. After we split up, the court ordered him to keep away from us. Thank God! When he went to America I thought that would be the last we'd hear from him.'

'I wonder how he got our address?'

Mary shook her head. 'God only knows. Unless he somehow managed to trick my mother into giving it to him.'

'I've got an idea. I can get loads of work up north – especially the north east. Why don't we all move up there?'

Mary sighed deeply. 'If he managed to get this address while he's living in the States, he wouldn't find it too difficult to trace us when he gets over here. No. Running away's not the answer.'

'What do we do then?'

'I wish I knew, Dave.' She let her head fall onto his shoulder, buried her face into his neck and sobbed. 'I wish I knew.'

***

'Cheers!' said Jason, sipping Mexican beer from the bottle.

Vanessa, who was having second thoughts about this date, raised her Bacardi and Coke glass and half-heartedly toasted him in silence.

'What's wrong, sweetheart?'

'I can't help thinking about Nicky. I feel guilty.'

Jason rewarded her with a cheeky smile, trying to charm her with his roguishness. 'No, you're not. Be honest. I think we're having fun. That's what life's all about. Having a laugh.'

Vanessa frowned, and echoing her thoughts, said, 'I'm not going out with you just to get at Nicky, you know.'

'Did I say you were?'

'Usually we get on quite well together.'

Jason shrugged. 'I wouldn't lose any sleep over it, if I were you.'

Vanessa stared thoughtfully into her glass, swirling the ice round with her little finger. 'I wouldn't like her to get hurt.'

'What the mind doesn't know,' grinned Jason.

Vanessa looked up sharply. 'You're very sure of yourself, aren't you?'

'Me? No. You've got me wrong. I'm really insecure.'

'Hah-hah! Pull the other one.'

'It's just that I really fancied you. Soon as you walked in that door.'

'Hang on!' Vanessa giggled. 'You were the one who walked through the door. You came to our house, remember?'

'Oh yeah. It must be the romantic in me. In my mind's eye I see you making an entrance, with a shaft of sunlight hitting you.'

Vanessa laughed and shook her head, then noticed he was staring at her intensely.

'What's wrong?'

'You're not going to like what's rushing through my head right now.'

'That depends what it is.'

'After we've had some food, why don't we go back to my flat?'

Vanessa's eyes widened. You don't believe in taking things slowly, do you?'

'That's not my style. And I know we could make beautiful music together.' Seeing Vanessa wince, he added, 'I wish I hadn't said that.'

'So do I. It was pretty crass.'

He laughed. 'That's me. A crass remark to end all crass remarks.'

Vanessa was suddenly distracted, and stared over his shoulder with a look of panic. 'Oh my God! Don't look round. It's a friend of Nicky's.'

But Jason had already turned round and been spotted by the girl standing at the bar with two other girls.

'Whoops!' he exclaimed as he turned back to face Vanessa. 'She knows me as well. She introduced me to Nicky at the party. Come on, let's finish our drinks and get out of here.'

Once they were out in the street, they fell against each other and Jason slid an arm about her waist. Both giggled at this heady feeling of treachery and forbidden fruit.

Jason stopped walking and brought his lips close to Vanessa's ear. 'When we've eaten,' he whispered, 'will you come back to my place? Please... will you?'

She kissed his cheek lightly. 'OK,' she whispered, almost imperceptibly.

Three

Nigel began to think he had made a grave error in bringing Jackie to the same Eastbourne teashop where he had brought Mary. It was almost six months ago, yet the same plump waitress who had served him then seemed to remember him, behaving in an over-familiar way.

'Buck rarebit, pot of tea for two and a selection of pastries, is it?' She smiled, pleased with her memory skills.

Colouring slightly, Nigel studied the menu deeply, then snapped it shut and declared loudly: 'An excellent recommendation.' He glanced at Jackie. 'Does that sound all right to you, darling? Or would you like something a bit more substantial?'

Jackie frowned abstractedly. 'No, that sounds fine.'

The waitress gave a self-satisfied, knowing nod, as if the order had been a foregone conclusion, before shuffling off to the kitchen. Jackie stared at Nigel, and he guessed what she was about to say.

'Have you been here before, Nigel?'

'I'm sorry. I should have mentioned it. I came here on several occasions with my ex-wife.'

'How long ago was that?'

Nigel made a show of trying to remember. 'Now let me see...'

'It must be quite some time ago.'

He tittered nervously. 'Yes, it must be many moons ago. I have to take my hat off to that waitress, she must have a wonderful memory.'

A note of suspicion crept in Jackie's voice. 'Have you been here more recently?'

'Well, if I'm out this way on business. I often pop in for a cream bun or something. You know me: I have an awfully sweet tooth.'

'Not only sweet. I've never known anyone pick at crisps and peanuts like you do,' she admonished him with a wag of her finger. 'Little pickers, bigger knickers!'

Relieved that the conversation had sailed into safer waters, Nigel grinned like a naughty but lovable child. He patted his stomach. 'I must start an exercise regime soon.'

'Yes,' Jackie leaned across the table and whispered, 'otherwise I'll be marrying a Mister Tubby Bear.'

'Not long to go now. Just another couple of weeks. Shame we couldn't have done it in early September as we first planned. And I thought it was going to be a quiet wedding. Now the guest list seems to be growing. Mainly with your side of the family.'

Jackie sighed. 'We've been through all this Nigel. It's only a dozen extra guests.'

'Only!' Nigel exclaimed forcefully.

Jackie looked round at the other tables. 'Ssh! Keep your voice down. And there's something I need to discuss with you... about the honeymoon.'

Nigel stared at her, almost resentfully, suspecting that he wasn't going to like what she had to say.

'We're not exactly... um... youngsters,' she continued falteringly. 'And as we still haven't made up our mind where to go on our honeymoon – as you claimed we might get a better deal on that last minute thingee – I thought we might have the honeymoon in November, when we might appreciate going somewhere sunny when it's gloomy and foggy over here.'

Nigel pouted like a sulky child. 'But a honeymoon's supposed to follow a wedding.'

Jackie laughed, and waved a dismissive hand, which irritated him.

'Yes but we've been there and done that – both of us – the first time. So why don't we treat this as a holiday?'

11

'I don't understand what the problem is of going away immediately after the wedding.'

Jackie shook her head emphatically. 'Because I can't go. I won't be available. I'll be rehearsing, and then in mid-November I'll be performing.'

Nigel stared at her, open-mouthed.

'I've joined the Royal Town Players, an amateur dramatic society.'

'So when did this all come about?'

'I told you: I auditioned for them the other night. I knew you weren't listening.'

Nigel fiddled with the salt cellar and scowled at it. 'Yes I was. Only I didn't think...'

'You didn't think I'd get the part?'

'Well, no... I mean... I hadn't really thought about it.'

'I'd have thought you'd have been pleased for me.'

Nigel looked up, giving her a feeble smile. 'Oh, I am. It's just that I'm disappointed about the honeymoon, that's all.'

'It's not as if it's cancelled. Just postponed.'

'And what about this play you're in?'

'What about it?'

'What sort of thing will you be doing?'

'Well, it's a romantic comedy. And I'm one of the leads.'

Nigel tugged thoughtfully at his lower lip. His voice was frosty when he spoke. 'I see. A romantic comedy. And does this involve kissing other men on stage?'

Jackie laughed. 'You're not jealous, are you?'

'Of course not. It's just that I'd like to know what I'm supposed to do with my evenings while you're out practising this play.'

'We don't call it practising,' said Jackie. 'It's called rehearsing.'

'Does it matter what it's called?' snapped Nigel. 'Does it matter?'

***

'Your guvnor in?' Tony Rice asked Mandy, Craig's shop assistant, who stopped shaking the scoop containing a freshly-cooked batch of jumbo sausages in batter and stared blankly at him, trying to decide whether he was friend or foe. He looked like a bailiff, like the one who came round that time her mum and dad were way behind on their council tax.

'I'll go and see,' she answered non-committally before disappearing into the back of the shop. Rice heard some whispered exchanges, then Craig appeared in the open doorway behind the counter, wiping his hands on a J-Cloth. He tried to look pleased to see Rice, but there was no disguising the insincerity of his over-hearty greeting.'

'Hello, mate! How's it going?'

A skeleton of a smile played on Rice's lips. 'Mustn't grumble. You got a minute?'

'Yeah – what can I do for you?'

'No, I mean...' Rice inclined his head in Mandy's direction as she squeezed past Craig and returned to the fish fryer. 'I'd like a word in private. There's a boozer round the corner we could...'

Craig shook his head. 'Sorry. Lunchtime on a Friday can get pretty busy.'

Rice stared at Craig without speaking. Mandy watched with interest this tacit exchange of wills between her employer and this stranger with his quietly threatening demeanour. After what seemed like an uncomfortably long silence, Craig backed down with a false laugh.

'As it happens, I could fancy a swift beer. I'll get my jacket. Can you manage for twenty minutes, Mandy?'

'Yeah. Go ahead,' said Mandy, while he collected his jacket from the back of the shop. She looked at Rice, who grinned and undressed her with his eyes. She shivered slightly and looked away.

Four

Tony Rice made random selections on the pub jukebox. The choice of music was irrelevant, since he was buying a convenient noise to cover their conversation in the near-empty pub.

'Cheers!' said Craig, raising his pint.

Rice nodded and came and sat opposite him. As soon as an unrecognisable track blasted from the jukebox, Rice got straight to the point.

'The working men's club you sussed out – I think it's a goer.'

A sudden twinge, a cold warning, shot through Craig's body. He took a large swig of beer before speaking.

'I'm not...' he began, faltering as he looked into Rice's dead eyes. 'I've decided I wanna go straight.'

'What's brought this on? Conscience bothering you?'

'I'm settled at the chippie now.'

Rice sneered. 'Yeah, an' I can smell the fish. How much an hour does he pay you?'

'My brother-in-law's dead. I'm the owner now.'

For some reason Craig regretted having to give Rice this information, but the ex-convict merely shrugged.

'Oh, so it ain't conscience but a change of circumstances. Fair enough. But you was the one who told me how easy it is to do the club. It was your idea.'

Craig started to speak, but Rice carried on talking, while glancing furtively around the pub.

'I've got someone else interested, as it happens. Someone who ain't got any form.'

Craig fidgeted with his glass. 'I don't understand. Why d'you need to tell me about the job if...'

Rice interrupted him. 'You've got form, my son. Soon as you do the club, filth's gonna come knocking on your door. I'm giving you a chance to get yourself a watertight alibi. I'm doing you a favour.'

Some favour, thought Craig.

'And another thing,' continued Rice. 'You was the one nominated me for membership at the club. They might just put us two and two together. So I'd like to think you ain't going to help with their enquiries. Understood?'

***

As he lifted the drinks off the bar of the Compasses pub, Alan Watson ached with tiredness. He was shattered, having done a very long shift at Pembury hospital, and would have given anything for a quiet night indoors. But a promise is a promise, and he had already agreed to a few drinks and a meal to celebrate his partner's new job, starting the following week.

Pran Kapoor watched him as he carried the drinks over, and saw him wince slightly as he put the drinks on the table.

'Cheers!' said Pran, raising his white wine. 'Does your arm still hurt?'

'Only when I laugh,' Alan replied, and slumped heavily onto his seat.

'A criminal record's not so funny, Alan.'

Alan shrugged. 'Obstructing a police officer?'

'Or worse: assaulting a police officer.'

'That'll never stick.'

'Don't be too sure.'

Alan sipped his lager and slammed the glass onto the table. 'I couldn't give a monkeys either way. I don't see why an innocent bloke, minding his own business, can't walk down the street without being picked on.'

Pran sighed impatiently. This was a recent argument regurgitated.

'They asked if they could search you. They didn't just suddenly jump on you.'

'That's not the point. The reason they searched me – for the second time in three weeks, is because I'm black.'

'I still maintain you should have complied, then put in a complaint afterwards.'

'Oh come on. Are you naïve or what?'

'I happen to think it's the other way round. Own up: you were just trying to make a statement about how butch you really are.'

Pran grinned at his partner, deliberately trying to wind him up.

'OK, let's drop the subject, shall we?' said Alan. 'We're not here to argue. This is supposed to be your celebratory drink and dinner. One of your last days as a free man. Here's wishing you luck for Monday.'

As they clinked glasses, Pran said, 'Yes, back to the grindstone, and all that commuting to London. I'd got used to loafing around over the last three weeks.'

'You said you were bored shitless.'

'I was. But I'd got used to it.'

'Pran, listen: when you start work tomorrow...'

Pran gave his partner a lopsided smile. 'I love it when you put on the oh-so-serious look.'

'Don't try and change the subject. And you know what I'm going to say, don't you? I want it to be different this time. I want you to be honest about who you are. And about us.'

Avoiding Alan's gaze, Pran stared into his drink.

'I mean it, Pran.'

'Yeah, yeah, yeah,' chanted Pran, parodying boredom.

Alan leant forward, glaring at his partner. 'Stop evading the issue. You can't live in a closet all your life.'

'Well, it's easy for you. Your parents... they've sort of accepted it, however reluctantly. Whereas I'm still getting the...' Pran adopted an exaggerated Asian accent. 'When-are-you going-to-find-a-nice-girl-and-settle-down routine.' He continued in his normal English voice. 'Given half the chance my father would arrange it for me, like he did for my sister. "A nice boy from a nice family," he said.'

'What's he like?'

'Don't ask! My sister suffers him in silence, like the good little Asian girl she is. It really winds me up. I can't stand him.'

'It won't go away, Pran. The problem's going to remain as long as your father's alive.'

'I know, I know. But a gay man from a Muslim family. I hate to think what he'd do if he found out. I know he'd have nothing more to do with me. And that hurts.'

Alan sighed and shook his head. 'I know. It's difficult. I can see that. But look, we're not talking about your parents finding out. We're talking about being open at work. My colleagues at the hospital accepted it. No problem. To begin with they didn't know how to handle it. Maybe they were embarrassed. But now...'

'Yeah. I know you're right,' Pran emphasised. 'But what do I do on my first day in the office? Make an announcement. Hey, everybody! I'm gay. Or do I send them all emails? Maybe I could pin it on the staff canteen notice board.'

'Seriously, Pran, you know damn well what to do. Someone's asks you about your home life – they're bound to – and you just tell them straight. You say you live with your partner Alan. You only have to tell one person and pretty soon everyone'll know.'

Pran shook his head disbelievingly. 'As simple as that, huh.'

'Yes, it is that simple,' Alan insisted. 'It's about being open and honest.'

Pran frowned thoughtfully before speaking. 'OK. I'll do it. I promise. But just remind me: if someone asks me about my home life, I say...?'

'That you live with your partner Alan.'

Pran took a pen out of the breast pocket of his shirt and offered it to Alan.

'Could you write that down for me, so that I don't forget?'

Alan looked confused, until he noticed the glint in his partner's eye. 'Come on,' he said. 'Let's go and eat.'

Five

Flexing the fingers of his right hand, Mike winced. 'It still hurts.'
Without looking up from her untidy mess of work strewn across the kitchen table, Claire said, 'The plaster's only been off a day. What did you expect?'

'Sympathy?'

Claire shook her head for his benefit. 'Men are such wimps when it comes to pain.'

'Don't start giving me that pain of childbirth lecture.'

'Well, it's true. Now shut up and let me finish my work.'

Mike tested his fingers, miming scissor movements. 'Another week and I should be able to start cutting again. My appointment book's actually looking quite healthy. I don't think I've lost too many customers. Maybe one or two.'

Claire ignored him, concentrating on proof reading an advertisement for country pub food. She sighed as she found another spelling mistake. Mike mistakenly took this as disapprobation over his coming out of the broken finger incident relatively unscathed as far as business was concerned.

'I know you think I deserve to lose more customers than I have done,' he grumbled, struggling to fit the plug into the electric kettle. 'I don't know what you want from me. I really don't.'

Claire's voice became brittle with suppressed anger. 'I want you to keep quiet while I finish off this work.'

'You're always bringing work home. We hardly ever get a chance to talk to each other these days.'

'And I suppose when you were busy cutting hair, and stopping off for a pint or six on the way home, I suppose we used to talk a lot then.'

'Well, I...'

Claire smiled, and gave Mike a look indicating that she had scored a point. But Mike was bored, and was determined to have the final word.

'Look, I know my drinking got a bit out of hand, but I can't put the clock back, can I? What's done is done. I'm doing my best to make it up to you.'

'Oh, really? By moping around the house, playing the helpless invalid, expecting me to mop your troubled brow?'

'That's not fair.'

'No, but it happens to be true. I came back from the office yesterday and you hadn't even put the breakfast things in the dishwasher.'

Mike took two mugs out of the cupboard and slammed the door hard. 'I already told you – I knew you weren't listening – I was making enquiries about Andrew's future.'

'And that took you all day, did it?'

'Yes, it did, as it happens.'

Claire suddenly felt like screaming. Clenching her teeth, she managed to control herself and said, 'Mike, why don't you pop out for a quick beer? I know you want one.'

Mike started to protest, so she added in a softer tone, 'You've done very well so far. You deserve a drink. And you don't have to go mad.'

Mike frowned , and looked down at his shoes, deliberating. 'I suppose I could just have a couple of pints.'

Claire smiled knowingly. 'Yes. And I can get on with my work.'

'OK. Shan't be long.'

As soon as he was out of the house, Claire sighed, and talked to the framed photograph of her deceased parents hanging on the wall by door.

'I know I'm asking for trouble, but I almost prefer the old Mike.'

***

Vanessa lay with her back towards Jason. He snuggled up close to her and stroked her hair.

'You awake?' he whispered, one eye on the bedside clock.

'Mm,' she purred contentedly. 'No rush is there?'

'Much as I'd like to spend Saturday in bed with you, I'm afraid I've got some work to do.'

'How long will you be?'

'What d'you mean?'

'Couldn't I stay here and wait for you?'

Jason sighed impatiently. 'I've no idea how long I'll be. Could be a couple of hours; or it could take all day.'

Vanessa gave him a voluptuous smile. 'I don't mind waiting. I could cook us a meal.'

He kissed her briefly on the cheek, rolled out of bed and grabbed his towelling bathrobe. 'Sorry, Vanessa, but you're going to have to run along. I've got a living to earn. I'll call you later.'

Wounded by the abruptness of his manner, this sudden change in her lover, Vanessa sat up in bed with the duvet wrapped around her protectively. She watched him, his back towards her, fiddling with a small black gadget on top of a chest of drawers.

'I hope this cordless razor's still got some life in the batteries,' he muttered by way of explanation. 'No time for a wet shave today.'

'Do you always work Saturdays?'

Jason turned around and grinned cockily. 'Not always. So I'll call you tomorrow. OK? By the way: what's your surname?'

'You ought to know. You're going out with my sister.'

Jason glanced impatiently at the clock. 'She never told me. So what is it?'

'Ingbarton.'

'Well, Vanessa Ingbarton, on this gloomy Saturday in September 2011, did you enjoy our lovemaking.'

'You know I did,' Vanessa replied, but slightly mystified by his strange way of asking.

Jason gave her a smug, self-satisfied smile. 'Yeah, me too.'

He turned his back on her, and she heard a click. Then she saw him slip the black gadget into his bathrobe pocket as he walked towards the door.

'What's that?' she asked.

He paused in the doorway. 'What?'

'In your pocket.'

He patted the side of his bathrobe. 'My cordless razor.'

Vanessa started to speak, but he interrupted her. 'I'm going to shower. I should have been out of here ten minutes ago. So if you don't mind...'

As soon as he had left the room, Vanessa climbed slowly out of bed, rescuing her crumpled clothing from a nearby chair. She frowned deeply. Something about Jason bothered her. The cordless razor had looked suspiciously like one of those miniature tape recorders. A dictating machine. But why would Jason want to record her saying she had enjoyed their lovemaking? Unless it was to feed his giant ego.

***

Brash music, discordant sound effects, blasted from the living room television set. Maggie went to the kitchen door and yelled:

'Daryl! Hannah! Turn it down. I can't hear myself think.'

Sitting at the breakfast bar, drinking from a can of Fosters, Craig laughed. 'Cartoons are bloody terrible when you're not watching them.'

'I said turn it down!' Maggie repeated. As soon as the volume dropped, she went and sat opposite her brother. 'They turn it up deliberately. Attention seeking. I'll be glad when it's Monday. It's been a hell of a week. What were you saying about the chippie, before we were so rudely interrupted?'

Craig coughed lightly before speaking. 'I was saying: if I sold the chippie, put the money into the wine bar, and became a sort of sleeping partner, I could also run the Maidstone chippie. Then, if you needed any extra finance for the wine bar...'

Maggie smiled warmly at her brother. 'I'm sorry, sweetheart.'

'What about?'

'You don't have to be a "sleeping partner". We've always got on well, I was just being stupid and snobby about the tattoos. And let's face it, most celebrities have them these days.' She offered Craig her hand. 'So here's to our partnership.'

Grinning, Craig shook her hand. 'Yeah, here's to the trendiest bar in the south east.'

'I've got an appointment with the solicitor first thing Monday. Come with me and we can sort it all out officially.'

'Tell you what,' said Craig, trying to sound casual, as if he'd just thought of what he was going to say. 'Why don't we have a meal out tonight; to celebrate.'

Maggie shook her head. 'I can't.'

'My treat.'

'I'm seeing someone. A fellah.'

Craig began to panic. He didn't have an alibi for tonight, and Tony Rice was planning to burgle the working men's club.

Noticing his downcast expression, Maggie asked him what was wrong.

'I just feel at a loose end, that's all.'

'Well, I could always do with a child minder for tonight. Save me having to drive the babysitter home afterwards.'

Craig looked relieved. 'Can I stay the night? Then you can stay out as long as you like. And if your date runs you home, you won't have to worry about how much you drink.'

'That sounds good to me.'

'Thanks, Maggs. Thanks.'

'What are you thanking me for? You're the one who's doing me a favour.'

Craig smiled twitchily. 'Oh, yeah.'

Maggie noticed his nervousness, but she put it down to the new partnership commitment and thought no more about it.

Six

Tony Rice finished his pint and checked his watch. Eight forty-five. Eyes down for bingo. And a bumper jackpot this week, so nearly everyone in the club would be playing. Upstairs, in the Gents toilet opposite the snooker room, his accomplice, 'Geordie' Pete, waited in the locked cubicle, having left the crowded bar five minutes earlier.

As soon as the bingo was under way, Rice left the bar and went upstairs. He glanced into the snooker room, making certain it was empty, then slipped quickly into the Gents, and tapped on the cubicle door.

'Out you come, Pete,' Rice said quietly. 'It's time to work.'

The bolt slid open and 'Geordie' Pete joined Rice under the loft hatch. Wasting no time, he climbed onto the ex-convict's shoulders and pushed open the hatch. The temperature had plummeted over the last few days and a cold blast of air hit him from inside the roof. He wished he'd worn a sweater on top of his polo shirt. But Coleman was young and fit, strong and wiry, having spent most of the ten years since he'd left school hod-carrying and digging, so what was a little cold air but a slight inconvenience. But now his strength, of which he was inordinately proud, was put to the test as he struggled to pull Rice up after him. And any minute someone might walk into the toilet.

Rice, with Coleman's co-ordinated strength, managed to leap and catch the edge of the opening. Coleman caught him under the arms, heaved and pulled, and Rice wriggled into the darkness of the loft as his breathless young accomplice slid back the hatch, plunging them into darkness, just seconds before someone walked into the toilet.

***

Bamber nearly shot through the ceiling when Donald tapped him on the shoulder. He glared at his partner before turning the volume down on the CD player.

'You nearly gave me a heart attack,' he complained. 'Creeping up on me like that.'

Donald gave his friend a lop-sided grin. 'Can I help it if you play this rubbish at mega decibels? It's a wonder you're not permanently deaf.'

'Pardon?'

Donald chuckled dutifully, then spotted empty crisp packets on the coffee table. 'What is the point of trying to keep this place tidy? Look at it! It's like a pig sty.'

'Oh come on. It's not that bad.'

'We can all tell where you've been sitting. Look at all the crumbs on the carpet. You might have hoovered before I came home.'

'I'm not your wife, you know.'

Bamber slumped into an easy chair and stared back at Donald with childlike defiance.

'Just a couch potato I feed and clothe.'

'I do my fair share.'

Donald raised his eyebrows mockingly.

'You forget. I'm convalescing.'

'You've been convalescing for as long as I've known you.'

'Had a hard day at the shop, have you?'

'Chance would be a fine thing.' Donald glanced at his watch. 'The sun is not yet over the yard-arm, but I could murder a gin and tonic.'

'You drink too much.'

'Hark at the pot calling the kettle beige.'

'In that case,' said Bamber, 'you can pour me one while you're at it.'

'I'll get the glasses and some ice and lemon ' Donald started for the kitchen, then stopped as if remembering something of minor

27

importance, and said, 'Oh, by the way, I forgot to ask you this morning: can you look after the shop for me on Monday?'

Bamber's eyes narrowed suspiciously. 'Why?'

'A Portobello Road dealer's clearing out of the business. I can buy her entire stock for a song.'

'Oh yes. And will this mean a visit to the theatre?'

Donald acted confusion. 'Theatre?'

'Yes, you know: those building where they put on Shakespeare plays.'

Smiling tolerantly, Donald said, 'I am not seeing Ted, if that's what you're thinking. I'm going up during the day. I haven't seen Ted in yonks. His wife's having a baby.'

A triumphant gleam blazed in Bamber's eyes. 'If you haven't seen him, how did you know about the baby?'

'I happened to bump into him in Sainsbury's a few weeks ago.'

'She's a bit old to be having a baby, isn't she?'

Donald laughed. 'I wouldn't mind being a fly on the wall once it's born.' Seeing the look of distaste on Bamber's face, he added, 'On second thoughts, I'll get the ice and lemon.'

As he past his coat hanging in the hallway, Donald took a small envelope from inside the pocket. If Bamber was suspicious, he wouldn't put it past the boy to go through his pockets. He'd have to find somewhere else to hide the theatre tickets this time. And he knew just the place. Under the sink, among the household cleaning items. Bamber could be relied on never to sully his hands by doing any household chores.

***

Rice shivered as he clicked on a pencil torch and peered at his watch.

'What time is it?' whispered Coleman.

'Time to get on with it.'

Coleman swore under his breath. 'I've never been so cold.'

Rice snorted. 'You can help yourself to a large brandy, my son.'

'I hope they ain't locked the door to the bog,' said Coleman. 'I noticed there was a lock on it.'

Rice patted his pocket. 'I'll soon have that open. Right, let's get on with it.'

'Can you hear anything?'

Rice listened. 'No. Let's go.' He shifted the loft hatch while Coleman held the torch. They both dropped stealthily onto the tiled floor of the Gents. Rice tried the door. 'It's not locked,' he whispered. 'Old Alex gets forgetful when he's had a skin-full.'

'Silly old bar steward!' Coleman laughed. 'Right! Let's go.'

Once they reached the downstairs bar, Coleman asked: 'You sure about the alarm?'

Rice gave a throaty chuckle. 'Everyone knows Alex come out the RAF in 1959, the year Buddy Holly died. He goes on about it often enough. The alarm's coded to assist Alex in his alcoholic amnesia.'

'You what?' said Coleman.

'Means he don't know what day it is.'

There was a sudden loud groan from a corner of the bar. Coleman gave a start.

'Jesus! What's that?'

The bar steward, who had been asleep on one of the padded benches, suddenly sat up, screaming, 'Who is it? What's going on?'

Rice grabbed the nearest weapon, a full and unopened bottle of Grouse, which was Alex's favourite tipple, and which he had left out to have a crafty drink should he wake in the night and suffer from alcoholic insomnia. When the litre of whisky came into contact with his skull, the bottle survived the impact. Unfortunately, his skull proved to be less resistant.

Seven

Curiosity rather than sympathy drew Vanessa to her sister's bedroom door when she heard snuffling, sobbing sounds. Vanessa tapped gently on the door before entering. She found Nicky sprawled across the bed, cuddling Polzeath, a well-worn teddy bear, named after a Cornish seaside resort; and memento of a family holiday, from a time when they were still a proper family.

'What's up?' Vanessa asked. Nicky carried on crying. Vanessa sighed and eased herself onto the edge of the bed, stroking her sister's hair. 'Tell me.'

Nicky lifted her head out of Polzeath's damp, threadbare fur. 'Where's Mummy?' she cried pathetically.

'Gone out. Shopping. Then she's going straight to the church hall to rehearse her play. She won't be back until quite late. You can tell me what's wrong, if you like.'

Nicky sniffed and wiped a hand over her smeared face. 'It's Jason.'

A cold feeling of guilt shot through Vanessa. 'What about him?'

'We've become... lovers. Only...'

'Go on.'

Tears filled Nicky's eyes again. Her voice trembled as she struggled to control herself. 'He was the first man in my life. The very first. It should have been special. But afterwards he couldn't wait to get me out of his flat. He was only after one thing. And now he's had it, he doesn't want to know.'

'Has he said he doesn't want to see you again?'

'Well, not in so many words... no. But I've been trying to contact him since yesterday and...'

Alarm bells rung in Vanessa's head. 'Saturday! Is that when you slept with him?'

'Well, I did sleep with him yesterday. But that wasn't the first time.'

Vanessa's voice became strident. 'What time was this?'

'Eleven o'clock. Why? What difference does it make?'

'Nothing. I just wondered.'

Vanessa chewed her bottom lip nervously and thought about Jason. No wonder he'd wanted her out of his flat by nine o'clock. He'd been seeing Nicky afterwards. Was this something he'd planned in advance? Had he known Vanessa would agree to go back to his flat on Friday night? He seemed so cocksure of himself. So arrogant. And what about his strange behaviour?

As if she could read her sister's thoughts, Nicky said, 'He was a bit weird.'

Vanessa frowned. She could almost guess what was coming. 'In what way?'

'Well, as a lover he seemed very – um, how can I put it? – he seemed very skilful. Very thoughtful, about taking precautions. It's just that afterwards, he brought out one of those little tape recorders – you know, one of those dictating machines. And he wanted me to say something about our loving.'

Vanessa's voice was barely a whisper when she spoke. 'What sort of thing did he want you to say?'

'Just that we'd made love on such and such a date. Like he wanted to keep a record of it.'

'Maybe he wanted proof.'

'What for?'

'I wish I knew.'

Nicky stared at her sister, frowning. 'What a peculiar thing to say.'

'How d'you mean?'

'You said you wish you knew like you were personally involved.'

Vanessa gave Nicky's hand a gentle squeeze and avoided her eyes. 'Well, you're my sister. And even though I'm younger than you, for some strange reason, I've always thought of you as "my little sister", as though I'm the older one. I suppose that's because... well, I'm not sure why, really.'

Vanessa stopped herself from saying it was because Nicky was so silly and babyish.

***

Late Monday morning, his mind racing from the sweet excitement of deception, Ted arrived home breathless after hurrying across the common burdened by rolls of wallpaper Marjorie had ordered.

'I'm in the kitchen,' Marjorie called out when she heard him come in. He went into the kitchen and found her sitting at the table, idly flicking through a Mothercare catalogue and sipping cream sherry.

'You shouldn't be drinking in your condition,' he said.

Marjorie gave him a sidelong glance. 'What would you know about it?'

'I do know that...' Ted began, but she interrupted him.

'A bit of what you fancy can't do any harm. Everything in moderation.'

Ted regarded the sherry bottle disapprovingly. 'Hmm!' he mumbled pointedly, which irritated Marjorie. She gave him the news he'd been anticipating.'

'They want you in this afternoon.'

'Who?'

'Who! Who d'you think? While you were out, they called from work.'

Ted acted out disappointment. 'Oh no!' It's a blooming nuisance having to work on my day off.'

'It's never bothered you before.'

'No, but I thought I could make a start on the nursery.'

32

Marjorie snapped the catalogue shut and thumped it down on the table. 'That's good quality wallpaper, that is. I know what your papering's like. I don't want one of your botched jobs. So I'm getting the proper man in.'

Ted glanced at his watch. 'Well, I'm going to need a lot of overtime then, to pay for it. Did they say what time they wanted me in?'

'As soon as you can make it. Staff shortages, they said. There's a lot of stomach bugs and flu going around. Change in the weather, I expect. So you'd better go back to the spare room for a while. I don't want to catch anything in my condition.'

Ted started edging towards the door. 'I'll be off then. I'll chuck my uniform in my bag and change at work.'

'Chap who telephoned,' said Marjorie, 'had a very posh voice.'

Ted looked at her blankly. 'Must be new.'

His heart racing, Ted dashed upstairs and bundled his uniform into his sports bag, called out goodbye to Marjorie and hurried out of the house. Donald's Volvo was parked, with the engine idling, just round the corner on Mount Ephraim. Ted threw his bag onto the back seat and settled into the passenger seat.

'Well,' smiled Donald, 'presumably she fell for it.'

'Hook, line and sinker. Only she thought you sounded posh.'

Donald laughed. 'Right! Twelfth Night here we come. We've loads of time to spare. But parking's going to be the problem.'

'What did you tell Bamber?' asked Ted.

'I told him I needed to buy someone's stock in Portobello Road, which is why we've got to drive to London.'

'Why can't we park at Tonbridge and catch the train?' suggested Ted.

'You don't know Bamber. He's probably noted the mileage on the clock of the Volvo, and will check it tomorrow.'

Donald laughed confidently, thinking he was one step ahead of his partner. But Bamber was at that moment lurking on the common, watching the Volvo as it pulled away from the kerb. All along he'd been suspicious about Donald's trip to London, so he'd closed the antique shop, and walked up towards where Ted lived, and now he'd been proved right.

Eight

Having just had an induction meeting with his manager, Pran returned to the large open-plan office and slid into his seat at the desk near Graham's. They were colleagues, working at the same level, but already Pran sensed some resentment because of this. Maybe it was because Graham was in his late thirties, and it had taken him longer to reach the grade that Pran had fast-tracked to in his last job. But Pran wondered if he was being paranoid. After all, Graham seemed to be making an effort to get to know him and put him at ease.

'And how's our line manager?' Graham asked with forced cheerfulness.

'Well, as I only started today, she just wanted to explain the routine.'

'It's going to be a hectic first week for you. We've quite a few deadlines to meet.'

'I don't mind.'

Graham stopped working at his computer, and swivelled to face Pran. 'Whereabouts d'you live, Pran?'

'Tunbridge Wells. On a good day it's only forty-five minutes on the fast train to Cannon Street.'

'You got your own place?'

Pran nodded. 'A flat.'

'You married?'

This was it. The questions Pran had been dreading. He breathed deeply, preparing himself for the revelation. 'No,' was all he could manage.

'Girlfriend?'

This was his opportunity to say "I live with my partner Alan", as they'd agreed. But he couldn't bring himself to say it.

'Not at the moment,' he said, feeling his mouth getting drier.

'So you live on your own.'

He hesitated, feeling as if he wanted to swivel away from Graham's probing stare. Eventually, in a voice that was almost inaudible, he said, 'I share with a flatmate. It keeps the cost down.'

But to Graham, this was just polite small-talk, and he returned his attention to his computer screen. 'Very sensible. The prices of places these days.'

Pran felt deeply ashamed. He could imagine what Alan would say about his weakness, and he dreaded facing the inevitable questions from his partner concerning his first day at work.

He cleared his throat, braving himself for a small confession. Perhaps he could just drop a hint to Graham, leaving him to read between the lines about his relationship with Alan. Oh to hell with it! Why not tell him?

'Graham,' he began tentatively, 'I think I ought to tell you...'

Jenny, their manager, marched up to their desks. A tall, striking blonde, with high cheekbones and wearing heavy make-up, she could sometimes be intimidating. She often practised being one of the lads, but only when it suited her.

'Why break the habits of a lifetime?' she said, flashing Graham a smile, which she panned effortlessly to include Pran. 'It's time we were propping up the bar.'

Graham grinned at her, then explained to Pran: 'We invariably go to the boozer after work. To forget that it's Monday.'

Jenny stared at Pran. 'It's become a ritual. When we're not working late, that is. D'you fancy joining us, Pran?'

'If it's just for a quickie.'

Graham snorted. 'And you might have time for a drink. Talking of which...' He looked up at Jenny. 'Have you clocked that new barman yet? Ooh, duckie!'

Jenny sniggered. 'I know. He's a real screamer.'

'He!' Graham almost shouted. 'Don't you mean she?'

'You're right. Talk about camp. Oh blast! I forgot my laptop. And I've got a budget outline to work on. I'll see you over the pub.'

She swept out of the office. Grinning, Graham turned to Pran and said, 'You couldn't ask for a better manager. She's all right is Jen. Oh, by the way: what were you going to say?'

Pran frowned. 'When?'

'Just before Jen come into the office.'

Pran stared down at his keyboard. 'Oh, it doesn't matter. I mean... I can't remember now.'

***

After drinking too much on Sunday night, Craig had overslept, and was hurriedly trying to make some coffee and toast before dashing off to open up the chippie, when the doorbell rang. And whoever was ringing it was assertive to the point of annoying, the way they kept their finger on the button. Craig strode out into the hall and threw the door open wide.

'Yes?' he snapped. But as soon as he saw them, he knew they were detectives. They showed him their warrant cards.

'Mr. Thomas? I'm DI Brooking. This is DS Browning. Mind if we ask you a few questions?'

Craig stared at them expressionlessly. In his mind he had rehearsed his responses, his stock answers, but this was different. For some reason unbeknown to Craig, this was no routine burglary enquiry from a low-ranking copper. This was the heavy brigade.

'What about?' he asked, after a brief pause.

'Just a routine enquiry, sir,' said the sergeant. 'Can we talk inside?'

Craig nodded and both brushed past him into the hall. He closed the door and showed them into his untidy combined living room and kitchen. He gestured towards chairs but they both ignored it and remained standing. The DI gave Craig a probing, hawk-like look before speaking.

'D'you know a Tony Rice?'

Craig paused slightly, as if trying to recall the name, but not overdoing it. 'Oh yeah. He turned up at my chippie about six months ago. Driving a taxi, he was. I hadn't seen him since I'd been inside. I didn't know him that well.'

'But you knew him well enough to nominate him for membership to the Working Men's Club.'

'Well, yeah. But that was six months ago. I ain't seen much of him since then.'

Did you go out on Saturday night?'

'I went to my sister's. To baby sit. Soon as I shut the chip shop I got a cab over there.'

'What time d'you shut the shop?'

'Just before nine. I usually get away before half-past. What's this all about?'

The DI ignored the question and let his eyes wander thoughtfully round the room. The sergeant produced a pen and notebook, saying: 'How long did you baby sit at your sister's?'

'From nine-thirty onwards. I stayed the night. Maggie – that's my sister – she never come home until the early hours.'

'We'll need your sister's confirmation for this. Can you let us have her details?'

Craig swallowed. His throat and lips felt dry and he needed some water. He was dehydrated after last night. 'Yeah... sure,' he said, keeping his voice steady. 'But what's this about?'

'We're investigating a murder,' said the DI, watching Craig's reaction.

'Murder?' Craig almost whispered. 'Who – ?'

'Alexander Benton. The bar steward at your club. He was beaten to death last night when he disturbed an intruder.'

Craig felt an unreal buzzing in his ears, and the two detective's faces seemed to go out of focus, like a dream sequence in a film. His head was swimming and a dizziness overcame him, so that he had trouble standing upright, and reached a hand onto the formica table to steady himself.

'You all right, sir?' asked the sergeant, in a voice heavy with suspicion.

Craig rubbed his eyes with a finger and thumb, trying to stem the flow of tears. 'I can't believe anyone could have done that to Alex,' he said. 'Everyone loved the geezer. Who could have done such a thing?'

'That's what we intend to find out,' said the DI, staring hard at Craig.

Nine

'I'm home!' Pran called out as he opened the front door, which led directly into the living room of their flat. Sitting on the sofa, a glass of white wine in his hand, Alan frowned as he looked up at Pran, then glanced pointedly at his watch.

'I was expecting you at least half an hour ago. Had you forgotten we were going to the pictures at Trinity tonight?'

Pouring himself a glass of wine, Pran said, 'We've still got plenty of time.'

'So how was your first day?'

'Mm. Not bad,' Pran said as he sipped his wine. 'Very busy day. Straight in at the deep end.'

'So what took you so long to get home?'

'I went for a drink after work.'

Alan gave him a long, hard look, waiting for an explanation.

'I couldn't get out of it, Al. It's a real pub culture there.'

'But why tonight, of all nights?'

'I was sort of railroaded into it.' Pran settled on the sofa next to Alan. 'Then I couldn't get out of it. It's the sort of place if you want to get on, you have to network.'

There was a pause, while a small, self-satisfied smile tugged the corners of Alan's mouth. Pran guessed what was coming.

'Still, no doubt the informal pub atmosphere gave you an opportunity to be open about your sexuality.'

Pran stared into his wine glass, sniffed it, then took another sip.

'Last week,' said Alan, 'when we went out for dinner, you promised you'd be open about it.'

'It was difficult. It's a real laddish culture. And you needn't worry about my coming home late, because I won't be going to the pub again. Not with that lot.'

Alan shook his head in disbelief. 'You've gone back on your word.'

'I couldn't help it.'

'Yes you can. It's about having the courage of your convictions, Pran.'

'You weren't there. You didn't hear the constant pub banter, the poof jokes flying around.'

Annoyed, Alan snatched the wine bottle and topped his glass up. 'Oh come on! Spare me! Once they know who you really are, Pran, that'll stop.'

'I'm not so sure. You should have heard some of the things they were saying to this gay barman. Not directly to him, but he couldn't fail to hear.'

'So what are you going to do?'

Pran shrugged, and his mind was swamped by a grubby tiredness. But Alan was relentless, and wouldn't let it rest.

'You can't just keep your head down, you know. It won't work.'

'It's finding the right time.'

'The longer you leave it, the worse it'll get. You need to deal with it. Soon.'

Pran felt like screaming. His neck and shoulders ached with tension, and he felt like slapping Alan. Sensing his partner's pent up anger, Alan got up and moved towards the kitchen.

'I've just got time to make us a sandwich before we go.'

'What's this film we're seeing?'

'Coriolanus.'

'Oh great! Heavy, heavy Shakespeare. That'll be a barrel of laughs.'

'You're such a philistine.'

'I'd sooner see Titanic in 3D.'

Alan smiled, a touch patronisingly. 'And you're such a child. It could be why I love you.'

***

Under the pretext of popping out to the corner shop to buy a magazine, Vanessa slipped out of the house and called Jason from her mobile. After having tried him several times since Saturday, and being fobbed off by his answering machine, she was surprised when he answered with a cursory 'Yes?' after only one ring.

'Jason,' she said hurriedly, as if she expected him to hang up. 'It's Vanessa here. I've been trying to get hold of you.'

A slight pause from his end, and then a quick intake of breath. Perhaps he'd been expecting someone else to call and she'd caught him unawares. But – she had to hand it to him – he recovered quickly. 'Hello, sweetheart. Let me guess why you're ringing. You've been wondering why I haven't been in touch. Fact is, I've been up to my eyes. Work and all that.'

'It's the "all that" I'm interested in. Why did you see Nicky on Saturday?'

'Well... because it was already arranged. I mean, before you and I...' He paused. 'Have you both been talking about me? Comparing notes?'

'Don't be stupid. Nicky doesn't know about you and me. She confided in me because she's the one who's supposed to be going out with you.' Infuriatingly, he laughed suddenly.

'What's so funny?'

'Well, I know we danced between the sheets on Saturday morning, just before I saw Nicky, but it takes two to tango, sweetheart.'

'I feel really guilty now. I wish I'd never... Nicky's been in floods of tears. She knows something's wrong.'

'So what d'you want me to do about it?'

Vanessa's voice rose a little higher. 'Well, for a start, you can tell me why you tape recorded her saying she'd slept with you.'

'Oh, she told you about that, did she?'

'You recorded me, as well.'

Jason's tone became defensive. 'What are you talking about?'

'You told me it was a cordless razor. It was a tape recorder, wasn't it?'

'Sorry?'

Vanessa began shouting. 'You recorded me saying how I'd slept with you on such and such a date...'

A couple walked by, giving Vanessa startled, surprised looks, before falling close against each other and giggling as they walked on.

'Look,' said Jason, 'I swear before Almighty God...'

'Don't give me that crap, Jason. Just give me the truth.'

'I'm telling you the truth. I didn't make a single tape recording when we were together.'

'You're lying.'

There was a brief pause before Jason said in a mid-Atlantic voice: 'I'm outa this.'

The line went dead. Vanessa gripped the phone tight. She felt like screaming, took great gulps of air, and eventually managed to control herself. As she stared at the mobile, she could imagine Jason's grinning, cocky face at the other disconnected end. 'I'll get you for this, Jason, that's a promise,' she said. 'I'll have your balls cut off!'

Then she burst into tears.

Ten

Maggie, having just put the children to bed, came into the kitchen and stared at her brother, her eyes frosty. Craig was sitting slumped at the breakfast bar, shoulders hunched, his head cradled in his hands. He loathed uncomfortable silences, and would sooner have had a blazing argument any day, but his sister was not about to let him off the hook, and she took her time as she stood leaning back against the sink, her lips tight with anger. When she eventually spoke, her voice dug into Craig like a knife.

'I've never known anyone as devious as you. The only reason you offered to baby sit for me was because you wanted an alibi. Sneaky little bastard.'

'I'm sorry.' Craig muttered lamely, avoiding her piercing glare.

Maggie snorted contemptuously. 'It's a bit late for that. You're involved in a murder enquiry.'

His eyes moist, Craig looked up at his sister. 'I had nothing to do with it, Maggs. Honest. Nothing at all.'

'No? So why d'you need an alibi?'

'Because of my track record.'

'Don't give me that. You knew, didn't you? You knew someone was going to rob that club.'

Craig nodded slowly. 'He's a dangerous bloke. Not the sort of person you grass on.'

'So how come you knew about it, if you weren't in on it?'

Craig shifted uncomfortably. 'It was my idea. I sort of planted it in his brain... without really meaning to. About six months ago, when I got a taxi to the club one night, this bloke picked me up... used to be in the same cell block as me. Then he kept coming round to the chippie. Wanted to know if I was interested in doing a job. That's when I told him how easy it was to do the club.'

Maggie sighed despairingly. 'Oh, Craig!'

'I was desperate.'

'Desperate? You had a job for Christ sake.'

'Oh yeah. Working all God's hours for five-fifty an hour.'

'So what stopped you robbing the club six months ago?'

'Well, I suppose I...' Craig's voice trailed off.

'Let me guess. Gary died and I gave you the chippie. And that's the only reason you decided to go straight. Am I right?'

Craig brushed a single tear away from his eye before replying. 'Maggs, I'm sorry. I never intended to rob the club. I really didn't. It was fantasy time... to get me through the day. I never thought...'

'Oh, stop feeling so sorry for yourself,' Maggie snapped. 'When I think how sneaky, how cunning you've been. Poor Daryl said he couldn't sleep on Saturday night. Said a noise woke him up. And you read him a story at half-one in the morning, deliberately keeping him awake so that you had a cast iron alibi. He boasted about it to the policemen when they questioned us; he said he saw the time on his bedside alarm clock. Which you, no doubt, made sure he was aware of. Sneaky bastard, using my kids like that.'

Craig stared at his sister with eyes that were glassy and pleading. 'Maggs, tell me: what was I supposed to do? I was in a no-win situation. You're overlooking the fact that I didn't do nothing. I'm innocent.'

'No, that's right. You didn't,' Maggie said sarcastically. 'You only planned it. Even if it was six months ago. And now a man's been killed. And you know who killed him. So what are you going to do about it, Craig?'

Craig shrugged helplessly. 'You haven't got any Paracetamol or Aspirin, have you? I've got a raging headache.'

***

Nigel stared into his bedroom mirror, coughed and cleared his throat. 'It's irritating,' he moaned, licking his fingers with a generous dollop of spittle and wiping them across a tuft of hair on the crown of his head. 'I'm going to have to do something about it.'

Jackie stood behind him, putting on her coat. 'It hardly notices,' she said. 'I'm sure if you went back to the barber's...'

'I'm not going back there. They're useless. Absolutely useless. And how d'you think this is going to look when we get married on Saturday?'

'Oh, I do think you're exaggerating, darling. Really – no one's going to notice that little bit of sticky-up hair. If you hadn't pointed it out to me, I would never have...'

'I don't care about that,' he wined petulantly. 'I can see that it sticks up, and that's what matters.' He could feel the sprout of hair popping up again as it dried out. 'I'm going to get Mike to cut it. And you'll just have to lump it.'

'Surely he's not the only decent barber around.'

'Hairdresser!' Nigel snapped. 'He's a hairdresser. That's why he cuts my hair properly. So that it doesn't stick up at the back.'

'There's no need to bit my head off.' She glanced at her watch. 'We're already late for our Bible class.'

Ignoring her, Nigel concentrated on vain attempts to spread the offending tuft in other directions.

'Darling!' Jackie sighed impatiently. 'For goodness sake get your hairdresser back again, if that's what you want. Only let's go. We're very late.'

Annoyed, Nigel gritted his teeth. 'That's why I hated going to church yesterday. This hair was annoying me.'

Jackie took his hand and squeezed it reassuringly. 'I'm sure God wouldn't have worried about a little bit of sticky-up hair.'

Nigel sniffed. 'Possibly not. But it wasn't God I was worried about. It was people in the pew behind us.'

***

Donald dropped Ted off at the top of his road, then drove home, ready with the excuse he would give Bamber, about the night spent haggling with a Portobello antique dealer, who wouldn't shift on the price, resulting in a "no sale".

As he parked the car, he noticed every light in the house seemed to be on, and wondered if Bamber had decided to honour his promise to thoroughly clean the house from top to bottom. But as soon as he fitted his front door key into the latch, he felt an icy stab of fear in his chest. He had no real reason to think anything was wrong, but it was a distant sound of water, rather like nights spent in the mountains or near a country stream, that was disturbing and unnerving. He pushed open the door and stepped inside, and his eyes alighted immediately on a sheet of A4 paper left on the hall table. The message was scrawled in blue felt-tip:

'Bastard. Goodbye. Don't try to find me.'

Then he noticed how loud the sound of running water was. He hurried down the hall towards the kitchen, and as he walked his feet made squelching sounds as he got nearer. Panic beating in his chest, he threw open the door and saw the sink overflowing, water cascading over the edge, flooding the kitchen floor. He ran over and pulled out the plug and turned the taps off, wondering why the overflow hadn't reduced much of the damage. That was when he noticed it had been carefully blocked with Blu-tack

He jumped as something cold and wet trickled onto his neck. He looked up with horror, screaming as he saw water dripping from the ceiling. The en-suite bathroom of their bedroom was directly above the kitchen, and Bamber must have blocked every basin in the house and turned all the taps full on.

As he ran upstairs, water swashing under his shoes, he wondered how Bamber had found out about their trip to the theatre. But what did it matter now? This was unforgivable. And if ever he got his hands on Bamber, he would slaughter him.

Eleven

Sitting in his part time secretary's swivel chair, Nigel looked up at Mike and smiled. 'I owe you an apology.'

'What for?' Mike carefully snipped the front of his client's hair.

'I had an interim cut at a barber shop. I regret that now. That bit sticking up at the back has driven me berserk.'

'Don't worry. I haven't been cutting hair for months.'

'Oh. Why's that then?'

Mike waved the hand with the scissors in front of Nigel's face. 'Hand's just come out of plaster. Had all my fingers broken.'

Nigel frowned, acting concerned. 'Oh dear! Nasty!' He sniggered suddenly. 'Who did you upset?'

'I think the bloke what done it was a professional breaker of bones.'

Nigel looked closely into Mike's face for signs of a leg-pull. 'You're having me on.'

Deadpan, Mike said, 'That's right. I'm pulling your plonker. I shut it in the car door.'

Nigel winced with imaginary pain. 'Ouch! So how have you managed? I mean financially.'

Mike shrugged. 'Had to dip into some savings.'

'Well, you'll need to top them up again. I've got just the thing if you're interested. A nice little sideline. Selling pet food direct to the customer. My son got me on to it. He's sold tons of it. And if a potential customer falters, guess what he does. He opens a tin of cat or dog food and eats it himself. Trouble is, he's putting on weight.' Nigel laughed uproariously. 'So how about it?'

'Thanks,' said Mike. 'But no thanks.'

***

'Hi, Lisa,' said Vanessa as she squeezed into the narrow gap between the fixed table and chair in the college snack bar. 'Anything to report?'

The girl seated opposite nodded gravely but there was a glint in her eye. 'Jason's friend Paul was in the Sussex last night, slightly worse for wear. He told me everything.'

Vanessa leaned forward. 'And?'

Lisa smiled, enjoying the moment. 'Are you ready for this?'

Vanessa drummed her fingers on the table. 'Lisa!' she warned. 'Where Jason's concerned, I don't have a lot of patience. And I don't have much time. I've got to go in a minute. So come on. Apart from working his way through all the female students at West Kent College, what's he up to?'

Lisa sniggered, tilting her head back. 'It's not just students. It's any girl he can get his dirty little paws on.'

'What's he trying to prove?'

'Ah-hah!'

Vanessa glanced at her watch irritably. 'Oh come on, Lisa. I know you're dying to tell me.'

Lisa fiddled with her Marlboro packet, trying to resist the temptation to go outside and light a cigarette. 'I like keeping you in suspense,' she teased.

'Lisa! I don't have the time. I've got to know before I get back.'

'You're still gunning for him then?'

'Well, aren't you?'

'I'd like to see him get his come-uppance, but...' Lisa tried to stifle a sudden giggle. 'I could have chosen my words a bit better. Then, seeing Vanessa's serious expression, added, 'I don't know why you're getting so obsessed with revenge. He's not the first bloke who wants to screw anything that moves.'

Vanessa dug her nails into her palms. Lisa could be infuriating. 'Just tell me what this Paul said.'

'If you ask me, Jason's one digit short of a phone number. Apparently he wants to get into the Guinness Book of Records as the bloke who can prove he's had the most number of women in a year.'

'I don't believe it.'

'I told you he had a screw loose.'

'So that's why he's recording all his conquests. He needs the proof.'

Lisa grinned and shook her head. 'If it wasn't so sad, it'd be funny.'

Vanessa's nostrils flared angrily. 'We're the ones who are sad, letting him use us like that.'

'So what are you going to do?'

'I'm not sure yet. But by the time I'm through with Jason, he'll wish he was celibate.'

Lisa grinned. 'Any help you need, you can rely on me. Whatever you decide to do to him.'

Vanessa looked at her watch, and stood up. 'I'd better go...'

'Another thing Paul told me,' said Lisa hurriedly. 'He said Jason had heard about that club owner, Peter Stringfellow, having had thousands of women, and he wanted to go one better.'

Lisa laughed and shook her head.

'What's so funny?'

'I don't think I told you, Vanessa, but Tom and I went up to London a couple of years back, and we went to see this Stomp show. We were walking along the Strand, past the theatre where Chicago is on, and Tom spotted Peter Stringfellow going in to see it, accompanied by this young twenty year old in a short skirt. She was all over him, and he must be old enough to be her grandfather.'

Vanessa frowned thoughtfully. 'If he wanted to impress a young girl, why Chicago? It's wasn't exactly a current show, even two years ago.'

Lisa laughed delightedly. 'Yes, it probably opened before the girl he was with was born.'

***

Donald surveyed the damage in the hall. The carpet was ruined. Fortunately the water hadn't spread as far as the living room, at least, not to any great extent, so he would only need to replace the hall carpet. The de-humidifiers he had hired, one for upstairs and one for downstairs, he would leave on, probably for the next three weeks, if not longer, until there was no trace of damp.

He felt tired. Drained. He had spent until the early hours with bucket and mop, attempting to soak up the worst of the flooding. Then, after he'd gone to bed, he spent hours tense and angry, cursing Bamber, and also cursing himself for being so stupid as to underestimate him, treating him like an idiot. Eventually he decided it was his own stupid fault, and he fell into a restless sleep. More like a doze, really. And now he was shattered, kept rubbing his eyes, and felt a strange buzzing in his ears. He decided he would have another strong espresso, then got down to the Pantiles shop and open up. There was nothing more he could do here.

The hall telephone rang and he picked it up. As soon as he had given the number, he heard nothing. He thought it was the pause before a sales call, was about to hang up, when he heard Bamber moaning.

'Oh, Donald! I'm sorry. I'm sorry. I didn't mean to... well, yes I did. It's just... I was so angry. Jealous.'

'You don't like Shakespeare!' Donald snapped incongruously. 'I just needed a friend to go to the theatre with, that's all it was.'

Bamber gave a dry, ironic laugh. 'Don't bullshit a bullshitter, Donald. I know there's more between you two. Am I right?'

Donald left too long a pause before answering. 'No, don't be a silly boy.'

He realised it sounded weak and Bamber pounced on it.'

'You're lying. I know you are. I can tell. Maybe at first, there was nothing in it. Just the two of you going out to the theatre. But not now. That's why I got so angry. Why didn't you tell me, instead of deceiving me like that? That's what I couldn't take. The lies. Treating me like an idiot. I'm sure the three of us could have worked something out.'

Donald's voice dropped to a whisper. 'What d'you mean?'

'You know very well. I'd sooner the three of us were having a bit of fun, instead of all that deception. So how about it?'

Donald cleared his throat softly. 'OK. Come back home and we'll talk about it.'

Twelve

Pran returned to his desk carrying a disposable plastic cup of water and took two Paracetamol tablets. Graham noticed and grinned.

'Rough night last night?'

Pran avoided eye contact with him and stared at his computer monitor. 'No, it's just a headache.'

Graham suspected he was lying and laughed. 'I had a couple of pints on the way home last night. Then my wife Jane and I did two bottles of wine. And I had the lion's share. But what's worrying is: I felt fine this morning. I think my body needs it. I can't sleep at night unless I've had a couple of drinks at least.'

Jenny came striding into the office, carrying a folder which she handed to Graham. 'Here's the budget outline for that community project. How did your conference go?'

Graham gave her a lopsided smile. 'Well, it was – interesting. But I should never have worn a pink shirt. Roger went on about it. You know what he's like. He said to me: "You shouldn't have worn pink, Graham. All the boys'll be queuing up to kiss you".' Graham flicked a limp wrist in front of Jenny and put on a camp voice. '"Why d'you think I'm wearing it?" I said.'

Jenny gave a little, snorting laugh. 'Oh, you know that chap... Michael I think his name is... used to work for the DTI. Did you know he's gay?'

Listening to this conversation, Pran could feel a tension in his shoulders.

Graham raised his eyebrows quizzically. 'Really? How d'you know he's gay?'

A triumphant gleam came into Jenny's eyes. 'Colin told me. Apparently this Michael's quite open about it.'

'He doesn't look like a shirt-lifter.'

Pran felt a pressure inside him, like a fear running through his body.

'I know,' Jenny went on. 'It's a shame. He's quite good looking.'

'Well, at least you don't have to worry about keeping your back to the wall.'

Jenny shook her head. 'I don't know. On the train home last night, this woman was giving me the eye.'

'You mean she was one of them. How could you tell?'

Jenny pursed her lips. 'I don't know. There was just something about her.'

Graham sniggered. 'Maybe it was the Doc Martens she was wearing.'

They both laughed. Suddenly something broke inside Pran. 'This is so unprofessional!' he yelled.

Stunned by the outburst, they both turned and stared at him. 'Sorry?' said Jenny, in a voice that was dangerously devoid of human feeling.

Committed now, Pran said, 'You're supposed to be a manager. And all these homophobic jokes are out of order. Unprofessional.'

Had Pran criticised her homophobic joke telling, it just might have been acceptable. But calling her unprofessional was something she resented with a hatred bordering on psychosis.

'There's no need to shout.' She cast her eyes around the large office. And sure enough, other workers were looking towards them. When they caught her eye, they looked away, pretending to get on with their work. But she could tell they were all listening.

Pran, realising that perhaps he hadn't handled this too well, began to back down and lowered his voice. 'I'm sorry. It's just that... we ought to watch our language. I mean, a fair percentage of our customers could be gay.'

Graham threw a glance at Jenny, a despairing look, before replying to Pran. 'Well, it's not as if they can hear us, is it?'

'No, but I can. And I find some of the things you say offensive.'

Suspicion crept into Graham's voice. 'Oh? Why?'

'Because I...' Pran faltered. He still couldn't bring himself to say it. 'Because I have some gay friends. And I don't like to hear them slandered. mean what you say in the pub is up to you, but...'

Jenny interrupted him. 'Well that's a small mercy.'

'Yeah,' Graham sneered. 'We don't have to answer to the thought police yet.' Pran glared at him. 'OK, OK. No more jokes while we're in the office. In future we'll mind our Ps and Qs.'

This was followed by an awkward silence. Jenny shuffled from foot to foot. Eventually, she excused herself. 'I've got a meeting in ten minutes. I'd better push on.'

Pran kept his focus on the computer monitor. He could feel waves of hatred emanating from them both, and he knew it was the "unprofessional" accusation that had done it.

Another job bites the dust, he thought.

***

Ted hovered outside Mothercare waiting for Marjorie, clutching a rolled-up copy of Big Issue. As soon as Marjorie emerged from the shop carrying a large carrier bag, she spotted the magazine and demanded, 'What's that you've got?'

'It's a copy of Big Issue.' Ted unrolled it and held it under her gaze. 'I bought it from the woman on the corner of Body Shop.'

Marjorie sniffed loudly. 'What d'you do that for?'

Ted gestured helplessly. 'I felt sorry for the woman. And she seemed pleasant enough.'

'You know I don't approve of these asylum people, getting handouts and begging.'

'She's not begging,' Ted sighed. 'She's selling something. Selling magazines to be precise.'

Marjorie stared at her husband, her eyes icy. 'Oh, and you're going to read that rubbish, are you?' She nodded at the picture of the Kaiser Chiefs on the front of the magazine.

'Well...' Ted began.

'I thought as much. It'll end up in the bin. And you say that's not begging.'

Ted shrugged. 'I might have a go at the crossword.'

But Marjorie had stopped listening. Her eyes widened as her attention was caught by two figures walking towards them.

'Hi there!' said Bamber, as he approached with Donald. He grinned at Ted, enjoying his discomfort. 'Long time no see.'

Marjorie glared at Donald, who looked and felt as awkward as Ted did.

Excuse us!' she blurted out after a brief and awkward hiatus. 'We're in a hurry.'

Ted gave Donald a slight, apologetic shrug, and caught up with Marjorie as she tore towards BHS. Once inside the store, she rounded on Ted.

'That man,' she hissed, 'was the one you was with in our house, asking questions about crisps and things. Pretending he was doing some sort of research. Right! That's it, Ted! We are going straight home after this. And you have got some explaining to do.'

Thirteen

Marjorie had been silent all the way back from the centre of Tunbridge Wells. Ted waited for the explosion he knew was coming but Marjorie kept him waiting, allowing time for her anger to grow. Each silent minute that ticked by pulled Ted's nerve ends to breaking point as he watched her going through the mail at the kitchen table.

'Cup of tea?' he offered in a hoarse whisper. She stared at him without replying, so he plugged the kettle in anyway.

Marjorie suddenly slammed the letters on to the table. 'Sit down!'

Almost cringing, as if expecting to be slapped across the face, Ted meekly slid into a chair at the table, well out of Marjorie's reach. She stared at him with repugnance, her mouth swept downwards with loathing, and visibly shuddered before speaking.

'You disgust me. Filthy disgusting worm!'

Ted opened his mouth to protest but was incapable of speech. He saw Marjorie shiver again.

'To think I let you...' she began, shaking her head at the incredulity of such a thought.

Ted cleared his throat hurriedly and found his voice. 'I know I lied to you, but it's not what you think.'

Marjorie's eyes narrowed into pinpricks of venomous hatred, a hooded cobra poised to strike. 'Go on then,' she hissed, 'tell me what I think. Well? Come on.'

'You think Donald and I are...' Ted was unable to complete the sentence.

'Oh-hoh,' she sneered. 'Donald, is it? Quite a little gathering that was in the precinct. You and your Donald and his fat friend.'

'He's not my Donald. We just happen to share the same interests, that's all.'

'Shakespeare. Pull the other one. What d'you take me for? I wasn't born yesterday, you know.'

'It's true. I told you before, we just like going to the theatre together.'

'If that's all it was, what was he doing round here that time? You and him, pretending he was interviewing you.' Marjorie's eyes widened with shock. 'You weren't...' She looked up at the ceiling. 'You and him wasn't... not in my house...'

'No!' Ted protested. 'Not here... I mean... not anywhere. He just came round here to arrange a trip to the theatre.'

Marjorie gave an elaborate shudder, an expression of her revulsion. 'This is my house. You can pack your bags and go. Now!'

Ted stared at her, open-mouthed. 'But... but what about our baby?'

'It's my baby, not yours. You're not coming within a mile of it when it's born. You're not fit to be its father. And I want you out of this house.'

'But w-where will I go?' Ted stammered.

'I couldn't care less.'

***

'Careful! Hold it still!' warned Dave as the stepladder moved a fraction.

Mary looked up and smiled. 'I've got it. Don't be such a baby.'

Dave slid the loft hatch across, then came hurriedly down the ladder. Mary giggled at the visible signs of relief showing on his face. 'A big baby!' she added.

'I never could stand heights.'

'It's not exactly Mount Everest.'

Dave looked serious. 'Like most fears, it's not rational. Why d'you think I didn't put them in the loft sooner? I had no one to hold the ladder for me.'

'And here was I just thinking you were holding on to your memories.'

'I was always torn between wanting to bury the past or resuscitate it. As you can imagine, the lad was mixed up.' He gave a nervous laugh. 'How many kids d'you know who had a woman for his father?'

Mary took his hand and squeezed. 'I'm sure your dad really loved you.'

'Oh, I know he did. I've often tried to put myself in his place, wondering what it must have been like. All the time he devoted to me and he couldn't say 'owt about our relationship.'

'I think it's better this way.' Mary glanced up at the loft. 'Healthier.'

'But it won't go away. I wish I had the guts to go public. What stops me is fear of ridicule. And for a comedian that should be a bonus.'

'But you want people to laugh at you, not feel sorry for you.'

'Comedy isn't just about telling jokes – which is what I do – it's about something absurd that people can recognize in themselves. If I had courage to stand up on stage and...' He stopped, his eyes becoming distant. A moment passed. Mary gave his hand another squeeze. He sighed deeply. 'Ah well – maybe one day.'

As he folded the ladder up, they heard the rattle of the letter box downstairs.

Mary froze. Dave noticed her anxiety.

'Don't worry. It's probably just a bill. Mind you, they can be pretty frightening sometimes.'

He leaned the ladder against the landing wall by the bathroom and went downstairs. Mary followed. She watched as he picked up a brightly coloured postcard from the front mat. She watched

60

closely as he read it, biting her lip. Then he looked into her eyes, frowning with concern.

'I'm sorry, sweetheart. It's from him.'

She took the card – a view of Disneyworld in Florida – and read it, her voice hoarse and tremulous. '"Hang out the bunting, baby, Ronnie's on his way home. Should arrive any day now. Love from your ever loving ex"' Her eyes were moist as she looked at Dave. 'This is a rational fear. He's a slime-ball. And dangerous. I'm going to dread that phone ringing.'

Then fate intruded. Bang on cue the telephone rang, making them both jump.

Fourteen

Dave answered the phone. Mary waited tensely at his side, and then relaxed when she heard him say: 'She's not here at the moment, Mrs. Parker. But I'll pass on the message. I'm sorry about that. I'll make sure she has a word with her little boy about it. Maybe if we can organise it so that they have the same thing in their lunch box it wouldn't matter.'

Mary watched Dave closely, as he frowned and tried to control his irritation. His voice rose a touch, with a deliberately patient tone, conveying to the caller that he was running short on goodwill.

'It was only a joke, Mrs. Parker. A joke. I'm sure we can sort it out. No problem. Bye now!'

He slammed down the phone. Mary ran a finger down the outside of his arm, relieved that it hadn't been Ronnie calling. 'What was all that about?'

Dave stared at the receiver, picturing the woman at the other end, who he imagined to be a snobby, dominating matriarch in twin-set and pearls. 'Some people,'

he shouted. 'Haven't they got anything better to do?'

'What's wrong?'

'I just don't believe I had a conversation with the stupid woman.'

Mary shook her head, and her mouth drew into a knowing smile. 'Let me guess. Was that Louise Parker's mother?'

'You know it was. You heard me talking to her.'

'What did she want?'

'Apparently her little treasure and Simon have done a swap with their lunch box meals. Simon prefers Louise's meals, and Louise prefers what you're feeding him.'

Mary shrugged and pouted. 'So big deal. Kids are kids. What can we do about that? If they want to eat each other's lunches, well...'

Dave rubbed at his eyes with a finger and thumb, indicating that he was tired, and this was a situation that was disturbing the imminent work on which he needed to focus. 'Louise has healthier options in her lunch box. Mummy forbids crisps and Kit-Kats and all the other bad things kids chuck into themselves. Like we never did that when we were kids. How many adults do you know who still eat the same junk food when they reach their thirties?'

Mary giggled. 'Plenty. Look around you. Loads of fat people; and loads of fast food outlets.'

'So what are we going to do about Mrs. Parker?'

Mary stood close to Dave and slid her arms around his waist. 'I'm glad you said "we". It makes me feel... well, that we're really a couple, and that you're sharing the responsibility of bringing up my boys. I just want you to know I appreciate that.'

'Thanks. But that still doesn't sort out the problem of Mrs. Parker's little treasure.'

A mischievous glint came into Mary's eye. 'Why don't I try to find out from Simon what Louise has in her lunchbox, then give him the same thing? That way we know he's going to eat his lunch, and poor Louise, who clearly doesn't like her stuck-up healthy options, will have to starve.'

Dave laughed. 'I think you're missing the point. This has nothing to do with food. This is early girl boy relationship developing. You show me yours and I'll show you mine.'

Mary's mouth gaped open. 'No! It can't be.'

'So how else d'you explain a kid giving up his crisps and sweets for Mrs. Snobby-git's rabbit food?'

Mary spluttered, then jumped as the phone rang again. When she answered it, Dave saw her shoulders tense, and the look of pain that scratched at her face.

'Ronnie,' she said, unable to disguise the tremor in her voice. 'How did you get this number?'

***

Maggie glanced at the kitchen clock. She frowned then looked questioningly at Craig.

'Yeah, I know what you're going to say,' he mumbled, staring at the floor and playing for sympathy. 'Why aren't I at the chippie?'

'It had occurred to me. There's no one in charge.'

Craig shrugged. 'There's no other way round it.'

Maggie's fist tightened around her coffee mug. 'Round what?'

Craig muttered something which she didn't catch. What was it?' she shouted. 'Come on, Craig. Talk to me.'

'I've left Mandy in charge. She's reliable. She can cash up. I might be gone some time.'

'Got an attack of conscience, have you?'

'Something like that.'

'So you're going to pop along to the local nick and turn yourself in, and to hell with all we've worked for.'

Craig stared at his sister, searching her expression for a clue to the way the conversation was heading.

'You can't bring the bloke back to life. You tell the police it was your idea, and with your record they'll do you good and proper.'

'Yeah, I'd already thought of that.'

Maggie gritted her teeth. 'Well then?'

'You've changed your tune, haven't you? You were all for me shopping Tony Rice earlier on.'

'Yeah, well, I've had time to think about it.'

'And?'

'I think you should forget it. Carry on as normal. It's not as if you've done anything wrong. You said so yourself.'

Craig shuffled uncomfortably and picked at a loose thread on his denim jacket. 'I couldn't live with myself if I didn't do nothing about Rice.'

Maggie snapped: 'Oh, come on, sweetheart, get real. This wine bar can be up and running in less than three months. We've already got a buyer interested in your chippie. Think what'll happen if you involve yourself in a murder enquiry.'

'I can't help thinking about old Alex though. Harmless old boy like that.'

'Are you feeling sorry for him or for yourself?'

Craig gave an ironic laugh. 'Both, I reckon.'

Maggie walked over to him and kissed his cheek. 'I know you feel guilty. But it's not your fault. Forget it. There's a lot at stake.'

Craig chuckled. 'I never realised before just how ambitious my big sister is.'

She smacked his shoulder playfully. 'Start comparing me to Gary and I'll beat you up.'

'Yeah, I believe you.' Craig frowned as he smelt the sweetness on her breath. 'Maggs, have you been drinking?'

'What, at half-eleven in the morning? Course not.'

She laughed lightly. But the way she behaved, Craig noticed, was contrived. The glib way she denied it; the way she avoided looking at him.

'Well, I'd better get down to the chippie,' he said. 'I'll see myself out. Thanks, Maggs.'

As soon as she heard the font door slam, Maggie opened one of the kitchen cupboards, took out a brandy bottle and poured herself a large measure.

Fifteen

Maria lay with her feet up on the sofa, staring at the telephone, willing it to ring. She glanced at her watch and sighed. 'He said he'd ring lunchtime. Maybe he smells a rat.'

Vanessa, sitting in the easy chair opposite, said, 'He'll ring. But he likes to play games. Make you think he's going to ring, then...'

Before she could finish her sentence, the telephone rang. Maria resisted the temptation to pick it up straight away and ran a hand over her bare midriff, toying with the ring in her pierced belly button. She let it ring three times before answering.

'Hi! Maria speaking.'

'Hi, Sweetheart. Jason.'

Maria smiled triumphantly at Vanessa. 'You only just caught me, darling,' she purred into the telephone. 'I was just about to leave.'

'Yeah. Sorry. Got held up on my last job. So how about it?'

She laughed, a throaty, sexy laugh. Dirty, even. 'Depends what you're referring to.'

'Dinner, of course,' he said with mock innocence, but matching the sexiness in his voice with hers.

'Of course,' she teased, 'I'd love to have a bite with you. I'll cook us something special.'

'But I've invited you out for dinner with me.'

'I'd sooner stay in. More intimate. And – if I say so myself – I'm a brilliant cook. So I'll see you at half-eight tomorrow. OK? Oh, you don't know where I live, do you?'

She gave him her address, then hung up and burst into laughter. 'You don't think I was over the top, do you?'

Vanessa shook her head and smiled. 'Let's face it, he's got such a big ego, you could have been twice as obvious and he wouldn't have been suspicious.'

'I can't wait for tomorrow night. 'm going to enjoy this.'

Vanessa's eyes glinted. 'Not half as much as I am.'

***

Ted followed the man up the narrow staircase. The man stopped suddenly as he ran out of breath, and coughed and spluttered. 'I ought to be in bed,' he complained. 'There's lots of bugs going round.'

On the top landing, he unlocked one of the two doors and held it open for Ted. 'This is it.'

Afraid of catching the man's germs, Ted squeezed past, holding his breath. The single room was depressingly small. And squalid, containing a single bed with a grubby candlewick bedspread of indeterminate colour, a cracked wash basin, an improvised wardrobe which was a limp curtain on a rail, and a rickety bedside table with an ancient table lamp. Beside the lamp lay an alternative red light bulb.

'Must have belonged to the other tenant,' the man explained.

Ted stared at it and frowned. Surely this room could not have been used for... Ted drove the thought out of his mind. After all, this was Tunbridge Wells. That sort of thing didn't go on here.

Seeing Ted hesitate, the man said, 'I know it's not exactly the Hilton Hotel, but that's reflected in the price.'

Ted felt nauseous. He wanted to get out of here. But this was it. This was all he could afford. Hobson's Choice.

'I'll... 'll take it,' he muttered reluctantly.

The man whipped out a filthy handkerchief and blew his nose copiously, before using the same rag to wipe beads of sweat from his balding head. Ted tried to swallow and almost gagged.

'What's your work situation?' the man asked as he closely examined the contents of his handkerchief.

'I work as a guard, on the railway.'

The man regarded Ted suspiciously. 'I see.'

'I've just left the wife.'

There was a pause while the man thought about this. 'Oh well, it happens. Not that it's any of my business. Right! Let's get downstairs and I'll do you up a rent book. I always give my tenants a rent book, just in case they lose their jobs. That way they've got something to give the unemployment benefits people.'

Sixteen

Rice inhaled deeply on his cigarette as the detectives returned to the interview room. He studied their expressions. He knew those looks; he'd seen them many times before. The half-smile and the glint in the eye that told him they were confident they'd got a result.

The detective sergeant gave Rice's solicitor a cursory nod, switched the tape recorder on and announced the continuation of the interview. Then the DI took over, going straight to the point.

'Mr. Coleman has made a statement naming you as his accomplice

in the burglary in the working men's club. In fact...'

Rice shrugged and interrupted him. 'I couldn't give a toss what Coleman

says. I told you: I left the club before the bingo started and went to Harvey Boyle's club in Hastings.'

'We've spoken to Mr. Boyle and he is unable to corroborate your alibi. He says he hardly knows you and that he wasn't with you on the night in question.'

Rice burned with anger, his head feeling as if it might ignite. He stared at the sergeant, who was wearing a provokingly smug grin, and he flipped, using every obscenity in his otherwise limited vocabulary to describe Harvey Boyle. His solicitor stared at the table.

'I don't think,' said the DI, 'that an alibi will do you much good, in any case. There's enough forensic evidence that proves you were up in that loft.'

Rice's eyes clouded over as he struggled to control himself. He still had one card left to play. 'I'm a professional. That's what I get for working with amateurs. If Coleman hadn't panicked, old Alex might still be alive.'

'Are you saying it was Coleman who killed the barman?'

Rice stared at the tape recorder and spoke clearly. 'I am. Coleman killed him. The bloke's an amateur and he panicked.'

***

After ringing the doorbell Donald pressed himself close to the front door, just in case Marjorie decided to look out of the window. If she saw who it was, he decided, it was unlikely that she would answer. He hummed quietly "March to the Scaffold" to keep his sense of humour alive. After an interminable wait, and thinking she must be out, he was about to abandon his foolhardy quest on behalf of his friend when the front door opened cautiously. And before Marjorie could slam it shut, Donald produced a dozen red roses from behind his back and handed them to her. This had never happened to her before and she was temporarily lost in wonder. A man giving her flowers!

Donald beamed at her. 'Congratulations! You must be overjoyed. And please give my best wishes to the father-to-be.'

Recovering slightly, Marjorie sniffed and said, 'He's not here. He's gone.'

'Do you mean "gone" as in moved out?'

Marjorie nodded.

'Oh dear! I hope I wasn't the cause of this... upset. If you could spare me just a few minutes of your time to explain, I'm sure we could sort things out.'

Marjorie turned, leaving the door open for him to follow. 'Thank you,' she murmured. 'I'll just go and put these in water.'

***

Craig scowled at each portion of fish as he dropped them into the sizzling oil. Mandy watched him closely. As soon as his plastic bucket was empty, she took it from him. 'What's wrong? It's your last week here. I'd have thought you'd be pleased, going on to bigger and better things.'

Craig gave her a half smile and a shrug. 'Yeah, well...'

'I thought you might be worried about me losing my job. But seeing as he new owners are keeping me on...'

'They'd have been stupid not to keep you on, Mandy. You're worth your weight...' Craig broke off.

'Are you trying to say I'm fat?'

'Of course not.'

Mandy smiled, teasing him. 'Just a bit on the large side, eh?'

Craig shook his head quickly. 'Well, you ain't exactly skinny. So what? You're great as you are.' Craig smiled awkwardly. 'Very tasty, in fact.'

Mandy giggled. 'Like fish and chips?'

'If you like.'

'So what's the problem?'

'Problem?'

'Yeah. I've often caught you looking at me in a certain way. I know because you was my employer, you wouldn't... but... well, now you're leaving...'

'Hold on a minute, Mandy. I know women are entitled to take the initiative these days, but...'

'But what?'

'This has nothing to do with you, Mandy. It's just I've got a lot on my mind.'

'Something to do with that bloke?'

Craig frowned, but guessed what she was going to say. 'He come round one morning... a few weeks ago. Wanted you to go to the pub. He seemed to have some sort of hold on you.'

Craig let his breath out slowly. 'How did you guess?'

'He was bad news. I could tell. You in trouble, Craig?'

'Sort of.'

'Anything I can do?'

Craig shook his head hurriedly and disappeared into the back room to fetch his jacket. When he returned, he left a bunch of keys on the counter.

'Will you lock up for me?'

Mandy looked concerned. 'How long will you be?'

'Haven't a clue.'

Mandy looked on the verge of tears, so Craig stroked her cheek affectionately with the back of his hand. 'Don't worry, love: I ain't done nothing wrong. I'm only helping them with their enquiries.'

Seventeen

Jason fumbled with the zip on the back of Maria's dress as they kissed. She pushed him away. 'No, you don't.'

'But you've been leading me on all night.' Jason looked like a toddler starved of sweets. 'Come on, baby. Why not?'

She let her eyelids close, then opened them again, as if trying to control herself. A melancholic performance. 'I can't,' she whispered.

Undeterred, Jason gave it another try. 'But you and me, we could make beautiful music together.'

Maria tried not to laugh or throw up. She controlled herself and said, 'It's not you, Jason. I want you. I really do. It's just that... I've got something wrong with me.'

He eased away from her on the sofa and discovered he'd been holding his breath. He let it out slowly before asking her what she meant.

'It's not what you're thinking,' she whispered, leaning across and kissing his cheek. 'I haven't got a sexually transmitted disease or anything.'

'Oh, I never thought...' he began, but she interrupted him.

'It's just that I've got... well... strange sexual preferences.'

A grin crept back onto Jason's face. 'Try me. As long as it's nothing painful. I'm game for anything.'

A creaking sound, coming from one of the bedrooms made Jason suspicious. 'What was that? I thought you said your flatmate was away.'

Maria pressed herself closer to him. 'She is. I expect that was the water heater in her room. It always makes that noise.' She ran a hand along his thigh. 'Now then: where were we?'

'You were about to tell me what turns you on.'

Maria giggled alluringly. 'I hope you're ready for this.'

***

As Mike hurried downstairs, he heard a snuffling sound coming from the living room. 'Claire?' he called out, poking his head round the door. 'Is that you?'

It took him a moment to spot her. She was squashed into a crumpled heap on the floor in a corner of the room. A sobbing mess, she looked as if she'd been that way for some time. He went over and knelt down beside her.

'What's wrong?'

She shook her head erratically. 'I don't know.'

'What d'you mean, you don't know?'

'I feel... so... so depressed.'

'What about?'

'Everything.'

Her body shook as she took great heaving gulps of air through her mouth. Mike tried to calm her by stroking her hair.'

'Please, please, sweetheart,' he pleaded soothingly, 'try to keep calm. There must be something wrong. Tell me about it.'

'I wish I knew. I really do. But I haven't a clue what's wrong with me.'

'Is it Andy. Or Chloe?'

'No. Andy's doing fine. He's sorted himself out. It's me who's....'

She stopped and stared into space, tormented by invisible demons.

Mike was torn. On the one hand, he was deeply concerned, but on the other, having glimpsed the time on his watch, he felt irritated that she was making him late for an appointment, and for no good reason that he could fathom.

'Why don't you see the doctor.'

'What can she do?'

Mike stood up, his patience wearing thin now. 'At least she might be able to suggest... or give you something for whatever it is that's wrong.'

'What?'

'How should I know? I'm not a doctor. But I've got to get off to work.'

She suddenly spat out vehemently: 'Oh, don't you worry about me. I don't want to make you late.'

'Look, I have to get going. If you won't tell me what's wrong.' He shrugged and pouted.

She stared at him, eyes filled with hatred, which surprised and frightened him. 'Well, go on then. Go.'

'I don't like leaving you this way.' He stopped in the doorway. 'Promise me you'll go to the doctor.'

'Yes, all right. If it makes you happy.'

It was on the tip of his tongue to say "no, it's to make you happy." Instead he muttered lamely, 'I'll call you later. See how you are.'

***

I feel stupid,' Jason protested, although he was panting excitedly.

'Come on, sweetie-pie,' Maria urged, 'don't give up on me now. You've come this far...' She drew bright pink lipstick carefully around his lips.

'I don't think I can contain myself much longer.'

'Shush. You're making me smudge it.'

'Hurry up.'

Maria put the lipstick down on the coffee table. 'That's it. I've finished.' He made a grab for her. 'No you don't. Keep your hands to yourself for just a minute. I want to see what you look like. Stand up. Move around.' She saw that he was about to object, so added breathily. 'Come on, Jason. I first got turned in by this when I went to see The Rocky Horror Show. I promise you it'll be worth it. I'm getting so turned on.'

Jason tottered precariously as he got up from the sofa, his size eight feet squashed painfully into Maria's size six high-heel shoes. He looked down at the stockings and suspenders he was wearing and discovered it was turning him on.

'OK,' Maria yelled. 'You can come in now.'

Jason's mouth fell open. He swivelled towards the door as Vanessa entered, followed by four other ex conquests of his from West Kent College. They all had digital cameras, and he faced a barrage of flashing bulbs.

'I'll get these photos run off in their hundreds,' said Vanessa.

Another girl giggled. 'We can email them to thousands of people.

'Have you ever seen such a wanker?' said Vanessa.

The other girls whooped and cheered and giggled.

Eighteen

Let's go through to the lounge,' said Marjorie in her best telephone voice.

'Allow me,' offered Donald, taking the tea tray. Best bone china, he noticed. Was she trying to impress, or had the flowers done the trick? Either way, he was in with a good chance of getting Ted off the hook.

As he entered the living room, he almost dropped the tray. That ghastly wallpaper! That hideous furniture! And in such a beautiful house. He felt like crying.

'Thank you. Put it on the coffee table,' said Marjorie.

Donald placed the tray carefully on the ceramic-tiled table top, his eyelids flickering rapidly as he caught sight of the design, a flamenco scene, complete with ubiquitous Spanish donkey. His hear sank. Did he really want to bring Ted back to this? He slid on to the pink Draylon sofa, hoping the static didn't raise his few remaining grey hairs.

'Milk and sugar?' asked Marjorie.

'Just milk, please.'

Marjorie poured the tea, handed him a cup, then settled into the chair opposite. 'Well, you've got a bit of a cheek, coming here like this, haven't you?'

She made it sound like a compliment, as though she admired him for having the nerve to confront her. He gave her a sly, knowing smile, as if they understood one another. He coughed delicately before speaking.

'I just wanted to reassure you that Ted and I just enjoy an occasional trip to the theatre. I don't want to come between husband and wife – especially someone in your condition.' He stopped to sip his tea. 'Men have hobbies. What's wrong with that?

And the child needs a devoted father.' He paused just long enough to give his next words dramatic impact. 'And uncle.'

'Uncle?'

'Yes, I love children. Spoil them rotten, I do. I only wish I could have them myself, but....'

Marjorie looked thoroughly confused now. This was too much to take in. She opened her mouth to speak but her mind was blank. During this hiatus, Donald decided it was time to push his luck.

'I hope you don't mind my saying how attractive this pregnancy is making you.'

Marjorie blushed and whispered,' Thank you.'

Donald congratulated himself. He had taken a calculated risk and it had paid off. If this woman was an Eskimo, he could have sold her a refrigerator.

***

A frosty reception greeted Nigel when he called to see his betrothed. Jackie flung open the door and spoke coolly. 'Oh, I wasn't expecting you.'

Nigel beamed at her, then produced a bunch of flowers and a pink envelope from behind his back. 'Own up: you thought I'd forgotten.'

Feeling guilty, Jackie accepted the flowers. 'Oh, they're lovely,' she said in a soft, whispery voice.

Leaning forward, Nigel gave her cheek a slobbery kiss. 'Many happy returns, birthday girl.'

Blushing, Jackie placed the flowers on the hall table and opened the envelope. 'I'm sorry... I thought... when the postman didn't bring a card from my loved one...'

'Who's that then?' Nigel teased.

'You know very well who.'

'No, I don't. For all I know it might be the milkman or window cleaner.'

Jackie tittered. 'Don't be silly.' She removed the card from the envelope and stopped herself from wincing. The design – a large, garishly painted bunch of flowers – left a lot to be desired. Nigel's taste in such things was sadly lacking. But Nigel was happily oblivious to his beloved's reaction to the card. Always one to flog a dead horse, Nigel was determined to keep the banter going for a bit longer.

'I'm not being silly,' he giggled. 'Unless you tell me who your loved one is, I might think it's someone other than yours truly.'

'All right,' she sighed. 'It's you, my darling. I think I'll put the kettle on.'

'Oh!' said Nigel, dropping back down to earth. 'I have an appointment in half an hour. I can't stop. I just wanted you to know I hadn't forgotten. And I've got another surprise for you. I'll give you your present over a candlelit dinner tonight.'

Jackie made an awkward expression with her mouth. 'Oh!'

Nigel frowned. 'What d'you mean "oh"?'

'I must have told you a thousand times. Rehearsals.'

'You didn't mention it.'

'I did. I told you.'

'But it's your birthday, for heaven's sake.'

Jackie laughed nervously. 'The show must go on, as Arnold says.'

Nigel put on an unpleasant-smell-under-the-nose expression. 'Is he this leading light of the amateur dramatics world?'

'You know very well who he is.'

'Yes, you've mentioned him often enough. I'm sick of hearing his name. Arnold this, Arnold that.'

'Now, now! Little green-eyed monster.'

'Well...' Nigel started to back away to the porch. 'I'm just disappointed, that's all. Can't you cancel the rehearsal?'

'It's the last one before the dress rehearsal. We open next week. You want it to be a good show, don't you?'

Nigel shrugged as if he couldn't care less.

'Why don't we pop out for nibbles after the rehearsals?' Jackie suggested.

'What time d'you think you'll be finished?'

'Oh... about ten.'

Without warning, Nigel suddenly metamorphosed into an overworked, overstressed, but very self-important business executive. 'Sorry, no can do.' He chopped the air with his hand. 'I have a presentation first thing in the morning.' He thrust back his sleeve and gave his watch an aggressive look. 'And I'm already running behind schedule...'

He turned and strode purposefully towards his car.

'Couldn't we go out tomorrow night instead?' Jackie called.

'I'm busy. Work to catch up on.'

'Then why not pop into rehearsals for a while? They know it's my birthday. Arnold let it slip.'

Nigel turned round, his face a cloud of suspicion. 'Arnold?'

'Yes. I told him it's my birthday. And I suspect they've arranged something. A cake, probably.'

Nigel hesitated, his hand on the car door. 'Oh, well, I'm not promising, but I'll try and make it. About what time?'

Jackie smiled triumphantly. 'Oh, about eight-ish.'

Nineteen

Craig stared at the no smoking sticker on the taxi window and inhaled deeply, imagining the warm smoke being sucked down into his lungs. It was nearly three years since he'd given up, but now he could really murder a cigarette.

'Nice day,' said the driver, attempting conversation for the second time.

Craig grunted and stared out of the window. The driver took the hint this time and turned up the radio, and began whistling tunelessly to a Coldplay recording. It began to grate on Craig's nerves, and he was relieved when the number ended and the local news began.

The driver pulled up close to Tonbridge Police Station. 'Here we are. The cop shop. That's thirteen-forty on the meter.'

Craig leaned forward across the front passenger seat, alert and listening. 'Hang about. I wanna hear this.'

The newsreader was saying: '...and two men have been charged in connection with the Tunbridge Wells Working Men's Club murder. Both men are local, and one of the men, who was released from prison just over six months ago, has been named as thirty-seven year old Anthony Rice from Tonbridge. Rice worked as a local cabby until recently. The other man has been named as father-of-two...'

Craig didn't catch the rest of it. The taxi driver gave a sudden whoop of recognition. 'Blimey! I remember him. He worked for our firm. What a nutter. Went smack into a BMW down near the Pantiles, and just walked away. Left 'is cab in the middle of the road. What a nutter.'

Craig leaned back in his seat. 'Keep the meter running. You've got another fare. I'm going back to the chip shop. I left something behind.'

'Chip shop to cop shop and cop shop to chip shop,' chortled the driver. 'Now the question is...'

'No,' Craig cut in. 'I ain't coming back here. No need.'

***

Mike stopped off at the White Hart for a lunchtime drink, and rang his home. After letting it ring for ages, he was about to hang up when his son answered, sounding breathless.

'Hi, Andy. It's Dad. You been running.'

'I was rushing to get to the phone. I heard it from outside.'

'Where's Mum?'

'Haven't a clue. If she was in, she'd have answered, wouldn't she? Hang on: there's a note here. It says she's gone up to Newcastle to see Chloe. And she's staying over.'

'She never mentioned she was going.'

Andrew chuckled. 'Does that mean we can have a Chinese takeaway tonight?'

'If you like. And I'll get in some beer.'

'How about hiring a DVD?'

'Don't push your luck.'

There was a brief pause, then Andrew said awkwardly, 'I suppose she is all right, isn't she?'

'What makes you say that?'

'This morning... I was waiting to use the bathroom, and she was in there ages. I thought I could hear her crying. Is Chloe in trouble again?'

'I don't think so. I think this is your mother's problem.'

'What's wrong with her?'

Without realizing he was doing it, Mike stroked and patted his beer stomach. 'Well, we're none of us getting any younger. I expect she's just going through that time of life.'

***

'You look terrible,' Donald told Ted when he met him outside the Opera House pub. 'Fleas keeping you awake, are they?'

Ted shivered and scratched his head. 'Don't joke about it. I think I'm infested.'

Donald took a giant sideways step away from him. 'Well, don't come near me.' Then, seeing the hurt, bewildered expression on his friend's face, he added, 'Come on – crack your face. It can't be that bad.'

'It's a hell-hole. I don't get any sleep.'

Donald smiled warmly. 'Cheer up! I'm here to tell you your worries are over. You may have sunk to the lower depths, but now you are reinstated. And it's all thanks to Uncle Donald.'

***

Dave slapped a bundle of paper money onto the kitchen table. 'Feast your peepers on that then. What a sight for sore eyes.'

Mary gave him a lukewarm smile. 'I'm very pleased for you.'

'Cheer up, sweetheart – it's not every day I get a yankee comes up. There's over two-hundred there. I'll get the kids a treat. We can go out, soon as they get home from school.'

Mary stood at the kitchen window and stared out at the neglected garden without replying. After an awkward silence, Dave sighed and said, 'Come on, love – when it's half term, you can come up to Blackpool for the week. The kids'll enjoy it. You will, an' all.'

'I just wish you weren't going.'

'We've been through all this. I've got to go. I've signed the contract.'

Mary turned to face him. 'You seem to think I'm exaggerating about Ronnie.'

'No, I don't. But it's a lot of water under the bridge. People change. Time being the healer, an' all that.'

'Not Ronnie. The bastard's consistent.'

'I thought you said he was unpredictable.'

'He's consistently unpredictable.'

Seeing a slight twinkle in Mary's eye, Dave laughed and came towards her. 'Is that a little smile I can see?' He put his arms round her. 'I love you. You know I wouldn't let anything happen...'

The doorbell rang.

'Saved by the bell,' said Mary, smiling now as she thought of the dishevelled return of her sons. 'They're home early for a change. I'll go.'

She walked down the hall, wearing her most welcoming smile, and threw open the front door. Her smile vanished instantly and it was like being punched in the stomach. He stood leaning nonchalantly against the porch, wearing that same arrogant expression she could never forget.

'Hi,' said Ronnie. 'I hope I haven't called at an inconvenient time.'

Twenty

Jenny sat in the staff canteen with Graham, discussing the "Pran situation" yet again. She stirred her latte thoughtfully, sipped the spoon, then shook her head at Graham.

'I mean, what was that outburst all about? Talk about over-reaction. Stupid prat.'

Graham pursed his lips. 'He's weird with a capital W. Uncommunicative.'

Jenny shrugged and turned her hands upwards on the table, as if Pran's attitude was beyond her comprehension. 'I like to think of us as a friendly team, but, when something like that happens, you feel you need to keep your distance from your staff. You see Martin, the team leader over there...'

Graham started to turn round.

'No, don't make it obvious – he'll know we're talking about him. Well, rumour has it that he told one of his managers not to have lunch with his staff. You'll lose your credibility as a manager, he said.'

Graham adopted a horrified expression. 'But that's terrible. It's so... so gradist.'

Jenny shook her head. 'Yes, but when you get pompous idiots like Pran shouting his disapproval across the office, it makes you wonder if you shouldn't keep your distance. They lose all respect for you otherwise.'

Graham examined his fingernails thoughtfully. 'At least we don't have any problems with anyone else on the team. D'you suppose it's because he's – how can I put this? – because he's got a chip on his shoulder?'

Jenny nodded emphatically. 'A lot of them have, if you catch my meaning.'

'Still,' said Graham, with a small shrug, 'I can't fault his work. He's very efficient. But it's his manner, and the bad atmosphere he creates in the office.'

'He should lighten up.'

'It's his personality, I suppose. He can't help being a miserable sod.'

Jenny looked around the canteen before leaning in to Graham. 'I mean, I try to be inclusive, as I know you do, Graham. That's why I've arranged a team building awayday next month.'

A new member of their team hovered near their table, trying to catch either Graham or Jenny's eye.

Jenny leaned even further in to Graham and dropped her voice. 'Oh look out! Bandits at ten o'clock. It's that new Admin Assistant looking for a table. I can't cope right now. If she comes over, tell her we're sorry, we've got an important agenda to discuss.'

Graham looked out the corner of his eye at the new assistant, then looked relieved. 'It's OK. She's found an empty table.'

Jenny smiled at Graham and sipped her coffee.

***

Mary opened her mouth, tried to speak, but her thoughts were jumbled. Ronnie watched her carefully, his manner deliberately laid-back, his smile calculating, enjoying her discomfort.

'Hello, Ronnie,' she muttered, after an uncomfortable silence.

Ronnie's grin widened. 'What would you say if you could speak?'

'Still using the same old lines, Ronnie?'

'Good ole reliable. That's me.'

'Oh, yes. So reliable, you go off to America for years.'

'Now don't start, baby. You were the one who got a court order preventing me from seeing the kids. So there didn't seem any point in sticking around.'

Mary's eyes narrowed as she stared suspiciously at her ex. 'So how d'you find out where I'm living now?'

Ronnie tapped the side of his nose. 'We have ways. Where are the kids?'

'They're not home from school yet.'

'You don't let them walk home on their own. Isn't that dangerous?'

'The school's at the end of the street. A hundred yards away.'

Ronnie frowned thoughtfully. 'Even so.'

A short stab of fear sliced into Mary's heart. 'The order... the court order,' she began burbling. 'It still stands, Ronnie. You can't expect...'

He put up a surrender hand to stop her. 'Whoa! It's a lot of water, baby. Can't we let bygones be bygones? People change, you know.'

'Not that much. Except your hair's grey now.'

Grinning, Ronnie ran a hand over his close-cropped hair. 'It's all the worry of missing you, babe.'

Mary stared at him, deadpan. He hadn't changed that much physically, apart from his grey hair, which had once been jet black. His eyebrows were still coal black. He was suntanned, and his neck was thicker, bullish, as if he worked out regularly. Apart from that, he was still exactly as she remembered him, conventionally handsome, although his eyes were rather small.

'You got my letter and postcard?' he asked.

'You warned me you were coming.'

He chuckled, knowing what she was thinking. 'I didn't mean to keep you in suspense, sweetheart. If I'd known you were going to worry...'

'You knew damn well I'd worry, Ronnie. More psychological tricks?'

Ronnie pantomimed innocence elaborately. 'May I be struck down dead if I tell a lie. I was detained on business. Had to take a trip to Mexico. But I'm here now.'

Mary sighed. 'Yes, you're here now.'

Dave, having heard most of this conversation from the kitchen, decided it was time to put in an appearance. Ronnie raised his eyebrows when he saw him.

'Well, well, well. Is this the new boyfriend?'

Mary introduced him and the two men shook hands briefly.

'You might as well come in and have a cup of tea or coffee,' said Dave. 'Then you can see the kids.'

He avoided eye contact with Mary, who was trying to flash him a warning. But Ronnie noticed it and grinned cockily at Mary as he entered.

***

Pran sat opposite Jenny in her office, and shifted uncomfortably in the silence as she flicked through the pages of his appraisals. His foot bumped against the desk and she looked over the papers at him.

'On the whole, you've not done too badly, but some of your box markings are a bit on the low side. There are some areas causing deep concern.'

Pran coughed lightly before speaking. 'Can you be more specific?'

'It's your communication skills, or rather your deficiency in this area. You seem to be withdrawn and surly. And your negative attitude creates a bad atmosphere in the team. You seem to have a chip on your shoulder about something. But let's face it, that's fairly typical of...'

She stopped speaking, caught herself just in time, and concentrated on reading the appraisal. Pran uncrossed his legs, and leaned forward across her desk.

'Typical of what?'

She refused to look at him, staring at the document. 'Let's talk about the previous box marking.'

Pran could feel himself burning with anger. 'What were you going to say just then? Let me guess. You were going to say that's fairly typical of an ethnic minority person, weren't you?'

She stared at him over the paper. 'Don't be ridiculous. I was going to say that it's fairly typical of someone with a negative attitude.'

Pran stood up and glared down at her. 'You liar!'

She exaggerated her shock-horror. 'Sorry?'

'You haven't even got the guts to say it.'

He started to leave the office.

'Just a minute,' she began. 'We haven't finished your...'

He slammed the door so hard behind him, the glass shattered in the door. As he strode across the open plan office, staff stopped working to watch him. There was no going back now, he realized. He had burnt his boats. Well and truly. And he dreaded going home to tell Alan he had walked out of his job.

Twenty-One

Vanessa hurried indoors and dumped her bag in the hall. She knew her mother was out at her amateur dramatics rehearsals. But Nicky was at home because she could hear pounding music coming from her bedroom. She hurried into the living room, thumbed through the phonebook on her mobile, found Mariaa's number and called. While she waited for the connection, she glanced upstairs through the open door to make certain the coast was clear. When she heard the ringing tones, she became more wound up.

'Hello, Maria speaking.'

She sounded as if she was talking through a mouthful of food.

'It's Vanessa here.'

'Oh hi, Vanessa. Can I call you back? I've just sat down to eat and it's...'

Vanessa interrupted her. 'I want to know what's going on..'

Genuine surprise from the other end. 'Sorry?'

'You know what I'm talking about.'

'Sweetie, intuitive I may be, telepathy I don't do.' Maria tittered at her own cleverness.

'I was taking some photographs in Dunorlan park today.'

There was a slight pause, then Maria recovered. Her voice was sweetness and light. 'Yes, it was a lovely bright day. Bit cold, but it was sunny.'

Vanessa ignored it. 'I was using a telephoto. I got a lovely shot of two lovebirds, clinging to each other as they walked by the lake. Then I recognised you both.'

Maria laughed. 'Well, we're both over the age of consent. And it's a free world.'

'But why Jason, of all people?'

'I felt sorry for him.'

'Felt sorry for the scumbag! What are you playing at, Maria? The guy's a creep. A wanker!'

'I think he's sweet. When we played that trick on him, I felt so guilty. Like I wanted to mother him.'

'It looked like you were doing more than mothering him this afternoon.'

'Well, he's quite sexy. I mean, you must know that, Vanessa. You went to bed with him.'

'Yes, along with dozens of other girls.'

Maria sighed loudly and deliberately. 'Look, Vanessa, d'you mind if we talk about this another time? Only I've...'

Vanessa was determined Maria wasn't going to get off lightly. 'I'm sorry, Maria, but I went to a lot of trouble to set Jason up like that. And he treated my sister pretty badly. The photos of him in drag will be in circulation by next week. No one will take him seriously again. Or anyone who goes out with him.'

Maria's voice suddenly had a harder edge to it. 'Well, that's where you're wrong, sweetie. Jason happens to be a Rocky Horror Show fan, and those photos will just show what a cool, fun-lovin' guy he is.'

Vanessa screamed down the phone. 'Why are you doing this?'

'I might ask you the same. What's all this revenge stuff?'

Vanessa clicked off the phone, hurled it across the room, making sure it had a soft landing on the sofa, then burst into tears. She jumped when Nicky spoke.

'Vanessa! What's wrong?'

Vanessa could feel herself going red. 'Oh, nothing. Just trouble with my coursework.'

***

'Haven't you got your front door key? Marjorie said, noticing how haggard Ted looked as he stood framed in the doorway.

'Yes, but I thought...'

'Oh, come in,' Marjorie said impatiently. 'Honestly, Ted, you bring on half this trouble on yourself.'

She closed the front door and Ted put his suitcase down. Marjorie put on what she thought was her softest, most forgiving, expression. It came narrowly close to Gloria Swanson's pose when she was expecting Mr. De Mille's close-up.

'I'm sorry, Ted,' she whispered. 'Let's patch it up.' She offered him her little finger. Ted entwined his own pinkie in hers and together they chanted: 'Make friends, make friends, never, never break friends.' Then Marjorie pulled him towards her and he bounced lightly off her protruding stomach.

'Ooh, what's that?' he said, after giving her a dutiful kiss.

'The baby. He just kicked you.'

'He?'

'Donald called him a "he". Donald says he's looking forward to playing football with him in the park.'

Ted stared at his wife, desperately trying to keep his expression deadpan.

Twenty-Two

Simon felt uncomfortable in his father's presence and regressed, moodily slouched against the kitchen cupboard, sucking the tip of his thumb. Thomas, being that much younger, held no grudges and found comfort leaning against his father's chair.

'Yup!' Ronnie said, a paternal arm draped around his young son's shoulders. 'It sure is a lotta water under the bridge.'

Mary stared at him coldly, hating him for intruding into her new life. 'You even sound like an American,' she said, deliberately needling him.

Dave threw her a warning look.

Ronnie's amiable expression froze, and his eyes flickered, but it was only for an instant, like a small wisp of cloud masking the sun, and the easy-going manner of his performance returned smoothly. He cast his eyes round the kitchen, like an estate agent making an inventory, and they finally came to rest on Dave.

'What is it you do, sport?'

Dave hesitated briefly before replying. 'I'm a comedian.'

'No kidding.'

'Well, quite a lot of kidding, actually.'

Dave hadn't intended this as a put-down, but Ronnie took it that way. 'Successful?' he asked pointedly.

'I get by.'

Ronnie looked critically at the state of the kitchen. 'Must be tough.'

Unthinkingly, Mary rushed to her lover's defence. 'Dave's got lots of work coming up at Blackpool soon.'

Ronnie's eyes narrowed, and his smile was far from friendly. 'How long you away for, sport?'

Dave glanced at Mary, knowing how vulnerable she was feeling. Ronnie stared at him, waiting for an answer. 'A couple of months,' he mumbled.

'That can't be much fun for your partner. Or are you two married now?'

Mary shook her head. 'We're all going up to Blackpool.'

Ronnie frowned, and feigned a puzzled expression. 'What about the kids' school?'

Mary spoke quickly, trying to cover her nervousness. 'During the school holidays, I mean. And I can probably keep them out of school one extra week.'

Ronnie knew he'd found a weakness and pursued his advantage. 'When are you leaving, Dave?'

'Next week.'

Mary could have kicked herself for being so stupid, for telling Ronnie about Blackpool. Her mind raced, trying to think of something to repair the damage. 'And next week's half term, so we'll definitely be going up then.'

Ronnie grinned confidently. 'But you'll have to come back soon after. They can't miss out on school. And all that time you'll be stuck here on your lonesome.'

His words were heavily loaded and Mary felt a crawling fear and her mouth was dry. 'I... I've got Simon and Thomas to keep me company.'

'Sure. But if you get sick of baby talk, just let me know.'

Dave frowned. 'How long you over here for?'

'Long enough to make peace with my ex wife and get to know my kids.'

Simon took his thumb out of his mouth and spat out, 'I don't talk like a baby.'

Ronnie laughed cruelly. 'No, but you sure as hell suck your thumb, kid.'

***

As he neared their flat, Pran decided not to tell Alan about walking out of his job. He knew it was cowardly, but just couldn't face it. Anything was better than having to deal with his partner's self-righteousness. That sanctimonious expression of disbelief that Pran hated, the precursor of a heated argument.

"Ace of Spades" assaulted him as he opened the flat door. It immediately set his teeth on edge. He entered the living room and, finding Alan sprawled along the sofa with his eyes closed, immediately crossed to the CD player and ejected the disc. Alan opened his eyes and glared at Pran.

'Hey! I was listening to that.'

'It was getting on my nerves.'

'Everything gets on your nerves these days.'

Pran slumped into an easy chair. 'You know I can't stand metal. Fascist white music.'

Alan sneered. 'A typical racist generalisation.'

Pran's head slumped forwards miserably, depression showing in his shoulders. 'It's just that it grates. That music makes me uptight.'

'Don't direct your anger at me, Pran. Leave your work problems where they belong. At work.'

'Who said anything about problems at work?'

Alan laughed humourlessly. 'Oh come on! Don't pull that one on me. Every day you come home in a bad mood. And you're taking it out on me. I have to put up with this shit because you won't confront your colleagues at work.'

Pran wanted to tell his partner that he had confronted his boss, and look where that had got him. He was now out of a job. He felt angry. How could Alan not see that he was in a no-win situation.

'And you know why you won't confront them,' Alan went on, throwing his legs off the sofa and sitting up. Cos you're a fuckin' wimp!'

Pran stood up. 'Right! That's it!'

'Where are you going?'

'Out!'

Pran stormed out of the room. Alan shouted after him:

'That's it! Run off to the pub and come home pissed, so you still don't have to face anything.'

The flat door slammed. Alan rubbed his fingers hard against his forehead. 'Shit!' he said. He went over to the stereo, but decided against playing anymore metal. It would probably set his nerves on edge, though it was not something he would ever admit to Pran.

***

Ronnie glanced at his watch. 'I have to hit the road.' He threw Simon a look. 'Unless you kids wanna take a ride with the old man?'

Simon shook his head, avoiding eye contact with his father.

'It's a real cool car, kid. A Chevrolet Corvette.'

'Cor! Can we, Mum?' said Thomas.

Mary shook her head. There was panic in her voice. 'I don't think that's a good idea.'

Ronnie stood up abruptly. 'Maybe another time.' He smiled at Dave. 'I don't wanna make waves. I come in peace.'

Rising, Dave said, 'I'm pleased to hear it. There's just one thing, Ronnie –'

'What's that?'

'Mary showed me the letter you wrote, in which you said you loved her till death – which you underlined.'

Ronnie walked to the door, turned and grinned at Mary. 'Didn't mean to worry you, babe. But, don't forget, we got married in a church, and we took the vows.'

Mary sniffed disparagingly. 'You were never religious, Ronnie.'

Ronnie shrugged. 'Even so. Well, I must be away. Be seeing you. Have fun in Blackpool, Dave. So long, kids.'

Simon ignored his father, staring down at the floor. Mary, Dave and Thomas saw Ronnie to the front door. The ex husband jerked his shoulders audaciously.

'He'll come round.'

'Not Simon,' said Mary forcefully. 'He's got a long memory.'

Ronnie shrugged it off with his catchphrase, 'Even so.' Then, without looking back, he hurried across the road, climbed into his Corvette, and drove off in high decibel style.

'Cool!' Thomas said.

'Yeah,' mused Dave. 'You can't hire cars like that. I wonder where he got it from?'

Mary gave his hand a comforting squeeze. 'Thank you for mentioning the letter.'

'Well, I couldn't let that one go.'

They returned to the kitchen to find Simon slumped over the table, sobbing. Mary cuddled him.

'It's all right, darling. He's gone now.'

'I hate him!' Simon cried.

Twenty-Three

Dead on the stroke of eight Nigel marched noisily into the church hall, causing the rehearsal cast to lose concentration before reaching the end of the first act. Jackie, especially, lost concentration and had to be prompted several times. The director scowled and scribbled furiously in his notebook.

Act One limped to a close, followed by a short embarrassed silence. Then Jackie introduced her fiancé and announced apologetically that he was visiting the rehearsal because it was her birthday. The director sighed petulantly before huffily mentioning that it was his intention to carry straight on with the rehearsal, so would they all please mind saving the birthday celebration and the cake until afterwards. The cast nodded gloomily and set up for the next act.

Jackie hurried over the Nigel and gave his hand a squeeze. 'I'm sorry, darling. I know you want to get away.'

Nigel's eyes darted in the leading man's direction. 'I suppose I don't mind waiting now I'm here.'

'But you'll see the end of the play. I don't want to spoil the opening night for you.'

'No fear of that,' Nigel replied, rather cryptically.

When rehearsals continued, Nigel laughed uproariously, but only it seemed whenever his fiancée had a funny line. He stared stonily at Arnold, the leading man, and didn't crack his face once. As soon as the play ended, Arnold tilted his head in Nigel's direction and said to Jackie, loudly for all to hear: 'We can tell who's got friends in tonight.'

In the pub later, Nigel bought drinks for everyone. It was a hefty round, but he felt a need to impress, especially in front of Arnold. And the leading man, he noticed, was overly tactile, mostly with Jackie.

The director asked Nigel what he thought of the rehearsal. Nigel looked towards Jackie, wondering whether he ought to be diplomatic. Then he glanced at Arnold, and thought about speaking his mind. And, when he saw the leading man touching his fiancée on the hand, he chose the latter option.

'I think,' he boomed, pausing for effect and claiming the attention of the assembled company, 'that it seemed unnatural, the way the actors behaved.'

The director felt a flush rising in his face. 'Could you elaborate?'

'The acting was – how shall I put it? – exaggerated. Unreal.'

In spite of remaining outwardly calm, the director felt cold waves of hatred as he stared at Nigel. 'But it's a naturalistic play.'

Nigel nodded in agreement, and there was a triumphant gleam in his eye.

'Let me get this straight,' the director went on, his voice several degrees colder now. 'Are you saying it was performed in the wrong style?'

Nigel chuckled. 'Oh, I don't know anything about styles. It made me laugh in places. It just didn't seem very real. But then I don't know much about the theatre.' He raised his glass at Jackie. 'Cheers, darling! Happy birthday!'

***

After reading Simon and Thomas a bedtime story, Dave returned to the kitchen and found Mary sitting at the kitchen table, staring into space. He sat opposite her and drummed his fingers on the table. Once he had her attention, he smiled.

'Have you forgotten? It's your favourite TV show tonight. Desperate Housewives.'

Mary pulled a face. 'You're looking at one.'

'Hey, come on! He didn't seem that bad to me.'

'How can you say that? Every time he opened his mouth, he...' She stopped and shuddered.

Dave smiled thinly and shrugged. 'OK. He proved he was an ace tosser. But he didn't do or say anything to make us think he might harm you or the kids.'

'He really scares me. God! How can you be so insensitive? Couldn't you see what he was up to?'

'Yeah, sure, he was playing mind games. But that's him, isn't it? I really don't think he meant anything by it.'

Mary shook her head forcefully. 'He's up to something. I know he is.'

'But why would he be? He's got a relationship with someone in the States. And why, after all this time, would he want to come back and... and what? It doesn't make any sense.'

'With Ronnie it's a power thing. And when the court ordered him to keep away from us, he lost that power. I think it's been festering in him ever since.'

Dave laughed nervously. 'Well, if you're that worried about it, why not call the police?'

Mary sighed with frustration. 'If you don't believe me, what chance do I have with the police?'

'It's not that I don't believe you.'

'But you think I'm exaggerating.'

Dave rubbed at his forehead. 'No, but I know where this is leading. I've signed that contract, Mary. If I don't honour it, they'll sue me. It's as simple as that.'

Mary sighed deeply. 'I know. It's just I'm scared. When we get home after half term, I'll be worried sick. I know I will.'

Dave took her hand. 'Look, Ronnie told us he's staying in Southend. He's got family there. He won't want to travel here that often.'

'Not at all if I can help it.'

'OK. We'll have a great time next week. And when you get back here, I'll phone you every night. You'll be fine. Just do as I suggested. Leave the answerphone on permanently and monitor the calls.'

'Great life I'm going to have.'

'A temporary measure. Until I get home.'

Suddenly, without warning, Mary's mood lifted. She giggled and gave Dave a mock punch on the jaw. 'What could you do to protect me against Ronnie? You'll have to go to the gym every day when you're in Blackpool. Build up those muscles.'

'Good idea. Keep me out of mischief and chorus girls.'

'You'd better not.'

He giggled mischievously and she knew she could trust him. He glanced at his watch.

'It's gone half-nine. I can just about afford a decent bottle of wine. Fancy a few glasses with some of those posh crisps while we watch the next episode?'

'I could kill for a glass of wine.'

'Steady on.'

'And there's no saying what I wouldn't do for a bag of those special crisps.'

Dave grinned at her. 'Looks like my luck might be in then.' He rose and grabbed his jacket from the back of the chair. 'I'll be a few minutes. I'll go up to the little Tesco's in Southborough.'

As soon as he was gone, the telephone rang. Mary was expecting a call from her mother, and dashed into the hall to answer it before it woke the children. But as soon as she picked up the receiver, a cold tingling sensation ran down her back.

'Hello? Who is this?'

Silence. She tried to speak again, but her voice caught in her throat. She could tell someone was listening at the other end, getting a kick out of her fear. She wanted to ask if it was Ronnie. That truly evil bastard. But she knew he'd left the house less than an hour ago, so it was unlikely he'd be back at Southend. Unless he was ringing from his mobile. She pressed the receiver close to her ear, listening for any background noises. But there was nothing. Just the silence. She slammed the phone down and burst into tears. She stood in the hall for a moment, shivering and sobbing, trying to compose herself. Once she had recovered, she knew she had to dial 1471 to trace the number. She thought the person would know enough to invalidate the trace by dialling 141, but it was worth a try. She was about to pick up the phone when it rang, making her jump. She hesitated, then grabbed the receiver angrily and hissed into the mouthpiece:

'Who is this?'

It was her mother.

'Have I called at a bad time, dear?'

Twenty-Four

B etty hurriedly crunched and swallowed a thirty per cent less fat crisp and managed to answer the telephone by the third ring. 'Good morning,' she sang in a ridiculously exaggerated rising inflection. 'Total Voice and Data. How may I help you?'

Nigel, who was on tenterhooks, waiting for the outcome of a recent tender, came tearing into the office. 'Who is it?' he whispered.

Betty covered the mouthpiece. 'It's your other half.'

'Oh!' Nigel found it difficult to disguise his disappointment. Besides, Jackie was the last person he wanted to speak to this morning. 'All right! I'll speak to her. Transfer it to my extension.'

Betty struggled with the buttons on her telephone as Nigel sat at his desk. The extension in the upstairs bedroom rang.

'Blast! Press and hold twenty-one.'

Betty tried to suppress her irritation. 'The last time I did that, I lost the call.'

Nigel tutted loudly. 'Oh here! I'll take it on your phone. The kettle's just boiled. I wouldn't mind an Earl Grey with two sugars.'

He leaned across Betty's desk and picked up the phone, furiously punching buttons to retrieve the call. Betty got up, throwing her boss a contemptuous look. For someone who sold telephone systems, how come he could never get to grips with his own four extensions? No wonder, she decided, his business was in decline.

As soon as she was out of earshot, Nigel dropped his voice to speak to his fiancée. 'Jackie, I have to be brief, I'm afraid. Got a busy day ahead of me.'

He heard Jackie snuffling. Was she getting a cold, or had she been crying?

'I hate you,' she said.

'Sorry?'

'It meant so much to me.'

'What did? What are you talking about?'

'You know very well. Last night you told the cast what you thought of them.'

'Oh – I see. That's what you're upset about. Well, I'm sorry – I only gave them my honest opinion. It's not my fault. That director chap asked me what I thought and I told him.

'You could have been nice instead of horrid.'

Nigel glanced at his watch and gritted his teeth. 'Lie, you mean.'

Jackie raised her voice. 'You have to make allowances, Nigel. They're not on the stage in the West End. They're doing it for a bit of fun.'

'They take themselves blooming seriously then.'

'Well, of course they do. Otherwise there wouldn't be much point in...'

Nigel interrupted, speaking hurriedly. 'Look, Jackie, I haven't got time to discuss this now. We'll talk about it later.'

'There won't be a later.'

'What d'you mean?'

'I mean the wedding's off.'

'But it's less than two weeks away.'

'I don't care,' Jackie blubbered. 'I never want to see you again.'

The line went dead. Stunned, Nigel replaced the receiver. Betty came into the room, carrying two mugs of tea.

'Problem?' she said.

Nigel nodded slowly, a dazed, faraway look in his eyes. 'I've just had an argument with Jackie. The wedding's off.'

Betty sat down and switched on the computer. 'What again!' she said.

***

'I called at the shop and you weren't there,' said Bamber, lighting another cigarette from the end of the one he'd almost finished.

'When was this?' asked Donald, deliberately busying himself plumping up the cushions on the sofa, and avoiding Bamber's probing eyes. Bamber could always tell when he was lying.

'Don't try to tell me you were out buying, because the Volvo's been parked outside all morning. So where did you go?'

Donald waved his arms about wildly and coughed dramatically. 'It's a disgusting habit. I don't care if you damage your own health, but why should I have to suffer?'

Watching his performance, Bamber smirked. 'Don't change the subject.'

'I'll answer you,' yelled Donald, 'when you put out that disgusting... thing.'

'And I'll put it out when you tell me where you've been all day.'

'This could go round in circles, you know.'

'I know. So you first. Tell me where you've been and I'll put it out.'

'No, you put it out first, then I'll tell you. See! I told you it would go round in circles.'

Bamber stuck the cigarette in his mouth and applauded Donald. Despite his uneasiness, Donald laughed.

'OK, I'll tell you on one condition. Promise me you'll have another go at giving up. You can get little patches you stick on your arm. They're supposed to be quite effective.'

'You're so transparent. Playing for time.'

'All you have to do is promise, and I'll tell you.'

Bamber shrugged. 'I promise. Now tell me.'

Donald hesitated. He decided he would tell his partner about going round to see Marjorie, telling him it was today instead of yesterday. 'I was at Ted's house. And before you say anything, he wasn't there. She's thrown him out. I went there to plead his case. See if the bitch would take him back.'

Bamber inhaled deeply on his cigarette and eyed Donald shrewdly. 'How did you know she'd thrown him out?'

'He phoned me at the shop. He was in a terrible state. But she's going to make it up with him. And you know why? Because she believes me about the occasional theatre visits.'

'Huh! More fool her.'

'It happens to be the truth. Ted and I are just good friends. It's all perfectly innocent. I promise you.'

'Yes,' muttered Bamber, 'and Elton John's not gay.'

'I wouldn't expect you to understand. You can never raise your mind above the level of your navel. Ted and I,' Donald stressed, 'are friends. Nothing more.'

Bamber stared at his partner and gave him a masturbatory gesture. Donald giggled suddenly.

'Well, that sort of thing does help to seal a friendship.'

Bamber frowned. 'I hope you're joking.'

'And another thing,' said Donald, starting to enjoy himself, because he knew he had the upper hand now. 'When his baby's born, I'm going to be the godfather. A very special uncle.'

Bamber looked pained. 'Oh, purlease! I think I might puke.'

Donald laughed loudly. 'We're going to be one big happy family.'

Angrily, Bamber dropped his cigarette into his coffee mug, knowing it would infuriate Donald, and moved towards the door.

'Where are you going?'

'Thought I'd take a walk on the common.'

Donald ground his teeth. 'Going cottaging, you mean.'

Bamber turned at the door, eyes glinting with minor triumph, knowing that the position of power had shifted again. 'It's all innocent. Like you and your theatre friend. You do believe me, don't you?'

Donald could feel the blood boiling in his face. 'I forbid you to go on the common.'

Grinning, Bamber came back and stood cockily in front of Donald. He took out his mobile and offered it to his partner.

'Ring your friend, get him round here, and let's all three of us have some fun.'

Donald went to take the mobile, then hesitated. 'I don't think he'll play ball. After all, he was straight until recently.'

'Was?'

Donald took the mobile and started to dial Ted's number. 'OK. But I don't think he'll like a heavy smoker any more than I do. Go and clean your teeth. And gargle with mouthwash. There's a good boy.'

Twenty-Five

Knowing Mary and his sons would be away in Blackpool, Ronnie arrived at Dave's house late one night, having parked the distinctive Chevrolet Corvette streets away.

He walked confidently into the narrow passageway beside the house, tried the back gate, and found it hadn't been bolted on the other side. He grinned confidently and thought about how stupid the comedian was, not even taking the precaution of bolting the back gate. As he felt his way along the wall towards the back door, he patted his coat pocket. The bulge was small, but it gave him a feeling of immense power. With these two little beauties, these two state-of-the-art, miniature camcorders, he'd be able to keep his eye on his ex-wife. He could watch her every move. It would freak her out. Oh yes, he had plans for the bitch. By the time he was through with her, she'd come crawling to him, begging to have him back. After all, they were two of a kind.. The perfect couple. They always had been, and always would be.

***

Nigel hastily finished his breakfast, dashed into the bathroom, and doused himself with cologne and after shave. He smiled optimistically at his reflection in the shaving mirror and inwardly congratulated himself. That champagne had been a masterstroke. So why hadn't she telephoned yet?

He went back downstairs, and was about to load his breakfast crockery in the dishwasher when the phone rang. Grinning, he dashed into the office and picked it up.

'Oh, Nigel,' said the loving, full-of-gratitude voice of his beloved. 'Thank you! That was a wonderful thing to do. The cast were thrilled.'

He chortled with delight. 'I hope you haven't drunk it all. It's for tonight. After the performance.'

She giggled, which was music to his ears.

'Of course we haven't drunk it. Mind you, there were a few of them who said they felt like getting sloshed after the dress rehearsal.'

'Oh dear!'

'Yes, it didn't go too well. People forgot their lines and the director shouted at us.'

'Huh! He's lucky to get you. You're the best thing in it, my sweet.'

'You're just saying that.'

'I'm not. I mean it. I can't wait for tonight.'

'And I can't wait for the week after next.'

'Why? What's happening then?' he teased.

'You know very well,' she giggled, playing along with him. 'There's something on television I want to watch.'

Nigel laughed loudly. 'Well, what's to stop you watching it?'

'Because I'll be all tucked up with my husband. Oh, I do love you, Nigel.'

'So do I,' said Nigel, caught sight of his reflection in his computer monitor and smoothed down his hair. 'I mean, of course, I love you. And after your performance tonight, I suggest we have a little celebration drinkie of our own. Just you and me. Back here, maybe.'

'Oh, but we're all of us going for a Chinese meal after the show. Cast and friends of the cast. It was Arnold's idea.'

Nigel felt himself go cold and he gnashed his teeth.

'Hello? Nigel? Are you still there?'

'Yes, I'm still here,' he said in a voice that had badly crashed.

***

Claire stared zombie-like at her bowl of muesli. Mike sat opposite her, trying to crunch his toast quietly in the stifling atmosphere.

'You haven't told me about your visit to Newcastle,' he said after a long silence.

'Haven't I?'

'No, you haven't.'

'Oh.'

Mike sighed, finding it difficult to conceal his irritation. 'Listen, Claire, if you won't see a doctor about this...'

'I'm going!' she snapped, cutting him short.

'When?'

'This morning.'

'What time?'

'Ten-fifteen.'

Mike glanced at the kitchen clock. 'You'd better eat your breakfast then.'

'I'm not hungry.'

'You must eat.'

'I said I'm not hungry.'

Mike stared at her, trying to suppress his growing anger. She hadn't moved from that position, or even looked up at him, for the past fifteen minutes. He felt like shaking her, shouting at her, but knew it wouldn't do any good. This was not self-indulgence on her part. This was real. Genuine depression.

'Let's hope the doctor can prescribe some happy pills,' he said with forced cheerfulness.

'I hope so.' She looked up at him suddenly. 'I don't want to be like this you know.'

'I never said you did.'

'Only I get the impression you think I'm putting it on.'

Licking the marmalade from his fingers, Mike got up from the table and took his plate over to the sink, trying to find room in the pile of dirty crockery. 'I've got to go and do some work. I'll do the washing up when I get home.'

'Don't martyr yourself, Mike.'

'I'm not. I'm trying to help.'

'Don't you think I want everything to be normal, just as they were?'

'Of course I do.'

'And, on top of it all, I've still got to write some stupid advertising feature on a new restaurant that's opening in Tunbridge Wells.'

'Well, you can do that on automatic pilot. You've done it before.'

'But they want me to attend their opening night, as well. Will you come with me? At least it'll be free food and wine.'

Mike smiled sympathetically, showing her he cared. 'What could be better? Whereabouts is this place?'

'Just off the High Street.'

'What is it? Italian? Chinese? Indian?'

'Well, it's a wine bar, actually.'

Mike frowned. Somewhere in the back of his mind a warning chord struck. 'What's it called, this wine bar?'

'I don't know. Does it matter?'

He picked up his haircutting bag and walked to the door. As he was about to leave, Claire said: 'I think it's called Maggie's Wine Bar. Very original, seeing as that's what the owner's name is.'

Mike went hot and cold suddenly. 'When are we supposed to be visiting this wine bar?'

'Tonight.'

'I'll see you later then.'

As soon as he left the house, Mike tried to call Maggie on her mobile. Although it was over between them, he had to let her know in advance that he would be showing up at her new wine bar with his wife, whom she had never met. For all he knew, she might handle it badly, and Claire might notice her behaviour, those tell-tale looks that pass between ex-lovers.

But Maggie's mobile was on voice mail and he didn't want to leave a message. Then he realised she was probably up to her eyes, what with it being the opening night of her wine bar. He glanced at his watch. He was already late for his first appointment. He would just have to hope and pray that Maggie was sensible enough not to allow her body language to reveal their past intimacy.

Twenty-Six

Nigel Dropped Jackie off outside the Victoria Hall, Southborough. She waited for him to park the car in one of the narrow streets opposite, frowning in concentration as she tried to remember her opening lines, which had mysteriously been obliterated from her brain.

'Nervous?' Nigel asked as he approached her, grinning broadly.

Jackie shook her head. 'I wish I'd never become involved now.'

Teasingly, Nigel tittered and said, 'Why? You're not nervous, are you?'

'Of course I am,' she snapped unintentionally.

Nigel squeezed her hand, kissed her cheek and said, 'You'll be all right.'

Then, looking at his watch added, 'I don't know what I'm going to do for the next hour. Why did you have to get here so early?'

'Because...oh, just because. Please try to understand.'

A note of petulance crept into Nigel's voice. 'It's a long time to hang around.'

'There's a pub opposite. Go and have a drink and a sandwich.'

'Can't you come with me?'

Jackie tutted. 'No, I daren't.'

Nigel's face screwed up into a puzzled frown. 'Daren't?'

'I daren't have any alcohol. I'll forget my lines.'

Nigel shrugged. 'Have a soft drink then. What's the problem?'

Jackie looked up at him, her eyes soft and appealing like a child's. When she spoke, it was with her helpless little girl's voice. 'I have to get backstage early, darling. Please try and understand.'

'OK,' he said, rather more abruptly than he intended. 'I'll see you afterwards.'

He turned and walked away. Slightly hurt, Jackie called after him, 'Aren't you going to wish me luck?'

113

He stopped and blew her a kiss. 'I hope it goes well. What is it they say?

Break your legs?'

Jackie giggled. 'I think it's just one leg, actually. And don't be late. It starts at seven-thirty.'

'Don't be daft. Why would I be late?'

'It's just that I know you.'

***

On his way home Mike rang Directory Enquiries to try to get the number of Maggie's Wine Bar, but either it wasn't listed yet or it was in another name. He wanted to warn her about turning up with Claire, but now it looked as if he was going to have to play everything by ear. The wine bar was only a fifteen minute walk from their house, so they agreed to walk there and catch a taxi home. As they were half way to the wine bar, Mike casually mentioned that he might know Maggie.

'You know that bloke Gary, who was killed in a car smash in Ashdown Forest?'

'When was this?'

'Nearly a year ago. I think it might be his missus who's running this wine bar.'

'What makes you think that?'

'I think her name was Maggie.'

'It's not an uncommon name. What makes you think it's her?'

'I was round there once, cutting his hair, and I remember them talking about opening a wine bar. It seems too much of a coincidence.'

Claire, who had up until now only been half listening, walking with her eyes fixed straight ahead, suddenly turned and looked at him, her eyes alert and demanding. 'Have you seen this Maggie since her husband died?'

Mike stared into the estate agent's window as they passed, suddenly showing great interest in house prices. Claire repeated her question.

'After her husband died, did you see this Maggie again?'

'Oh, didn't I tell you what happened? I thought I did. It was embarrassing. I turned up to cut Gary's hair only a week after the funeral. He had an appointment...'

'Well, you weren't to know.'

'All the same. It was awkward.'

'So what happened?'

'What d'you mean what happened?'

'When you confronted the grieving widow like that.'

'Well, what could I say? I just apologised and went away.'

'And did you see her again?'

Mike overdid a puzzled expression, frowning furiously, and laughed lightly.

'Of course not. Why would I see her again?'

'Well, Tunbridge Wells is not that big a town. You could have bumped into her on your travels.'

'Yes, well... I didn't.'

Mike's mouth felt dry. He realised he had made a mistake. He should never have mentioned Maggie in this way. He had alerted his wife, aroused her suspicion, and now it was too late to backtrack. He just hoped Maggie said all the right things.

And he prayed her body language didn't give Claire any further clues.

'Well, we'll soon see,' said Claire, 'whether this is the same Maggie or not.'

Mike shivered. The way Claire had spoken indicated that she was going to be watching for every little look exchanged between him and Maggie.

***

Nigel was ten minutes late for the performance. He had walked down to the Cross Keys, and it was further than he thought, and while he was there, he overheard a customer talking about the need for a new telephone switchboard, and had seized the opportunity to do some selling. After an hour long discussion on the pros and cons of various systems, Nigel stared at the pub clock and it suddenly hit him that he was late.

He offered the potential client a card, then ran all the way back up the hill to Southborough, and caused an upheaval as he pushed his way to his seat in the third row of the Victoria Hall. He made up for his lateness by laughing loudly at every joke. He laughed so loudly at one of Jackie's lines that a woman sitting nearby stared at him as if he was mad. It hadn't been that funny. Noticing her stare, Nigel gave her a wide grin. 'It's my fiancée,' he explained proudly.

***

When Alan got back from work, he found Pran lying on the sofa, staring at the Pointless. His eyes were distant, and he was clearly not taking anything in. Alan summoned up all his patience in an effort to be sympathetic and understanding.

'So how d'you feel?'

Pran rubbed at his forehead. 'Bloody awful.'

'What did the doctor say?'

Alan noticed his partner was deliberately avoiding eye contact with him, staring with a fixed expression at the television screen. Well?' he demanded, the sympathy starting to wither.

'Not much really,' said Pran, his voice deliberately monotone.

'He must have said something.'

'He said he couldn't find anything wrong with me. He said the headaches could be caused by depression.'

Alan tried to check his impatience by breathing out evenly. 'And that's it?'

'Yeah, that's about it.'

'And did he sign you off?'

Pran didn't answer, continued to stare at the TV screen as if he had found an item of interest.

'Pran, I'm talking to you. What are you doing about work? You've been off for three days now. That's why you need a doctor's certificate.'

'I've already written to them at work. I've handed in my notice.'

'You what?'

Alan couldn't believe what he was hearing. He felt the anger rising in his body, about to erupt like a volcano. As he looked at his partner stretched out on the sofa, he wanted nothing more than to smash the little shit's head in.

Twenty-Seven

'Are you pissing me about, or what?' yelled Alan, standing between the sofa and the television set, blocking his partner's view.

'I've walked out. I'm not going back there.'

'I don't believe this. You've just walked out of a bloody good job.'

Pran rubbed his eyes and mumbled through his hands. 'I couldn't stand it. It was doing my head in.'

Alan stared disbelievingly at his partner, trying to control himself. 'It was doing your head in! I don't believe I'm hearing this. You walked out of there on Monday, and you lied to me. Made out you were ill.'

Pran looked up at Alan, a pleading, sorrowful look in his eyes. 'I didn't lie to you. I really did feel ill.'

Alan laughed humourlessly. 'Oh! A bantering remark brought on one of your headaches, did it?'

'It wasn't that. It was my manager. Racist cow! We were doing my quarterly appraisals and she said I had bad communication skills, then said it was fairly typical of an ethnic minority person.'

Alan frowned and shook his head. 'She said that? If you'd stayed put and made a complaint...'

Pran looked away guiltily and dropped his voice. 'Well, she didn't actually get as far as saying it. She stopped herself in time. Hypocritical bitch. But I knew what she was going to say.'

Alan sighed deeply, picked up the remote control and switched off the television. 'So now what are you going to do?'

'I'll sort something out.'

'Oh yes, having walked out of a job, they're going to welcome you with open arms wherever you choose to work. And what about our trip this summer? Three weeks on the west coast of America. I suppose that's out the window now.'

Pran's lip quivered and he dropped his head onto his chest. 'Well I can't afford it. You'll have to go on your own.'

Pran seemed to be revelling in his misery, which provoked Alan's anger. 'Thanks a bundle. I was looking forward to this holiday. It's why I've been putting in extra hours at the hospital. And now...'

Knowing it would inflame the situation, Pran stared confrontationally at his partner as he interrupted him. 'You selfish bastard!'

'What did you say?'

'You heard. That's all you care about. "My holiday". You're pathetic.'

Alan moved towards Pran, his fists clenched. His partner flinched and said, 'Go on then: hit me, if it makes you feel better.'

Alan stopped, controlling himself. 'What? And give you more ammunition to play the self-pitying martyr. No way, mate.'

He went to the door. Pran suddenly felt insecure, wanting to undo what he had just said. Wanting to apologise, tell Alan how much he loved him, and how sorry he was for any hurt he had caused him; but all he could think of saying was a feeble: 'Where're you going?'

There was a sneering expression on Alan's face as he stared back at him from the doorway. 'It's my turn to go to the pub and come home pissed. With a slight difference. I can afford it. Because I still have a job.'

He turned and left. As the flat door slammed shut, Pran put his head in his hands and sobbed.

***

119

After the performance, the cast assembled in the bar of the Victoria Hall. Josh, the stage manager, bushy-bearded in tatty denims, with an enormous bunch of keys dangling from his hip, cleared his throat loudly and made an announcement.

'Ladies and gentlemen, and those of you who aren't sure.' – polite titters – 'If I could just have your attention for one minute. As you all know, Jackie is getting spliced next week, and her betrothed has very kindly provided us with a case of champagne,' – mutters of approval – 'which I put in the fridge prior to the performance; so without any further ado, and with her fiancé's permission,' – 'indulgent smile from Nigel – 'I will get uncorking. And can I ask you all to wash up your own glasses afterwards?'

After everyone had toasted the happy couple, the director, who seemed to have forgotten Nigel's severe criticism of the rehearsal, asked him what he thought. Jackie looked up at her fiancé, nervously chewing her lip.

'Best thing I've ever seen in a theatre,' Nigel enthused loudly. 'I thought it was wonderful. Terrific!'

There was a slight hiatus, as everyone now thought he might be sending them up. Arnold, who hadn't forgotten or forgiven Nigel's comments took advantage of the silence to get his own back.

'I thought you said this was champagne, Josh,' he said to the stage manager, picking up a bottle and closely scrutinising the label. 'This is sparkling white wine, my old son.'

Twenty-Eight

Craig cast his eyes around the wine bar, his lips moving silently as he counted. 'Unlucky thirteen,' he muttered.

'What are you on about?' Maggie asked, struggling to uncork a bottle of house red.

'Thirteen measly punters,' Craig complained. 'You'd think at least the free nosh would've attracted more than this.'

'Customers,' Maggie corrected him, 'not punters. And we've talked about this. What did you expect for a Tuesday night?'

'We should've opened at the weekend.'

Maggie yanked the last bit of cork out and sighed impatiently. 'If we'd opened at the weekend, we wouldn't have given ourselves a chance. It would've been baptism by fire. At least this a nice and easy way to open.'

Craig looked unconvinced.

'We've got to give it time for word of mouth to get around,' said Maggie. 'You wait! By Saturday you won't be able to move in here. Then you'll be complaining you're overworked.'

Craig tilted his head back, letting his eyes wander thoughtfully across the ceiling. 'All this bric-a-brac. Must be worth a few bob. I s'pose if the worst comes to the worst...'

Maggie cut in. 'Don't be such a pessimist. In a few years' time we'll be selling the whole caboodle, good will of business – everything – for a small fortune.'

'That's if you haven't drunk away the profits.'

'What's that supposed to mean?'

'Well, I've noticed, you ain't half knocking back the brandy lately.'

'Stop nagging. This is our opening night. It's a special occasion.'

Craig had stopped listening, distracted by two new customers entering. 'Good evening,' he said brightly as they approached the bar.

Maggie, who had turned away to pour some wine, hadn't seen them enter. When she turned back and saw Mike standing at the bar with Claire, she almost fainted from shock.

***

Rice glared at the cell door as it slammed shut. Bastard screw! Bastard had been goading him. Giving him details of the Tonbridge robbery. Just a stone's throw from his flat. How often he'd passed that building near Kwik-Fit, never given it a second look. And inside it was all that money. Over fifty million quid in banknotes. He almost got a hard-on thinking about it. Fifty-three fucking million! A staggering sum. The sort of heist he'd only ever dreamed about. Money to fucking burn. Years ago, he remembered reading about the Great Train Robbery, one of the few books he'd read in detail. There were still some blokes – three in all – who'd never been caught. Got clean away. But when he thought about that farm, where they set fire to pound notes to light their fags – Jesus! That was one he'd have like to have been in on. And the way that screw just now had rubbed his nose in it, telling him there were geezers who'd get clean away with the Tonbridge robbery, and how he was up on a murder charge for doing a shitty little working men's club.

That's when his whole useless fucking life passed before him. That bastard screw was right. All he'd ever done was dream about those sorts of jobs. He'd lived in Tonbridge most of his life, and had never come near to getting a sniff of the sort of geezers who'd include him on that sort of heist. Class crime like that. The sort of jobs he could only ever think of in his fantasy. The writing on the wall spelled out what a useless small-time fucker he was. Small crimes and small people. And now he was facing a murder charge. And for what? Nicking some booze from a club.

He stared at the pencil and paper. They'd allowed him that much. Couldn't do any harm. Or could it? He could damn himself totally. Make a pact with the devil. Go out in a blaze of hatred. Revenge for all the pettiness he'd had to suffer. Revenge! The most evil act of all. The final nail in the coffin.

***

Recovering quickly, Maggie threw Mike an exaggerated look of recognition. 'Hi, Mike. How've you been?' Then she looked at Claire and smiled. 'It's a small world.'

'You can say that again,' Claire answered cryptically.

'Your husband used to cut my Gary's hair.'

Claire nodded seriously. 'Yes, he's already told me.'

Maggie looked confused and began wiping the bar with a tea towel.

'When Claire told me it was called Maggie's Wine bar,' Mike said hastily, 'I guessed it might be you. I remember you and Gary talking about it.'

Maggie laughed nervously. 'You've got a good memory.'

'He remembers what he wants to remember,' said Claire. 'D'you mind if we sit down, Mike?'

Claire turned away abruptly and made for a table in a far corner of the bar. Maggie called after her: 'Everything's on the house. Order what you like from the menu on the blackboard.'

She stared into Mike's eyes, wondering if she still found him appealing. He seemed to have put on weight, and wasn't looking too good, but she wondered if there was a spark, something left of what attracted her to him in the first place. Now that Claire was no longer standing next to him, he grinned confidently, almost cockily, sending her an obvious signal that he wanted her. And the look in his eyes spoke volumes.

She gave him a sexy, meaningful smile. 'Would you like red or white wine?'

'Well, Claire only drinks white wine.'

'White wine it is then.'

As Maggie watched him retreating to the corner of the bar to join his wife, Craig muttered under his breath, 'His missus was a barrel of laughs. Miserable cow.'

Maggie felt the effects of the last brandy had long since worn off, leaving her feeling jaded. As there was a bottle in the kitchen, she said to her brother, 'I'm going to have a word with Martin. Will you get Mike and his wife their wine and take their order?'

From the corner of his eye, Mike saw Maggie disappearing through the door behind the bar. As Claire was watching him carefully, he tilted his head back, looking up at the ceiling.

'They must have gone round every antique and junk shop in Kent for this lot.' Claire just stared at him, which he found unnerving, and added with false brightness, 'Still, it's quite effective.'

Claire sniffed disdainfully. 'It's a bit over the top, if you ask me. But then again, that Maggie looked over the top. And all this junk attached to the ceiling, it's been done before. That pub in High Brooms, where I went that time with Sally... talk about unoriginal.'

Suddenly, without warning, tears filled her eyes. She hurriedly rummaged in her handbag, brought out a tissue and dabbed her cheeks.

'What's wrong?' Mike asked.

'I don't know. I just don't know. I wish we hadn't come here. I thought it would help. But somehow it's even more depressing than being at home. And that Maggie. That didn't help.'

Mike frowned. 'How d'you mean?'

She stared into his eyes, a look filled with venom. 'You tell me, Mike. You tell me.'

His mouth suddenly felt dry. 'I'm not sure... what the hell are you talking about?'

She looked down at her handbag, and snapped it shut, closing the conversation, but showing a mysterious threat in her attitude. 'It doesn't matter. It really doesn't matter.'

***

When they opened Rice's cell door in the morning, they found he'd cut both wrists and had bled to death. They never did discover how he'd managed to get hold of the small razor blade. He'd left a suicide note, abandoned on the floor as far away from the bed as possible. Presumably, so that it wouldn't get covered in blood.

The note was Rice's final, evil act. The pact with the devil. It said:

I never killed old Alex. It was Geordie Pete who killed him. But I was there, so I was responsible. But I swear it's the truth. It was Pete Coleman who killed him.

Twenty-Nine

'Mum!' Thomas complained. 'Simon pushed me on purpose.' Simon jabbed his younger brother with a finger. 'Wally!' he sneered.

'Stop it! Both of you,' Mary said, her voice tired, drained of emotion, as she struggled to fit the key into the front door.

It had been one hell of a journey from Blackpool, due to engineering works. The children hadn't stopped complaining that they were bored or tired or hungry. Never again would she travel by rail on a Sunday.

She eased open the door, the bottom of it scuffing against a pile of letters and leaflets on the mat. Bills no doubt. Mary sighed and stooped to pick them up as the children barged past, their hostilities forgotten now they were home.

'Have we got any biscuits?' said Thomas, racing towards the kitchen, dumping his backpack in the middle of the hall.

'Don't eat the last one, else I'll kill you,' said Simon, following his brother.

Mary closed the front door and breathed a sigh of relief as she put her suitcase down. She took the bundle of letters through to the kitchen. They were all addressed to Dave, and she was right – they were mostly bills. As she dropped them onto the table, she noticed a blank audio cassette tape, propped against the salt cellar, which she didn't remember leaving before she left. She remembered the last minute check to see that everything was switched off, but she couldn't recall seeing the tape on the table. She knew Dave often used audio tapes to record and learn musical numbers, which he played on the cheap portable radio and cassette player in the kitchen, but there was something alarming about the way this tape had been left on the table, like a message, as if it had some sort of meaning. She picked it up slowly, frowning, wondering if it had some significance, or if she was being paranoid.

'What's that?' Thomas asked through a mouthful of biscuit.

'Tape, stupid,' said Simon. 'Can we use it to record on, Mum, with Uncle Dave's recorder?'

Mary opened the cassette box. 'I don't remember this being here before we left.'

'I expect it's Uncle Dave's,' said Thomas casually, who was more interested in rummaging through the biscuit tin and anything else he could find in the food cupboard.

Simon snatched the tape out of his mother's hand. 'Why don't we play it and find out?'

While he slotted it into the tape player, Mary went to the sink and filled the kettle. As soon as the tape began playing, Simon noticed the tension in his mother's back, just as if she had received an electric shock. She slammed the kettle onto the work surface and spun round.

'Turn it off!'

Simon was confused. He could tell his mother was upset, the way her voice was hoarse and strained, but it was, after all, only some guitar playing something he didn't recognise.

'Why? What's wrong?' he said.

'I just don't like this song, that's all. Please – there's a good boy – switch it off.'

Sensitive to his mother's genuine distress, Simon shrugged and clicked the off switch, just as Eric Clapton began singing.

Mary tried to control her fear, but cold clammy hands made a ghostly assault on her body, sending shock waves through her skull.

'Wonderful Tonight' was their song. Ronnie used to play it when they first went out together. She knew that somehow or other he had managed to get into the house while they were away.

***

Nigel tugged the Windsor knot on his tie and spoke to Jackie's reflection in his hall mirror. 'It'll make a change from the morning service.'

'I only wanted us to go to the morning service because I don't like to think of you working so hard.'

'I had to get off some urgent quotations before we fly off into the sunset.'

Jackie tittered shyly like a young girl. 'Our flight is mid morning.'

'Metaphorically speaking,' said Nigel, turning to face Jackie. He held her hands. 'We get married on Wednesday, fly off on Thursday, which only gives me two days to finish off a mountain of work.'

Jackie shook her head disapprovingly. 'You'll have a nervous breakdown if you carry on like this.'

Nigel smirked. 'Won't be the first time.'

'It's nothing to be proud of.'

'I know, but I've got a living to make. And it doesn't get any easier.'

'But you've had quite a good year haven't you?'

Nigel looked up at the ceiling, deliberating. 'Hmm. Not really. Only forty-five K profit last year.'

'That doesn't sound bad to me.'

'I can do a lot better. It should be double that. There's still a great killing to be made out there.'

'It all sounds a bit...'

Nigel sensed her disapproval, and irritation slipped into his tone. 'What?' he demanded.

'Well, a bit thrusting.'

Nigel frowned deeply. 'Thrusting? What on earth d'you mean, thrusting? Unless it's something you've got in mind for the honeymoon.'

She smacked his arm playfully, frowning to indicate that she was serious. 'You can be very obtuse when you want to be. I just mean that we mustn't get too greedy. Too materialistic.'

'There's nothing wrong with trying to carve out a decent living.'

'I'm not saying there is.' She picked up her handbag from the hall table. 'We'd better go. We'll be late.'

Nigel pulled a face, his lips puckering, as if there was a bad smell under his nose. 'I mean, you wouldn't want me to end up like that Arnold creature.'

Jackie smiled sadly. 'Poor chap.'

Nigel almost exploded. 'Poor chap! He's downright ignorant.'

'I must admit that business about the sparkling wine was terrible behaviour.'

'Intolerable!' said Nigel, then added: 'And the sparkling wine I selected is as good as champagne. You couldn't tell the difference. In this test they did with wine experts....'

'Yes, yes, yes,' said Jackie impatiently, glancing at her watch. 'There was nothing wrong with the champagne. I was really disappointed in Arnold. He showed himself in his true colours. But don't you see, darling, he was jealous of you. Apart from his amateur dramatics, he's got very little in his life. Fifty years old, and he still works at the counter selling motor car parts. We really ought to be tolerant and pray for him tonight.'

Nigel grinned suddenly, and his eyes lit up mischievously. 'As long as he doesn't find salvation at the church we attend.'

***

Mary had just got the children to bed when the phone rang. She hurried to answer it, thinking it might be Dave to see if she had arrived safely. It was Ronnie.

'Just got the kids to bed, sweetheart?'

She felt herself grow numb with fear.

'You there, sweetheart? I hope you liked the song. Our song. Remember?'

Mary's voice was hoarse once she started to speak. 'Ronnie, can't you get it into your head, we are finished. A long time ago.'

'Oh come on, sweetheart. I saw the way you looked at me, when I came round. Like you was in love all over again. Loads of couples realise they've made a mistake by splitting up. And I can't get you out of my mind. You can't deny we had something special going for us.' His voice dropped to a whisper. 'And tonight, I know you'll be lying in bed thinking of me. But I'll be with you sweetheart. I'll be right by your side. I don't mind if you touch yourself, in those places you liked to be touched by me. Goodnight, sweetheart. I'll be there with you.'

She was about to hang up, but Ronnie anticipated it and the line went dead. She stood in the hall, numb with shock and fear, wondering what to do next. She stared at the telephone, wondering how soon she could get the number changed.

Thirty

Vanessa and Nicky sat at the kitchen table, their postures signifying boredom. Vanessa actually yawned noisily, which irritated Jackie.

'You might make more of an effort,' she snapped, her voice husky from tension.

'Effort?' questioned Vanessa, giving her mother a confused frown. 'What are we supposed to do? Jump up and down?'

Nicky giggled.

'You might at least say something nice.' Jackie's voice rose a notch. 'Something encouraging, instead of just sitting there criticising.'

'I haven't said a word,' Vanessa said.

'Exactly.'

Nicky looked at her sister and grinned. 'We can't win.'

Jackie glanced at the microwave clock. 'Nigel's cutting it fine. We're supposed to be at the registry office in less than an hour. And we've got to find somewhere to park.'

'Maybe he's done a bunk,' said Nicky. Then, seeing the pain in her mother's eyes, added: 'Only joking. He's probably stuck in traffic.'

Vanessa grinned maliciously. 'Yes, Tunbridge Wells is the car jam capital of the south east. He could be gone hours.'

Jackie ignored this obvious wind-up, walked over to the sink, squeezed out the dishcloth and wiped the draining board, which already gleamed from her recent state of obsessive cleaning and tidying. Vanessa recognised her mother's behaviour as an obvious displacement activity, and felt slightly guilty for the attempted inappropriate tease.

'When is his son due here?' she said.

'Well, he should have been here by now. Nigel's picking him up at Tonbridge station, because there's more choice of trains.'

'What happens if the trains are delayed?' said Nicky.

'Then we'll just have to get married without him,' said Jackie more forcefully than she intended.

A key rattled in the front door. Vanessa, frowning, stared at her mother. 'Since when has he had his own front door key?'

Jackie glared at Vanessa. 'Since I agreed to marry him,' she hissed.

'He's always rung the doorbell before.'

'Yes, well, now things are different. So you'd better get used to it.'

Nigel came into the kitchen, wearing an expensive suit with a red carnation in the buttonhole. His eyes looked tired, bloodshot and hurt.

'Darling! What's wrong,' said Jackie, fearing the worst.

'Martin's not coming. He called me on my mobile. Said he couldn't make it. Something unexpected has turned up the last minute.'

'Oh, darling. I'm sorry.'

'Yes, well, you'd think he could have made an effort.' Nigel waved his hands about helplessly. 'And why didn't he call me at home. Why did he have to wait until I got to the station, almost as if it was deliberate?'

Jackie tried to sound sympathetic, but she was more concerned for her own situation as the impending marriage drew closer. 'I'm sure it couldn't be helped. Can't he make the wedding breakfast either?'

Nigel shrugged.

'Shame,' said Vanessa. 'I was dying to meet him.'

Nicky sniggered. 'You'd go for anything in trousers.'

Vanessa smiled knowingly. 'Or even without trousers.'

'Especially without trousers,' added Nicky.

'I think we'd better be off,' said Jackie, hastily.

***

Clutching a small, plastic bag containing a sweet treat from Marks & Spencer's, Marjorie dashed indoors to answer the telephone before the caller hung up. It was her friend Freda, ringing with gossip about her neighbour, who had just been prosecuted for indecent exposure in Dunorlan Park.

'Guess what I've just heard,' she began. 'You know the family who moved into your old house, Robbie and Angela Barings...'

Getting no response, other than heavy breathing, Freda stopped to ask: 'You all right, Marj?'

Marjorie felt her whole body pounding, like a pulse beating out a giant rhythm . 'It's that hill,' she wheezed. 'It's really done me in.'

Freda, who had always been jealous of her friend's change of circumstances, couldn't resist the opportunity to get in a friendly dig. 'Serves you right for hob-nobbing with all them rich people.'

'It's not our fault, Freda. We inherited it.'

'Well, if you're not happy, you could always sell it.'

'I might just do that, after the baby's born.'

'Does Ted know?'

'Not yet.'

Freda chuckled. 'Poor sod's not got much say in it, I don't s'pose.'

'Well, it is my house, Freda.'

'That's what I mean.'

Marjorie placed a hand on her stomach and rubbed gently. 'Still, there'll be plenty of time to think about that after it's born.'

Freda cackled dirtily. 'Fancy Ted getting you up the duff at your age. He's a dark horse, that one. Alec thinks it's for stirring his tea with. We only do it about three times a year. Ted'll have to come round to give 'im lessons. Oh yes: I was telling you about Robbie Barings. He's been done for flashing to some French students in Dunorlan Park.' Freda sniggered. 'They was in a boat on the lake. So they was what you might call a captive audience, Alec said. Robbie Barings stood on the bank, took it out and – you know – he was doing it to himself. So one of the students...'

Noticing the lack of response from Marjorie's end, Freda stopped relating her story to ask: 'Marj? You still there?'

Marjorie looked down. She felt peculiar but quite calm. 'Would you do me a favour, Freda? Would you hang up and make two phone calls for me?'

'Why? What's happened?'

'Me waters've broken.'

'Oh my God!' yelled Freda. 'Alec! She's having the baby. Try not to panic, Marj.'

'I'm not. Would you call an ambulance for me, then call Ted on his mobile? He's at work.'

'You must try and keep calm,' shouted Freda.

Marjorie felt her heart pumping hard. She tried not to let her friend's sense of urgency and near panic get to her. She was determined to stay in control.

'Freda,' she said, her voice tremulous. 'I'll be all right if you phone. I'm just bloody annoyed, that's all.'

'Annoyed,' Freda repeated. 'What you annoyed about?'

'That me waters never broke in Marks and Sparks. I've heard they give you all kinds of maternity clothes free of charge if that happens.

Thirty-One

As soon as Marjorie was helped onto the bed in the delivery room, she was overcome with fear and regret. Her eyes had the fearful expression of a cornered animal, and her breathing was shallow and quick.

'Try to breathe deeply and slowly,' the staff nurse advised.

'Where's Ted?' Marjorie demanded.

'Your husband?'

'Of course.'

'I think he's on his way.'

'But where is he? I want him here.'

The staff nurse sighed, then smiled comfortingly at Marjorie as she propped up her pillows. 'I expect he'll be here any minute now.'

'Huh!' Marjorie exclaimed loudly, deliberately showing the staff nurse what she thought of her husband.

The nurse turned away to conceal an amused smile.

***

Ted was at Charing Cross station when he received news that his wife had gone into labour. He immediately telephoned Donald at the antique shop to share the news, but Bamber answered. Ted paused, pressing the mobile close to his ear, then asked if he could speak to Donald.

'Who wants him?' Bamber enunciated carefully, as if demanding a password.

Ted paused again. 'It's Ted here.'

'Ah,' Bamber chuckled. 'I thought I could hear trains being announced in the background. Are you Donald's Shakespeare friend?'

'Er – ye-es,' said Ted, guardedly.

'Sorry? You'll have to speak up. All I heard was a loudspeaker announcing the next train for Dover.'

'Yes!' yelled Ted, looking around foolishly at the people milling about him on the platform. 'I'm Donald's Shakespeare friend.'

Bamber sniggered. 'But soft, what light through yonder window breaks? It is the East and Donald is the sun. D'you like that, Ted?'

Ted was at a loss. 'Um – I have some news to tell Donald. Can I speak to him, please?'

'He's not here. He's gone out buying.'

'Could you give him a message for me? Can you tell him my wife's gone into labour?'

'I'll tell him on one condition.'

'What's that?'

'Come round soon and let's have that threesome.'

Ted was about to speak, to tell Bamber he had to get back on his train, but he was numbed by the thoughts running through his head. Intriguing and deliciously tempting, an invitation to explore things which he had only fantasized about. He was brought back to reality by Bamber's harsh laugh.

'Didn't my partner tell you? I asked him to.'

Ted cleared his throat. 'I think he may have mentioned it.'

Bamber chuckled delightedly. 'Well?'

'Yes. All right. But I really do have to get back on this train. Be sure to give Donald my message.'

'I will. And I look forward to meeting you properly, Ted.'

Ted hung up quickly and boarded the train.

***

'Say cheese for a cheesy grin,' giggled Nigel, his arm round Jackie's waist. She snuggled up to him and sighed contentedly.

'Oh, Nigel.'

Vanessa and Nicky exchanged pained expressions, which the photographer caught as he took the picture. 'Just one more like that,' he coaxed. 'And could the girls try to look happy this time.'

Several of Jackie's relatives and friends stopped smiling and stared at Vanessa and Nicky with enquiring expressions. Nigel sniggered. He was too full of his own satisfaction to worry about his wife's daughters. The ceremony had gone well, and he had managed to banish the disappointment he felt at his own son not attending, and hadn't given it another thought since they had arrived at the registry office.

'Come on, you two,' he said, heartily. 'Don't be miserable all your life. Have a day off.'

Jackie smacked him playfully on the bottom. 'Behave yourself, you.'

Vanessa, not wanting to be thought of as a complete killjoy, grinned artificially and said, 'I think he's got over-excited.'

The photographer gritted his teeth. He had a far more interesting assignment to attend soon and he was becoming anxious. He clapped his hands together and shouted: 'Come on now, everyone! Big smile! Here we go!'

They all posed, grinning at the lens. Even Nigel's uncle, who was well into his eighties, and not known for his high spirits, managed a lopsided grin. Unfortunately the camera was unable to capture evidence of this rare smile. The instant was lost as he raised a hand in front of his face to wipe a dew drop from his nose.

***

As soon as Ted walked into the delivery room, Marjorie took the mask away from her face. 'You took your time,' she panted. 'Where've you been?'

'I didn't think you'd want me here in uniform,' he said. 'So I went home to change first.'

'You've got about as much sense as...' she began. Then, unable to think of a suitable analogy, she smacked the mask back over her mouth and inhaled deeply.

Ted sank unobtrusively into a chair by her bedside.

'I'll leave you to it for a minute,' said the nurse.

Ted looked panic stricken at her departure. 'But what about...'

The nurse turned at the door and smiled. 'I don't think anything's likely to happen for a while. I won't be far away if you need me.'

As soon as they were alone, Marjorie glared at her husband over the top of the mask. Ted felt he had to make some sort of gesture of affection, so he stroked her hand gently, but she found his touch feeble, more irritating than comforting, and snatched it away.

'I'm sorry,' Ted said.

***

Jackie held Nigel's hand under the table and beamed at her guests; but as she looked around the table, the smile faded, giving way to a puzzled frown. She hadn't thought about it up until now, but why did Nigel only have one decrepit old uncle attending? It was odd to go through life without making any friends. No wonder he had moaned about her having eleven guests, not counting Vanessa and Nicky, to attend the wedding. It wasn't so much a reluctance to pay a hefty bill for the wedding breakfast, she realised, more a feeling of inadequacy. It showed him to lack popularity. She had been going out for almost a year with a man who had no friends, and she had never noticed up until now

Nigel smiled at the waiter who had taken all the orders except for the bride and groom. 'My wife...' He stopped to give Jackie

138

a possessively loving glance before continuing. 'Will have prawn cocktail, followed by the Dover sole. And I'll have the prawn cocktail to start off with, followed by a sirloin steak.'

Jackie frowned. 'Is that wise, darling?'

'Is what wise?'

'Steak.'

Nigel frowned back at her. 'What's wrong with steak?' He looked pointedly at some of Jackie's other guests, the ones who had ordered steak.

'Well...' Jackie dropped her voice, and glanced shyly up at the waiter, hoping he would come to her rescue.

'Nothing wrong with the beef, madam,' he said. 'Only the best. We've never had any complaints.'

Jackie coloured slightly. 'No, I'm sure it's perfectly... but we don't normally eat red meat.'

Nigel snorted. 'Speak for yourself.' He followed this with a bellowing laugh, lest others thought him serious.

'I mean,' Jackie went on, becoming more flustered, 'that fish is far healthier. And Nicky's practically vegetarian. Aren't you, Nicky?'

'I don't mind fish,' said Nicky.

'Oh, well,' Nigel said, reluctantly, 'I seem to be outnumbered. I may as well have the sole too. But I warn you, I'm going to be hungry again by dinner time.'

After the orders had been taken, Vanessa stood up and raised her champagne glass, inviting the guests to toast the happy couple. Gratefully, Jackie smiled warmly at her daughter as they all raised their glasses and wished them happiness. And then she noticed that Nicky, who was sitting opposite her, was staring pensively at her glass and hadn't joined in with the toast. Jackie leaned forward and asked her if anything was wrong.

'I was just thinking...' said Nicky.

'I thought I could smell burning,' laughed Nigel.

Nicky gave him a withering glance before continuing. 'I wondered where we're going to live now you're both married.'

'Well,' said Jackie, taking a delicate sip of champagne, 'Nigel and I have talked about selling our house and moving into his house.'

'But what about us?' demanded Nicky, rather forcefully.

'There's enough room for all of us.'

Without warning, Nicky burst into tears. 'But I'm going to miss my room. I've always lived where we are now. I don't want to move. And you can't make me.'

She pushed her chair back from the table and ran out of the dining room. The other guests offered Jackie expressions of concern and sympathy, some of them shaking their heads disapprovingly at her daughter's behaviour. The only one not to have noticed anything was amiss was Nigel's uncle, who had busied himself with blowing his nose loudly during the exchange, and was now closely examining the discharge in his handkerchief.

Thirty-Two

Ted flinched as Marjorie dug her nails into the back of his hand. He wanted to understand, to be sympathetic, but he felt nauseated by her stale, sweat-drenched smell, which occasionally made him want to heave.

A young Australian doctor leant forward between Marjorie's legs and peered closely. 'Meconium,' he told the nurse. 'The baby's in distress.'

A rasping, strangled cry came from deep within Marjorie's chest. 'It's OK,' the doctor assured her, 'your baby's passing a black substance called meconium – which is not so surprising after struggling to get out into the world for the past thirteen hours. I think we ought to assist it.'

'He means a caesarean section,' the nurse explained, throwing the doctor a sidelong, irritated glance.

The young Australian grinned back at her. 'Oh, so that's what it's called.' He glanced at Ted, wondering why the husband seemed so detached, so unemotionally involved. 'Right! You understand what's involved, Mrs. Blackburn?'

Marjorie nodded, relieved now that the pain would soon end and she could sleep, and allow someone else the responsibility. Soon it would be out of her hands.

***

Nicky and Vanessa sat together on the sofa, watching a crime film with a convoluted plot which they both found difficult to follow. Vanessa yawned and glanced at her watch, wondering if she would sleep if she went to bed this early.

'Have you ever done anything bad, something you regret, but can't do anything to change?' Nicky asked.

Vanessa thought about Jason. He'd been Nicky's boyfriend until she stepped in.

'Have you?' Nicky persisted.

Vanessa nodded. 'Yes, but I'm not in the mood for confessions. What about you?'

Nicky looked suddenly desperate, and her eyes filled with tears.

'What's wrong?' asked Vanessa.

'Oh God! What have I done? I only wanted to get at him. Not at Mum. But she's the one who'll suffer.'

Vanessa sat up excitedly and turned towards Nicky. She found it difficult to suppress the intrigued smile that was spreading across her face. 'What have you done? Tell me.'

'I did it without even thinking. I found his passport on the floor of the car. It must have dropped out of his jacket pocket when it was draped over the back seat. So I took it.'

Vanessa looked disappointed. 'Oh, is that all? Well, they're not leaving until mid morning tomorrow. You can phone him and tell him you found it here.'

Nicky's voice began to tremble and tears ran down her cheeks. 'No, I can't. I cut it into bits with a pair of scissors.'

'You did what?'

Nicky nodded slowly and looked into the distance through a veil of tears. 'I can't believe I did it. I was so angry. I cut it into tiny bits and chucked it in the bin.'

'Shit!' Vanessa said, and there was a degree of admiration in her exclamation. For the first time in ages she almost admired her sister. She herself would never have had the nerve to go that far.

***

Beaming happily, almost as if it was her baby, the auxiliary nurse told Ted he was the proud father of a perfectly healthy girl. 'We'll just clean her up and weigh her,' she said, 'then you can hold her.'

He watched while they wrapped and placed the tiny bundle on the scales. She seemed quiet. He had expected there would be much crying and bawling, like he'd seen in films.

'Seven pounds, two ounces,' the nurse told him. She brought over the bundle for him to hold. He took it carefully, accepting it as one might a precious gift. Then he looked down into his daughter's vivid blue eyes. She seemed to know who he was. Had he imagined it? Was there a brief glimmer of recognition?

'I'm seeing her before Marjorie, aren't I?' he said.

'Yes,' the nurse replied. 'Your wife hasn't come round yet. It's a shame, but there we are.'

Ted smiled, a look of triumph in his eyes. He didn't think it was a shame at all. He was pleased to be seeing his daughter before Marjorie. He gave her a wicked grin.

'Who's Daddy's girl, then? he crooned softly.

His grin widened. He couldn't wait to share his news with Donald. Soon he would be free to go round to Donald's place, while Marjorie and his baby were in hospital. And he would be free to indulge himself with both Donald and Bamber. Suddenly he felt no remorse. No guilt. Life was becoming exciting and different.

Thirty-Three

Pran blinked the sleep from his eyes as his blurred vision adjusted to the brightness of his surroundings. He felt a swaying sensation as a hand gently but firmly shook him by the shoulder. It took him a moment to get his bearings. He was still in the pub, which was now almost empty.

'Come on, sir,' said the manager. 'Time to go home.'

Pran felt a buzzing sensation in his head, and he stared woozily at the table in front of him. 'I could have sworn I had a glass of wine.'

The manager sighed and looked pointedly at his watch. 'You did have, but you finished it.'

'Are you sure?'

'Positive. Time you went home.'

Pran shrugged and tried to get up, but his legs seemed to fail him. Using the table for support, he pulled himself up. The table tilted precariously, and would have toppled but for the manager holding it down. Losing patience, the manager grabbed Pran by the arm and escorted him to the door.

'Goodnight, sir. Thank you so much for your custom.'

Pran missed the sarcasm of the manager's tone as the door closed behind him. He staggered and weaved across the pavement, and automatic pilot guided him back to his flat. As soon as he was indoors, he flopped back onto the sofa and fell asleep Alan, who had heard him arriving home, got out of bed and went into the living room. When he saw his partner sleeping fully clothed, mouth wide open and snoring loudly, he looked disgusted.

'That's it!' he said. 'I've had it, Pran. I can't take any more.'

***

Jackie shielded her eyes from the bright morning sunshine as she watched Nigel searching the back of his car. In her stomach she felt fluttering wings of panic. 'Find it?' she called.

Nigel returned to the house, shaking his head. 'It's not there.'

'Are you sure?'

Nigel clenched his teeth. God! She could be irritating at times. 'Of course I'm sure,' he snapped.

'It might have fallen behind the back seat.'

'What d'you think I've bloody well been doing all this time?'

Tears appeared in her eyes. 'Nigel!' she admonished softly, as a child might scold her father.

'Sorry,' he mumbled, scowling. He slammed the front door shut and strode into the kitchen. Jackie followed, treading softly, her shoulders carrying an invisible weight.

'Now what do we do?' he said, gesturing helplessly with open palms.

'I think we ought to go over to my place,' said Jackie.

Nigel waved his hands about frantically. 'I left my jacket in the car,' he explained slowly, as if to a half-wit. 'My passport was in my jacket pocket. And the jacket didn't leave the car.'

'Yes! All right!' Jackie snapped. 'But one of the girls might have picked it up and taken it indoors.'

'Why on earth would they do that?'

'I don't know. If you found a passport on the floor, you wouldn't just leave it there, would you?'

'But you'd tell someone you'd found it, wouldn't you?'

'Well...' Jackie hesitated. 'You know what they're like.'

Nigel made a downwards sweep with his mouth, an expression Jackie detested. 'Oh yes,' he said. 'Only too well.'

'Well don't blame them because you've lost your passport.'

'I can't think where else it could be. You'd better go and phone them.'

***

Nicky came tearing out of her room when the telephone rang, crying, 'Vanessa! Wake up! I bet that's them.'

Yawning, bleary-eyed, Vanessa eased open her door, being irritatingly slow. 'Oh God!' she complained. 'I need this like a hole in the head.'

'But you promised,' Nicky pleaded. 'Please, Vanessa.'

'OK, OK, I'm going,' said Vanessa, regretting that she had reluctantly agreed to deal with the inevitable phone call. It must have been because she still felt guilty about the fling with Jason; either that or because she had wanted to silence her sister's irritating blubbering in the early hours of the morning. Eventually Vanessa would have agreed to anything just to shut her up.

As she started down the stairs, Vanessa gave Nicky a wry smile. 'Wish me luck. This'll be an Oscar winning performance.'

***

Ted blinked in the bright sunshine as he opened the door. Donald stood framed in the light, the sun seeming to form a halo around him. 'Are congratulations in order?' he said, cheerfully.

Ted rubbed the sleep out of his eyes then noticed the champagne in Donald's hands. 'How did you know. Did Bamber tell you?'

Donald smiled. 'He did. And he also said something about you agreeing to the three of us...'

Embarrassed, Ted interrupted hastily. 'I know, but I've been thinking about that, and I don't know if now is the time... what I mean to say is... can I think about it? Put it on hold. Put it on the back burner.'

Donald laughed. 'Take a rain check. Know any more clichés, Ted? Or have you been reading very little Shakespeare of late?'

'I'm serious...' began Ted.

Donald waved his objection aside. 'Don't worry, dear boy. Bamber's gone to Lewes. He'll be gone some time. His mother's in a bad way. It looks as if she's not long for this world. One leaves as a new one arrives. So don't keep me in suspense. What did you have?'

'A girl.'

Donald's smile broadened. 'Thank goodness for that. Now I shan't have to kick a silly ball about. s she beautiful, Ted?'

Ted nodded enthusiastically. 'Out of this world.'

'Well, we'd better wet the baby's head, hadn't we?'

Ted stepped aside for Donald to enter, saying, 'It's a bit early to be drinking, isn't it?'

'Special occasion, dear boy. Now why don't you run yourself a refreshing bath while I open the bubbly, then I'll bring you up a glass.'

***

Nigel was leaning against the sink, staring at his feet, when Jackie returned to the kitchen. 'They didn't find it, did they?' he muttered.

Jackie sighed and shook her head.

'Well, I suppose that's that,' said Nigel. 'I hope the insurance will cover loss of passport.'

'Perhaps you lost it in the restaurant, or outside the registry office. We could try ringing round. Someone may have handed it in to the police.'

Nigel looked at his watch, and made another irritating downward sweep with his mouth. 'We're supposed to be at Gatwick in an hour and a half. It's not going to happen. You can go on your own, if you like.'

'On my own?'

'Why not? I could spend the day at the passport office, sorting out another emergency application, then join you tomorrow or the day after or something.'

Jackie sank heavily into a chair by the kitchen table. 'I don't want to go without you, Nigel.'

'Well,' he murmured, 'it was just a thought.'

Jackie sat upright suddenly, as if the weight had lifted from her shoulders. 'I've just had an idea. We could explain to the travel agent what's happened. And, as you say, we might be covered by the insurance. We could go somewhere else. Cornwall or Devon. Wales. The Lake District. It'll be fun just taking off without planning anything. Who knows where we might end up.'

Nigel beamed at her. 'What a great idea. And I'll be able to finish that call centre system proposal before we go. Then I can drive back from wherever we are on Monday, to do an important demo.'

'Darling!' Jackie said. 'It's our honeymoon.'

The thought suddenly struck her that Nigel might be lying about his passport, pretending to have lost it, so that he could carry on with his work.

Thirty-Four

Nicky yawned as she shuffled into the kitchen, scratching her head sleepily. Vanessa was at the breakfast table, noisily slurping the remaining milk from the bottom of her cereal bowl.

'Anything for me?' Nicky asked, indicating the pile of unopened mail on the table.

'Don't think so. You expecting anything?'

'Well, no, not really. Maybe a postcard from Mummy.'

Vanessa smirked. 'You don't deserve a card from her, after what you did.'

Nicky slumped into a chair opposite her sister. 'Oh, don't remind me. I'll always feel guilty about that. Till the day I die.'

'No, you won't. This time next year you won't give it another thought..'

'Oh, well,' Nicky nodded, with a small sigh. 'You're probably right. And at least it wasn't a total disaster. I wonder where they went in the end.'

Vanessa shrugged, pushed her cereal bowl aside and picked up the mail. 'Junk mail, bill, bill, junk mail,' she chanted as she sorted through them. 'Ah, but this looks like an invitation.'

'Who's it for?'

'Me!' Vanessa tore open the envelope and tugged out a gold-edged card. 'It's a wedding invitation.'

'I couldn't face another wedding right now,' Nicky said.

Vanessa sniggered. 'Especially this one.'

Nicky stared at her sister, frowning hard. 'What d'you mean?'

'My friend Mariaa's getting married to Jason.'

'Jason?'

'Yes, you know, that slime-ball you went out with for a while.'

'I didn't know you knew Jason.'

'Oh, I'm sorry – I should have told you. bumped into him by accident in the pub one day, and I introduced him to Maria. They started going out together. I should have told you, I suppose. But I thought you'd be upset.'

'I can't believe you've known Jason and your best friend were going out together all this time, but you never said anything.'

Vanessa shrugged carelessly, then looked her sister straight in the eye and smiled. 'It's a small world,' she said.

***

Ted crept around the house in case he woke the baby, who was sleeping peacefully in the nursery. She seemed to do nothing but sleep. After the birth, it was a sudden gut-wrenching anti-climax. Every so often, he tip-toed into her room to make sure she was all right, and to convince himself she was real, but all she did was sleep.

Having spent most of the morning getting the house ship-shape, Ted now felt exhausted. Marjorie was upstairs, running herself a bath, and he thought he might indulge in a quiet sit down with a read of The Tempest.

Marjorie suddenly appeared in the living room doorway, holding up an empty champagne bottle as if it was a urine sample. 'What's this?' she demanded.

Ted could feel the blood drain from his face. How had he overlooked the bathroom? He'd been shaving and showering in there for the past three days, so how had he missed it? Too much on his mind, probably. What with the baby, seeing Donald, and having to work a late shift. Perhaps it was the tiredness. How on earth had me missed a champagne bottle standing on the edge of the bath. But there it was. Now that Marjorie had confronted him with it, he could see in his mind's eye the champagne bottle glaring obviously at him from where he and Donald had...

'Well?' said Marjorie.

He realised the silence had stretched to an unbelievably unrealistic length while she waited for his explanation.

'I... um ...' he began. 'I just wanted to wet the baby's head.'

'You drank a whole bottle yourself?'

Ted nodded silently.

Marjorie's lip curled triumphantly. 'Then why are there two glasses in the bathroom?'

Thirty-Five

Ted stared at Marjorie, his mind a blank. After a long silence, he said, 'I'm not with you.' He realised it was weak, but he continued holding eye contact with her, keeping his face expressionless.

Marjorie's eyes narrowed as she repeated her accusation. 'Why are there two glasses in the bathroom?'

Ted shrugged and pursed his lips. He suddenly felt sure of himself. 'I couldn't drink a whole bottle of champagne in one go. I expect I took another glass up the next day.'

Marjorie deliberately let her mouth open in a parody of amazement. 'You lay in the bath two days running and polished off a whole bottle of champagne?'

'Nothing wrong with that, is there?'

Marjorie sniffed disapprovingly. 'All that hot water's costly. What's wrong with the shower?'

Ted giggled audaciously. 'The water gets into the champagne.'

Marjorie felt she was losing ground. She waved the empty champagne bottle in front of Ted and raised her voice. 'You're turning into a right boozer. How much did this set you back?'

'Oh, um, not much. It was on special offer.'

'That's not what I said. How much exactly?'

'I can't really remember. It was just under twelve pounds.'

Marjorie looked as if she had been hit with something cold and wet. 'Twelve pounds!'

'Well, perhaps not as much as that,' Ted began, hastily.

Marjorie glared at the worthless empty bottle. Sadness and longing crept into her voice. 'You've never bought me any champagne. Not once. Not ever. Not even when we got married. You could have waited till I got home.'

'I thought you weren't supposed to have alcohol.'

'That was before I had her.'

Ted was struck by a sudden bright idea, a way of changing the subject, once and for all. 'That's a point.'

'What?' Marjorie snapped, her eyes hard and piercing.

'We haven't decided on a name for her. Oh, I know we talked about it before...'

Marjorie broke in. 'I think I've settled on calling her after my mum.'

Ted looked horrified.

'What you looking at me like that for?'

'Your mother's name was Doris.'

'What's wrong with that?'

'Nothing. It's just that... well, it's a bit old fashioned.'

'Some of these old names are coming back into fashion now.'

Ted shook his head violently. 'Yes but not Doris. She's not a Doris. What about Portia? Or Olivia?'

Marjorie looked as if she could smell something unpleasant. 'Oh no, if we're going to have something old fashioned, it's got to be Doris.'

'In that case,' said Ted, snatching the champagne bottle from her hand, 'we'll have to give her something a bit more up to date.'

Ted started to leave the room. Marjorie, unused to such assertive behaviour in her husband, shrugged and relented. 'Perhaps you're right. Something a bit more modern Like Tracey.'

The tall distinguished man with greying hair and old-fashioned film star looks, handed Craig an American Express card. From behind the counter, as she poured two glasses of house red, Maggie caught the man staring at her brother's tattoos. A burning sensation of shame and embarrassment surged from deep inside her. Craig turned as he walked away from the table and flashed her a smile. She glared back at him.

'What's wrong, Maggs?' he asked, as he reached the bar.

'Nothing.'

Maggie's eyes darted over to the customer, who was talking unashamedly loudly to his lady friend in the rich flat vowel sounds of the upper classes, that made Maggie want to cringe.

'You're a wonderful brother to have.' Maggie came around the bar and moved close to Craig, rubbing his arm, as if giving his tattoos a seal of approval. 'I'm proud of you.'

Craig looked into his sister's smiling face, thrown by this sudden mood swing. He thought he detected a stale sweetness on her breath.

'Maggs,' he said, frowning, 'you been drinking?'

She stiffened, then broke away from him, and returned behind the bar. 'No, I haven't.' She avoided looking at him. 'We've been too busy. When am I supposed to have had a drink, Craig? Hmm? When?'

'I don't know. I just thought...'

She silenced him with a warning look, picked up two bottles of house red and carried them over to two men in a far corner of the wine bar.

'Your food won't be long,' she said. One of the men, wearing a suit that fitted him in a way that advertised bespoke tailoring, smiled at her as he broke off his discussion about exporting copper tubing, and she smiled back at him.

'I hope you like our house red.'

The glass slipped in her hand. She tried to catch it, but would have been better off if she had let if fall. She knocked it flying into the man's lap.

Thirty-Six

Something inside Mike snapped. 'I can't stand this any longer,' he yelled. 'Will somebody please tell me what I've done to deserve this?'

'Shouting won't do any good,' Claire said, her voice a dead echo from a paralysed mind.

Mike clenched and unclenched his fists, fighting to control his temper. Tears sprang into his eyes and his voice became choked. 'If only you knew what this depression of yours is doing to us. If only you knew how contagious it is.'

'Infectious,' said Claire automatically. 'Contagious is when it's spread by physical contact.'

'Yeah well...' shouted Mike, floundering. 'That's exactly what I do mean. Everything you touch in this house becomes depressed. You pass it on to the house itself. You can feel it in the walls. And we hardly ever see Andrew these days. He locks himself in his room. He's scared to come out.'

Zombie-like, Claire stared at the untouched cup of tea on the table before her. She wanted to speak; to tell Mike how sorry she was; how much she loved him. But the numbness in her mind was like a niggling toothache. She wanted to crawl away like a wounded animal and huddle in a corner until the depression went away, but she knew it wouldn't, even though she was aware that she needed to seek help.

'I'll go this morning,' she said, as if replying to something Mike had just said, something different.

'Go?'

'To see the doctor.'

'You should have gone weeks ago.'

'I know.'

'Well, why didn't you?'

'I'm going this morning. All right? I promise.'

'What time?'

'I don't know. I'll ring them up.'

'Tell them it's urgent. They have to see you.'

Almost imperceptibly, Claire nodded and continued to stare at the tea cup. Mike sighed deeply and tremulously. 'I'll ring them if you like.'

Claire looked up at him. 'Why? Don't you trust me?'

'It's not that I don't trust you. But I get the impression that as soon as I'm out the door, you'll just sit there staring at that cup.'

'I said I'd go. I don't need you to hold my bloody hand.'

He noticed how she had raised her voice slightly in irritation, and felt this was a good sign. Anything was better than having to suffer her unemotional staring into the distance. He glanced at his watch.

'Well I'd better be off. I'll come straight home after my last appointment, to see how you go on at the doctor's. Be some time after four I expect.'

Claire didn't reply. She continued to stare into the distance, as if she was trying to escape the present. Mike was almost tempted to yell out something like:

Come on, pull yourself together! He almost smiled to himself as he permitted himself this small fantasy of what not to say to someone in a clinically depressed state. But the truth of it was: it was how he really felt. He felt depression was an indulgence on the part of the sufferer, as if they were deliberately trying to punish those around them.

His jaw clamped tight with tension, he shuffled quietly out of the house, got into his car, and drove recklessly away from his street. He felt like driving dangerously fast to get the anger out of his system, but as soon as he was onto the main road, the rush hour traffic brought him to a halt. Instead, he took his anger out on every four-by-four vehicle waiting to move out into the traffic.

'I'm not letting you out, you bastard,' he said, avoiding eye contact with the driver. 'Gas guzzling wanker!'

***

Picking up his suitcase, Alan opened the front door, then turned awkwardly round to acknowledge Pran.

'So this is it,' said Pran, a pleading, dog-like expression in his eyes. 'Now who's not facing up to things? Now who's running away?'

Alan cleared his throat gently before he spoke. 'We've been over and over it, Pran, until I'm sick and tired of the same arguments. Everyone's got a breaking point.'

'What if I said I'd get a job? Stack shelves at Sainsbury's. Anything.'

'It wouldn't work.'

'How d'you know, if you won't give it a try?'

'It's been weeks now since you packed in your job. And in all that time, it's been sheer hell. And I can't take any more of it.'

Pran grabbed Alan's arm. 'Everyone deserves a second chance.'

'You're dragging me down. The only way I can pick myself up again, is if we split up.'

Although the morning was warm and sunny, Pran shivered from a sleepless cold. He'd been dreading this morning, and now the moment of parting had arrived, he felt a great numb confusion, unable to cope with his emotions. He was adrift now, floating listlessly, and there seemed no point to anything.

Releasing Alan's arm, he said, 'How the hell am I going to afford this flat on my own?'

Alan shrugged. 'You'll have to do what I'm doing. Find somewhere else.'

'You can't just chuck away the four years we've lived together.'

'This is not impulsive, you know. We've spent weekends arguing, and I feel exhausted. Drained. Like I've not had any sleep. And my work is suffering. If I don't watch it, any promotion I was expecting will go right out the window.'

'So you're putting your career first, is that it?'

Alan stared at Pran with a look of disgust before turning away and starting down the flight of stone steps. 'I'll be back to pick up my things. Soon as I can hire a van.'

'Phone first,' said Pran. 'So I don't have to be here.'

Pran watched as Alan pulled the handle out of his suitcase. Then his ex-partner walked away, wheeling the suitcase behind him, and did not look back.

***

When Mike returned in the early evening, he found Claire sitting at the kitchen table in the exact same spot, still staring at the cold cup of tea. He wanted to hit her, but restrained himself by clenching his fists and breathing deeply.

'So you didn't get to the doctor's.'

Silence. She leant forward and held her head in her hands, quietly sobbing.

'Jesus, Claire! What the hell is this all about?'

Mike felt no compassion for his wife as the quiet sobbing continued. If anything, it had the opposite effect, and he found himself shouting. 'I told you to go to the doctor's. You're destroying this family. And for what? I'm fucked if I know. But don't expect me to stay in and suffer your misery. I'm going out. And if I come home pissed – too bad!'

Mike stormed out of the house, slamming the door. As soon as he was in the street, he stopped, wondering where to go. He hadn't had any lunch, and he was hungry. He felt a deceitful urge to splash out, treat himself to an expensive meal, with plenty to drink. Then he remembered Maggie's Wine Bar. He would go there, and try to rekindle the relationship with his ex-lover.

Thirty-Seven

Simon and Thomas were engrossed in watching The Simpsons when the telephone rang. Mary was expecting Dave to call, but then something about the time of call, and the ring tone seemed to signal a telepathic warning. As soon as she answered the call, her apprehension turned to fear.

'Hi, Babe. I think you missed me last night.'

'Ronnie!' she almost screamed. 'I don't want you to call me again.'

'Am I supposed to have done something wrong?'

'You know bloody well you have. That tape for a start. How did you get in the house?'

'It was a piece of cake, kid. You want to get Mister Funny Man to make the place secure. I mean, anyone could get in. It's not difficult. Think what might have happened if it'd been anyone but me.'

Mary shivered and her hand gripped the receiver tightly. 'Now listen, Ronnie: I don't need all this. Not after all this time. If you continue to pester me, I shall have to call the police. And I'm changing this phone number.'

She heard him laugh, a deliberately provocative chuckle, false and devoid of humour. She struggled between the desire to slam down the phone or keep listening.

Before she could decide, his laugh broke off, like a light being switched off.

'Don't waste your time changing the number,' he said. 'All that hassle, and I'll get the new one.'

'How can you do that.'

He laughed again. 'I've got ways. I work for the Americans now. All hush-hush stuff. So I'd watch it if I were you. We know everything you get up to. And last night, as you tossed and turned

160

in your bed, who were you thinking of when you enjoyed yourself. Not Mister Funny Man, was it? Or were you thinking about us? About the great times we had between the sheets. I'll always be the best lover you ever had, babe. Was it me you were fantasising about last night? You pulled the duvet right back as you pleasured yourself. Jesus! It got me horny. So horny, I thought...'

She slammed the phone down hard, stood bent over the hall table as if she'd been hit in the stomach, and found it difficult to breathe. How had he known? How had Ronnie known about what she did last night? Or was it just a coincidence? Was he just guessing?***

Arriving breathlessly at the wine bar, Maggie headed straight for the cold cabinet, uncapped a Perrier and swigged from the bottle. Craig appeared in the kitchen doorway.

'Dehydrated, are we?'

Maggie jumped slightly, spilling water down the front of her Fort Lauderdale T-shirt. Craig gave a deliberate, self-righteous and sneering laugh.

'Sorry if I made you jump.'

'I didn't think you'd be in yet.'

'Someone's got to do the clearing up.'

Maggie sucked in her breath. 'Yes, all right! You were the one who insisted I went home early. You know how difficult it is for me, what with picking up the kids from school. And I like to see something of them.'

'I'm not arguing about that.'

Maggie pouted. 'Oh. So this is an argument, is it?'

'If you like. I think it's time we had a serious word.'

'Come on, Craig. Now's not the time. We open in five minutes. If you've got something on your mind, save it for later.'

'It might have escaped your notice, Maggs,' said Craig, waving a hand towards the tables, 'that everything's been done...'

'What do you want? A medal? I told you...'

Craig interrupted her, raising his voice. 'This has nothing to do with you taking time off to be with the kids.'

'There's no need to shout.'

'I'm not shouting.'

Maggie giggled lamely, trying to turn it into a joke. 'Sorry? I can't hear you.'

Craig stared at her, coldly.

'Oh, come on, little brother,' Maggie sighed, 'and give us a break. Lighten up, will you?'

'You know bloody well what this is about, don't you?'

'Yeah, yeah, yeah.'

'Maggie! I'm trying to help. You've got a problem. You're knocking back the hard stuff.'

'What's the point of running a wine bar if I can't have a couple of drinks to be sociable?

'It's not just a couple of drinks, and we both know it.'

Maggie took another swig of Perrier

'I think you're drinking on the quiet,' Craig went on. 'I can smell it on your breath, Maggs. And that incident with the wine yesterday...'

'Don't give me any grief about that. It was an accident.'

'I know we all have accidents from time to time...'

Maggie stared at her brother, parodying an adoring expression. 'Except my wonderful young brother, who never does anything wrong.'

Craig's face flushed with sudden anger. 'Why don't you admit you've got a drink problem, sweetheart? You don't fool anyone except yourself. Even Dad's mentioned it to me.'

Maggie looked suddenly alarmed. 'What did he say?'

'Oh, just that he thinks you might be overdoing it. But I know what he meant. You've got to get a grip, Maggs.'

Maggie sighed, pouting, and let her head fall contritely onto her chest. 'I'll try,' she muttered. 'But...'

'But what?'

'I don't think I can cope anymore. I wish I'd never got into this wine bar business.'

Craig stared at her disbelievingly. 'But we're doing all right, Maggs. We're going great guns.'

'Yeah, financially. But I just don't think I can cope. It's like there's something missing from my life. There's an emptiness. A gap. It's difficult to explain.'

At that precise moment there was a tap on the glass of the entrance door. Outside stood Mike, grinning and looking though the window at them. He held up his wrist watch and tapped the glass of it pointedly.

Maggie grinned back at him. 'Better open up,' she told Craig.

Thirty-Eight

As Mike stood at the wine bar counter, smiling at Maggie, Craig sensed there was something between them. He detected that undercurrent that runs between lovers, the secret mutual appeal they think is latent but is clearly noticeable by others.

'Hi,' said Mike. 'How've you been?'

Maggie's body language became openly inviting, as she returned his smile, and brushed her hands back across her stomach until they rested on her hips.

'It's been a bit hectic,' she said. 'What can I get you?'

'I'll have a bottle of Beck's.'

Craig nodded approvingly at Mike, then went into the kitchen, pleased that perhaps Maggie might rekindle an old love, which he knew would be far healthier than her drink problem.

Maggie handed Mike his beer, and he toasted her with the bottle before taking a small sip.

'I've missed you,' he said. 'I don't think I can live without you. I know you said you didn't want to ruin my marriage or come between me and my wife, but... well, these things happen. I want you, Maggie. I can't stop thinking about you.'

Maggie knew then that she had to make a choice. Either ignore her brother's warning, and carry on destroying herself, or choose to embrace the positive aspect of being desired, and finding a new strength through a burgeoning relationship.

'Mike,' she said softly, having made her choice, 'I want you too. I never really wanted for us to split up. If you want to give me a ring tomorrow morning, after I've taken the kids to school...'

Mike's grin widened. 'I'll do that. Maybe I can call round.'

'OK,' she said. 'Though I might have to be here just before lunchtime. Let's see how it goes.'

'I'll drink to that,' he smiled, raising his bottle of Beck's.

Maggie frowned at the allusion to alcohol. She opened the cold cabinet, grabbed a bottle of Perrier, flipped off the top, and clinked bottles with Mike. Already she felt better about herself, thinking positively about what lay ahead in her life.

***

After Simon and Thomas were asleep, Mary sat watching a drama about young homosexuals on BBC2. There was a permanent frown on her face and she wasn't really paying much attention to the programme; but she was distracted from her worrying thoughts when she saw the explicit homosexual love scenes between the leading character in the programme and another attractive young man. She found herself becoming curiously aroused by the scene, and wondered if there was something disturbingly wrong about becoming stimulated by homosexual sex. Then she surrendered to the lubricious enjoyment, knowing that it was because the actors were so good looking. A sex scene between two ugly male actors would have been different.

As she began to relax back into the sofa, her frown softening, a growling engine sound came from the street outside. It sounded like a car that was brash and aggressive, large and flashy, like the American car that Ronnie had driven. Frowning again, she got up off the sofa, and crossed to the window. Holding her breath she tugged the curtain back a foot. There in the shadows opposite the house was Ronnie's Chevrolet Corvette. The engine of the car rumbled and died, and an eerie silence accentuated her fear. Suddenly, from the hall, the telephone rang, piercing and alarming, and she shuddered. Perhaps it was Dave. He had promised to ring as soon as his show had finished. She needed him. God! How she needed him. She would beg him to come home, even if only for the night. She dashed out into the hall and grabbed the phone.

'Darling!' she said with a quick intake of breath, expecting it to be the comforting warmth of her partner's voice, but her expectation turned to ice as she heard the humourless laugh from the other end.

'You haven't called me that in years. Now I know I'm in with a chance.'

'Ronnie!' she said. 'I told you not to call me. It's over between us.'

'Then why did you do that just now?'

In spite of wanting to slam down the phone, her curiosity was aroused, wanting to know what he meant. 'Why did I do what?'

'Give me the signal just now. Pull back the curtain as arranged. Letting me know you were ready for me.'

'I didn't!' Her voice rasped as she tried to stop herself from shouting and screaming, in case she woke the children. 'I heard your car, that was all. I had to see who it was.'

'Could have been any old car. Don't give me that, babe. You were waiting for me. So now I'm here. You going to let me in or not?'

Mary slammed the phone down, ran to the front door and slid the bolt across the top. Then she tore out to the kitchen and tried to do the same with the bolt at the bottom of the door, but the bolt was rusty and hadn't been used in years. It wouldn't budge. Panicking, because she knew Ronnie had somehow managed to enter the house when they were away in Blackpool, Mary dashed back into the hall and dialled the emergency services. She asked for the police, saying she was under attack from an intruder. And then she heard Ronnie's car starting up, and heard it's heavy roaring sound as it drove past the front door. Dazed, she stood listening to it's diminishing roar as it distanced itself from the house.

She stood like a statue, unable to move, numb from the fear of knowing that Ronnie had the upper hand. What could she tell the police when they arrived? And, more to the point, what could they do to stop him?

Tears trickled down her cheeks as she stood helplessly clutching the hall table for support, waiting, growing colder and colder, and more desperate as the minutes ticked by.

Thirty-Nine

As soon as Maggie got home, having dropped the children at school, the telephone rang. It was Mike, talking in hushed tones on his mobile. He hurriedly explained that his wife was suffering from depression, and he was having to accompany her to the doctor's, and couldn't get out of it. Then he hurriedly ended the conversation, saying he would try to call in at the wine bar later that night.

As soon as he had hung up, Maggie felt let down. She had dared to indulge in the luxury of anticipating her ex lover's arrival, and the possibility of some frantic and hurried lovemaking, the sort of forbidden-fruit quickie that is exciting at the beginning of a relationship. Now she felt truly disappointed, especially as she had promised herself that this time their relationship might become deeper, more lasting and committed.

Later in the afternoon, having struggled with her demons while she watched her customers knocking back wine, she succumbed to the temptation to pour herself a large Chardonnay. First she had to get rid of Craig, so she told him to have a few hours deserved break. Glad of the excuse to get away from his sister for a while, and under no illusions why she wanted him out of the way, Craig decided to walk back to his flat in High Brooms and have a relaxing soak in the bath. He met his old employee, Mandy, as he set off up Mount Pleasant.

'Hi, Mandy,' he said, his voice leaping with surprise and pleasure.

She smiled at him, her eyes warm and twinkling as she registered how genuinely delighted he seemed at this chance meeting.

'Hello, Craig. I've missed you these last weeks.'

'Have you?'

She nodded solemnly. 'It's not the same any more. I don't think I'll ever have a boss as good as you was.'

'What's the new owner like?'

'I'm thinking of jacking it in, when I get something better.'

'Why what's wrong?'

'Mario's a sneaky, dirty little git. As soon as his missus ain't around, he comes on really strong.'

Craig laughed.

'It ain't funny. I can't stand him.'

'Sorry,' said Craig, looking suitably contrite. 'It's just I can't imagine it. He's like Danny De Vito. Tiny little runt. I should think you could eat him alive.'

'I ain't that fat, Craig.'

Craig blushed. 'No, I'm sorry. I didn't mean...'

'So how's tricks at the wine bar?' Mandy asked hastily, to save his embarrassment.

'It's doing pretty well. It was a slow start. But now I think we've cracked it.'

'Good. I'm really pleased for you.'

Looking deep into her eyes, Craig believed he could read her thoughts. He was certain he was getting a clear signal that she wanted him; that she was his for the asking. But then Craig always felt insecure where women were concerned, and never made the first move for fear of rejection.

He swallowed noisily, then started to speak. 'I... um...'

Mandy smiled warmly, attracted by what she thought of as his disarming shyness. 'What were you going to say?'

Craig shrugged nonchalantly and looked away from her. 'I've got the rest of the afternoon off. I was just about to wander back to my gaff and have a nice long soak in the bath.'

Mandy waited for him to look at her before she spoke. 'I was just about to do the same thing myself.' She licked her top lip and smiled at him. 'Of course, we could always save on the water.'

An enormous grin spread across Craig's face. 'Especially as there's almost a drought on. Sounds good to me. Wanna come back to my place?'

Mandy quickly slid her hand into Craig's. 'I thought you'd never ask.'

'I was going to walk back. It's a good twenty minute walk.'

'That's OK. It's a nice day.'

'Yeah, but I don't know about you: I'd sooner get there as quick as we can. Let's go back to the station and get a cab.'

She could sense his urgency now as they hurried along towards the taxi rank. She squeezed his hand and smiled knowingly to herself.

***

Ted gazed lovingly at his little bundle in her cot and gently tugged back the sheet to allow her to breathe more freely. He sighed contentedly and gave her his secret smile, reserved for her and no one else. Then a deep frown clouded his expression as he contemplated the name. Tracey. She was definitely not a Tracey. He had set his heart on Portia or Olivia. Lavinia even.

'What are you up to?'

Ted straightened up, like puppet having its strings jerked, and turned around to face Marjorie as she shuffled into the nursery.

'Shh!' Ted put a finger to his lips. 'She's still asleep.'

Marjorie gave him a patronising smile. 'Of course she's asleep. She's been fed. But you can feed her in future.'

Ted looked shocked. 'Me!'

'I don't think I can carry on giving her the breast.'

'But isn't it...' Ted began.

'What?'

'More... well, better for her.'

Marjorie snorted. 'Load of old rubbish. It don't make the slightest bit of difference. My mother was all skin and bone, had no milk to speak of. And she put me on the bottle pretty damn quick. And it didn't do me no harm.'

Ted paused while he thought about a witty rejoinder he might make to this but thought better of it. 'Well, if you're sure,' he said, lamely.

'Of course I'm sure.'

Marjorie suddenly spotted the large soft Donald Duck at the end of the cot. 'What's that?' she demanded in a harsh whisper.

'It's a soft toy.'

'I can see what it is. What's it doing there?'

'I bought it. Babies like cuddly toys.'

'But why Donald Duck?'

Ted shrugged. 'No reason.'

'I mean, why not a teddy bear or a lion or a dog. Why d'you pick Donald Duck?'

'I just thought...' Ted stopped, unable to think of an explanation.

'What?' demanded Marjorie forcefully.

Ted tutted with frustration. 'I saw it I the shop, so I bought it. I don't know why.'

Marjorie's eyes narrowed suspiciously. The doorbell chimed. Relieved, Ted began tip-toeing towards the door.

'No you don't,' whispered Marjorie. 'I'll get it. You go and make up Tracy's feed.'

Ted stopped and frowned. 'How?'

'Everything you need's on the kitchen table. Just follow the instructions. You can't go wrong.'

Forty

At first Marjorie was taken aback when she opened the front door and found Donald, wearing a beatific smile and a twinkle in his eye like a roguish monk. But she recovered quickly when she spotted the enormous bunch of red roses he was carrying, which he suddenly thrust towards her, almost as if they were lovers.

'Oh!' she exclaimed, then noticed the boastfully large Donald Duck he held in his other hand. 'That's strange.'

Donald raised an eyebrow, an expression he had perfected over the years. 'I'm sorry?'

'Ted bought her a Donald Duck as well.' Her eyes narrowed suspiciously. 'And your name's Donald.'

Donald chuckled. 'Two minds but a single thought. I'm her Uncle Donald. Her wicked Uncle Donald.'

'So you're going to be Tracey's uncle, are you?'

'Tracey!' Donald looked ill. 'Is that what you've called her? Tracey?'

'What's wrong with that?'

'Nothing, but I just thought something more suitable for the little angel might be more...'

Marjorie interrupted him. 'You haven't seen her yet.'

'No, but I can imagine how beautiful she must be. Your little treasure.'

'Hmm,' said Marjorie as she sniffed the roses, almost hoping they might bring on a bout of hay fever.

Donald smiled hugely. 'Your Ted's besotted by her.'

'Is he? When did he tell you that?'

Donald shrugged off her questions. 'Can I come in and see her?'

'Marjorie stepped aside reluctantly. 'I suppose so.'

'Thanks,' said Donald, noticing the strong smell of boiled fish and lavender floral air spray as he stepped inside. Marjorie grasped his arm in a claw-like grip as he shut the door.

'What about your friend?'

'Friend?'

'Yeah. The one with the funny name.'

'Oh! Bamber!'

'Yeah. Him.'

Donald laughed uneasily. 'Don't suppose you've ever watched University Challenge?'

'I might have done. A few times. If there was nothing else on. What about it?'

'Bamber's mother named him after the quizmaster. Bamber Gascoine. She was a fan, you see.'

'Oh,' said Marjorie, releasing her grip on Donald's arm. 'And what does he think of all this?'

Donald frowned deliberately. 'Bamber, you mean? I'm not with you.'

'What does he think about you and my husband going out together?'

'He's... er... well, put it this way – Bamber prefers the mind-numbing, mindless thud of rock music to the seductive language of the bard.'

'Seductive?' Marjorie questioned, peering suspiciously at Donald.

'Er, just an expression.'

Ted appeared at the top of the stairs. He blushed when he saw Donald.

'Hello. Ted,' enthused Donald. 'Once again – congratulations!' He waved Donald Duck in the air. 'Look what I've got for... er... Tracey.'

Ted giggled sheepishly. 'I got her one as well.'

173

'Not quite the same,' said Marjorie, sniffing disdainfully. 'Donald's one is much bigger than yours.'

Donald looked down at the floor. He didn't dare catch Ted's eye.

***

Although it was late afternoon, Pran still felt shaky and unsteady on his feet. He didn't have a definable headache, but somewhere inside his head a swarm of something decidedly painful buzzed around in an endless and disturbingly unreal aggravation. When the doorbell rang, he struggled to pull himself into a sitting position on the sofa, fumbled for the remote, and clicked off Deal Or No Deal.

When he eased open his flat door, he was puzzled to discover an extremely attractive mixed-race girl. Not that he was attracted to the opposite sex in any way, shape or form. But he could see she was a lovely looking, with a figure that many women would have died for.

'Mr. Kapoor?' she said.

He nodded, puzzled and unable to comprehend any discernible reason for her visit. Surely the creditors were not on to him already? He was aware that his unemployment was eating into his savings, but as far as he knew he was still afloat.

She gave him a wonderfully warm and gleaming white smile from a perfect set of teeth before she spoke. 'I've tracked you down, from your previous employment. I took over your job after you walked out. And I've had terrible problems with my manager. t was so bad, I took the organisation to an industrial tribunal. I'm taking them to court to try to get compensation. So I'd like to talk to you about the problems you had with her.'

Pran's hangover seemed to vanish instantly. This was the revenge he'd been waiting for, being handed to him on a plate. He grinned at his visitor.

'You'd better come in. I'm happy to talk to anyone who can get even with that bitch.'

Forty-One

'There you go. Tina, isn't it?'

Pran's attractive visitor nodded as he handed her a mug of coffee. She noticed how shaky his hands were, and wondered if he was nervous; but while he'd been out in the kitchen brewing coffee, she had noticed the two empty wine bottles on the coffee table and decided he probably had a hangover.

Pran sat in a chair opposite her, and gave her a shy smile. 'You said you wanted to talk about my experiences in the organisation.'

She blew on her coffee and nodded. 'That's right. I've brought an industrial action against them on grounds of racial discrimination.'

Pran frowned, and his eyes took on a determined steely look. 'It's about time someone did. You know I walked out of the job.'

'Yes, I heard rumours. Then a colleague of yours confirmed it for me.'

'It was stupid of me. Walking out like that. I should have done what you're doing.'

'Maybe you still can.'

Pran shook his head. 'It's probably too late now, but any help I can give you... I mean, I can't tell you how much I regret walking out. The times I've fantasised about getting my own back on them. Revenge would be so sweet. So any help I can give you...'

'Thanks. So what went on must have been pretty extreme, if you just walked out like that.'

'It had been building up from week one. I hated every day I spent in that office. Then all it took was one more remark and I flipped. Lost it completely.'

'Well, I suppose if you'd been subjected to racist comments for six months...'

Pran shook his head emphatically and cut in. 'No, there was only one racist comment. That was when I walked out. That bitch

176

of a manager accused me of having a chip on my shoulder, said it was typical of...' Pran broke off, gestured both palms upwards, offering it to his visitor to guess the rest.

'Of what?' said Tina. 'Ethnic minority people.'

'She didn't actually say it. She stopped herself in time.'

Tina banged her coffee mug onto the table. 'Oh damn! I wonder if a tribunal would interpret the first part of her comment as a racist one she was about to make. I doubt it. She'd just deny that's what she was going to say.' She looked at Pran with a puzzled frown. 'So what was the build up to this incident. What was going on?'

There was a pause while Pran thought about this. 'I'm gay,' he said, watching carefully her reaction. Her expression remained blank.

'And they discriminated against you for it?' she said.

'They didn't know. They thought I was straight. It was the banter and homophobic remarks that got to me. My partner at the time, Alan, was furious I hadn't outed myself. We broke up because of it.'

'So it cost you your job and relationship?'

Pran nodded sombrely. 'At least now I've got the chance to do something positive. Help with your case.'

'But if you're going to tell the tribunal about all the inappropriate remarks and behaviour, you might have to admit...' She stopped herself, and let Pran pick up the cue.

'That I'm gay. Yes, I'd thought about that.'

'But if you couldn't say so at the time...'

Pran shrugged. 'Why now, you mean? I suppose it's because I've no more pride left. I've nothing to lose.'

'But these things can sometimes snowball, you know. Make headlines.'

Pran stared down into his coffee cup and muttered: 'That's the one part that bothers me. If it becomes public, my parents...'

Tina leaned forward, looking concerned. 'Don't they know?'

'I think it would destroy my father, if he knew.'

'Oh my God! Nothing's worth that risk.'

Pran looked up, staring across at her, fire in his eyes.

'Yes, it is. I'll do it. I'm not going to end up like my sister, denying my true feelings. If my father has a problem with my sexuality – then tough! I'm not going to hide. Not anymore.'

***

When Craig arrived back at the wine bar in the early evening, Maggie couldn't help but notice how relaxed and happy he looked, even though he seemed remote, lost in his secret thoughts. He didn't even nag her about the large white wine she was drinking.

'It's amazing,' she said, 'what difference a few hours break and a nice long soak in the bath can make.'

He grinned, poured himself a red wine, and clinked glasses with her. 'Cheers! If you can't beat 'em.'

Maggie frowned thoughtfully and stared at her brother. Never had she seen such a rapid change in him before. He had gone off after the afternoon session looking moody and irritable, and now he was like another person.

'Did you meet anyone while you were out?' she asked lightly.

'I think I've sorted out our staff problems.'

'How d'you mean?'

'Remember Mandy, used to work for me at the chippie?'

'Vaguely.'

'I bumped into her on the way home. She's still there, working for the new owner. You know, that little toe-rag you couldn't stand.'

'At least he made us an offer we didn't refuse.'

'Yeah, well, Mandy ain't too happy working for him.'

Maggie slammed her glass onto the bar. Several customers looked round. Maggie leaned close to Craig and spoke through gritted teeth. 'You haven't offered her a job, have you?'

Craig was startled by her sudden vehemence. 'What's wrong with that?'

'Oh, Craig!'

'So what's wrong with Mandy? It saves us having to advertise.'

'I just wish you'd consulted me first.'

'I thought you'd be pleased.'

Maggie pulled a face. 'Oh, I'm delighted.'

Craig's jaw tightened. 'D'you mind telling me what you've got against Mandy?'

'I've got nothing against her personally; I hardly know her. I just don't think she's right for this type of wine bar, that's all.'

'I don't believe I'm hearing this.'

'I just think we ought to keep our options open, Craig. You can't just go around offering jobs to anyone you happen to bump into in the street. It's unprofessional.'

'I haven't offered it to her. I just said there was a good chance of a job. And she's coming to see us on Monday morning.'

'Well that's something, I suppose. I only hope she doesn't think it's a foregone conclusion. I think we ought to see a few more applicants first.'

Craig shook his head with irritation. 'We haven't got any.'

'We were planning to advertise. I still think we ought to.'

Craig's voice rose a trace. 'Why waste the money? Mandy's a good little worker.'

Maggie looked long and hard into her brother's eyes. 'Are you and this Mandy... have you got a thing going for her.'

Craig shrugged and looked down into his glass. 'Well...'

Maggie sighed loudly. 'Oh, Craig! That is definitely not a good idea to employ someone who...' She left the sentence pointedly incomplete.

Craig could feel tears of disappointment pricking the back of his eyes. 'Well at least give her a chance.'

Maggie suddenly felt guilty, and squeezed his hand. 'OK. We'll see her Monday. And who knows? It might work out.

Let's wait and see.'

***

Mary had just tucked Simon and Thomas in for the night, and was coming out onto the landing, when she heard the letter box opening and something landing on the doormat. She frowned. It was a bit late for one of the free papers to be delivered.

From the top of the stairs she saw the A4 brown envelope lying on the mat, and right away she had a bad feeling about it. She hurried downstairs and picked it up. There was nothing written on the envelope. She went into the kitchen and tore it open. Inside was a photograph of her in the bedroom wearing nothing but bra and panties. Something screamed inside her brain as panic seized her. She dropped the photograph onto the table and rushed upstairs to the bedroom. She looked on top of the wardrobe, tried to find anywhere there might be a hidden camera, as she thought about the angle of the picture, but she found nothing.

In the street outside, several hundred yards away from the house, Ronnie sat in his car. So far so good. Everything was going according to plan. He had broken into the house the night before, removed the camera, then left leaving no traces. He loved these sorts of mind games, knowing how much it would unsettle her.

Tomorrow he would activate the next part of his plan. Then soon she would be his again.

Forty-Two

Mike stood at the cash machine waiting for his money to be dispensed, all the time thinking about another visit to Maggie's wine bar, to see if he could persuade her to meet him again. He regretted having had to postpone their last assignation and only hoped she wouldn't change her mind about becoming his lover once again.

He stuffed the dispensed hundred pounds into his wallet, waited for his receipt, then grabbed it and walked along the High Street towards the wine bar. He glanced down at the receipt, and what he saw made him stop in his tracks. The account should have been in credit, at least to the tune of fifteen hundred pounds. Instead, it was overdrawn by over two hundred. Well within their agreed overdraft limit, but still overdrawn when it should have been in credit. What was going on?

He hesitated, dying to pay Maggie another visit, but now he needed to know why he and Claire's account was overdrawn. Had she taken a great deal of money out of the account, and for what purpose? Reluctantly, he turned away from Maggie's wine bar, and began walking in the direction of home, intent on finding out what had happened to the money in the account. Their joint account. As he strode purposefully up Mount Pleasant, breathing heavily from the exertion, he cursed the day he had agreed they should have a joint bank account.

***

The photograph of Mary had been printed on ordinary copying paper, obviously printed off from a computer. She stood over the kitchen sink, held the match under the picture, and watched as it caught fire, curling slowly at the edges, until the flame

swept upwards and destroyed her image. She let it fall into the sink, then ran the tap to wash away the ashes, so that there was nothing left of the remains. It was gone.

When she first saw the photograph, she felt dirty, even though she hadn't posed for it. It was the creeping feeling of being watched she couldn't take. It made her flesh creep. Ronnie watching her. But from where? She'd checked the bedroom thoroughly and could find no hidden cameras. And that was when it occurred to her that he'd been in the house again, just like the time he'd left the cassette tape behind. Deliberately letting her know that he could come and go as he liked; and she knew that if she had the locks changed it wouldn't do any good. Ronnie would find another way to get at her. He was that sort of man. Manipulative. Evil. He liked to play games. Nasty, evil games.

She stared down into the sink, feeling slightly better now that the photograph had vanished. Cleansed by fire. If only she could find out where Ronnie lived. Get a can of petrol while he was asleep. Set fire to his house or flat, then watch while the flames wiped him out of her life for good. Then she would feel truly cleansed.

She looked at the kitchen clock. It was ten-fifteen. She wanted to phone Dave, and tell him what was going on, but she knew that if she stood in the hall using the landline, and began raising her voice, she would probably wake Simon and Thomas. That's if they were asleep. She certainly didn't want to worry them. Her handbag was on the kitchen table, so she took out her mobile and dialled Dave's number.

'Hello, sweetheart,' he said when she made the connection. 'I'm in a noisy pub. I'll just walk outside.'

She could hear music and laughter in the background, then a whoosh of sound like air escaping, and some cars hooting and traffic noises.

'That's better,' Dave shouted. 'Marginally. I miss you, Mary.'

'Dave,' she said, 'he's been in here again.'

'Who?'

'Who d'you think? Ronnie of course.' She told him about the photograph, and how she couldn't find a camera in the bedroom.

After a brief pause, he said, 'First thing tomorrow, get along to Tonbridge Police Station. You've got the evidence to nail the bastard.'

'What evidence?'

'The photo.'

Tears swam into her eyes as she said, 'I burnt it.'

'What!'

'I couldn't stand the thought of him watching me like that. I had to destroy it.'

'You idiot! That's the first thing the police are going to ask for.'

'Dave!' she cried. 'Please come home.'

A brief pause before he answered. 'You know that's out of the question.'

'I need you, Dave.'

A tired, overly patient voice. 'You know I can't. I can't break my contract. We've been through all this.'

She sobbed openly, letting him know how distraught she was. It was intended to make him feel sorry for her, enough perhaps to make him leave Blackpool and rush back to her side. Instead, it had the opposite effect. A remote, coldness crept into his tone.

'Mary, I have to go. And I don't know how much help I could be even if I was back in Tunbridge Wells. It's the police that need to deal with this.'

'I know,' she cried, 'but I need your support. I can't handle this on my own.'

'Sweetheart, listen, my battery's almost run out. Any minute now. That's why I said I had to go. Get along to the cop shop first thing tomorrow, and I'll give you a call once my battery's been recharged. Then we'll see about...'

He deliberately clicked the cancel on his mobile, then switched it off. He hated doing it, and lying about his battery, but what could he do? His hands were tied. Why couldn't she realise: a contract is a contract. And besides, domestic issues shouldn't interfere with work.

He went back into the pub and joined his colleagues.

***

Claire gave Mike a warm smile as he came into the kitchen, went over and kissed him on the lips, then stood back and examined the fierce expression on his face.

'What's wrong? I thought it was quiz night at the White Hart tonight. I wasn't expecting you to stagger back until almost midnight.'

'I needed some cash, so I went to the hole in the wall and drew some out. When I got my receipt, it said we were two hundred pounds overdrawn.'

Claire frowned and nodded. 'I was going to tell you, but...'

'But it slipped your mind? How can seventeen hundred disappear from our account?'

Claire did her best to look contrite as she slid into a chair by the kitchen table, but she seemed infuriatingly calm. Content almost.

'I think you'd better sit down, Mike, while I explain.'

He sat opposite her, staring hard, trying to catch her eye, but she avoided prolonged eye contact, almost as if she couldn't stand his piercing, probing look.

'As you can see, I've been making progress over the last couple of weeks. And I'm over the depression.'

'Are you trying to tell me you've been paying some psychiatrist privately for a cure.'

'Not a shrink – no way. Psychiatric practices are detrimental to an individual's health.'

'Since when?'

'Since I saw the light.'

Mike frowned deeply. 'Saw the light! What sort of mumbo-jumbo are you into?'

Claire smiled beatifically. 'You know that American friend of mine. Lucy. Well, she's helped me out enormously. No more depression. I feel great, Mike. And I've recognised my potential and turned all my negatives into positives.'

'Just what has she done that's cost us a five figure sum?'

'Don't think of it in terms of money. She's brought me onto the path of enlightenment.'

Mike's voice rose angrily. 'Don't give me that shit? What's happened?'

There was a pause while she calmly examined a cuticle. Then she said: 'I've joined the Church of Scientology.'

Forty-Three

Maggie stared at Mandy, trying hard not to look her up and down. 'We have got one or two other people to see,' she said. 'So we'll contact you one way or the other very soon. OK, Mandy?'

It was said dismissively. Mandy looked at Craig for reassurance, but he was embarrassed and was staring out of the wine bar window. Maybe he'd changed his mind about offering her the job and didn't know how to tell her.

Maggie stood up abruptly, bringing the interview to an end. 'So if you'll excuse us, we've got a busy lunchtime ahead.'

'Er, yeah, fine,' Mandy mumbled, colouring slightly as she rose from the table. She felt depressed, and suddenly nauseous, as if she was losing control physically. The disappointment had proved too much for her. Craig had promised. The job was hers, he'd said. But the job interview with his sister had seemed so formal.

Craig walked with her to the door, unlocked it, and let her out into the street. 'I'll give you a bell later,' he said with exaggerated sweetness and winked at her.

The door clicked shut and Mandy found herself walking in a daze towards Mount Pleasant, confused and miserable. Just days ago she and Craig had made frenzied, desperate love together before lying, nakedly entwined, lost in each other's hopes and promises. How false those promises seemed now.

***

Mary looked at the kitchen clock and panicked. 'Hurry up, Thomas! You're going to be late for school.'

He slurped the dregs of milk from the bottom of his cereal bowl. Mary sighed with frustration and raised her voice. 'How many times have I got to tell you? Do not drink from the bowl like that.'

Thomas, who had heard this many times before, grinned at his mother and wiped the back of his hand across his mouth.

'He does it to wind you up,' said Simon, sounding wearily grown up.

The doorbell rang. 'Blast!' said Mary. 'Come on, you two. It's probably the postman.'

They hurried down the hall, and Mary threw open the door. The postman held a registered packet out. Mary frowned with confusion. The packet looked reasonably bulky, so she didn't think it could be a bill. And it was addressed to her and not Dave.

She stared at it, making no move to take it from the postman.

'What is it?' asked Simon.

'How should I know?'

'Registered packet,' the postman informed her in a tired, even tone. 'I'll need a signature.'

Reluctantly, and suspiciously, she accepted the letter and signed for it. She ignored the postman as he made a glib remark about the hot weather, before hurrying towards the house next door.

Mary stared at the letter. 'I wonder what it is?'

Simon laughed. 'You only have to open it to find out.'

She tore open the seal, and her heart jumped as she spotted the edge of a bundle of paper nestling in the darkness of the envelope. It looked like a wad of money. She slipped her hand inside and drew it out. It was money alright. A large bundle of twenty pound notes, crisp and new.

'Wow!' said Thomas. 'That looks like a lot of money. Who's sending us that?'

Simon was scowling suspiciously. He had been through too many hard times and hard knocks to appreciate that something for nothing always comes with a price to pay.

There was a note with the money. Mary frowned as she read it. The note was handwritten in a scrawl she recognised from years ago.

Hi Babe. Thanks for the photo which I will cherish. All I wanted was a little souvenir. And I don't take liberties. I pay for what I want. So this is yours to enjoy. Be seeing you.

Ronnie.

'Who's sending us that money?' said Simon.

'Your father.'

'You're not going to take it, are you?'

Thomas's mouth fell open, almost a parody of shock. 'We can't give it back. We can't, Mum. We can't.'

Simon, who had developed a cynicism that far outstripped his years, said, 'She will. I know her.'

Mary was jolted from the sudden shock of the dichotomy of good fortune and bad news. 'Come on,' she said. 'You'll be late for school.'

As they hurried along the street, Thomas kept pestering her by asking if they were going to keep the money. Every time he asked her, she always gave him the stock response.

'We'll see.'

Forty-Four

After the hectic lunchtime session, Maggie paused behind the bar and poured herself a large Chardonnay. She made a show of huffing noisily at a wisp of hair trailing across her forehead. As he cleared tables, Craig glanced disapprovingly in her direction.

'You still sulking?' Maggie said as he placed a row of dirty glasses on the counter.

'At least Mandy don't drink,' he replied, his jaw tight with suppressed anger.

'Well bully for her!'

'I still don't see what you've got against her.'

'Nothing personal.'

'So what's the problem?'

Maggie shrugged irritatingly and took a sip of wine.

'Well?' Craig demanded, his eyes boring into hers.

'If you've got something going with this girl,' Maggie said, 'I don't think a boss employee relationship would work.'

'Why not? What about you and Gary? You were a husband and wife running a business, like thousands of other couples do.'

'Yeah, and Gary and me were always at each other's throat. Anyway, you're talking about a family run business. That's different.'

Craig gave her a lopsided, ironic smile. 'Yeah, you can say that again. It's worse. A lot worse.'

Maggie turned away impatiently. 'Just because you can't get your own way, little brother.'

'It's not a question of getting my own way.'

Maggie spun back to face him. 'Shh! Keep your voice down.'

'I'm sorry. It's just that...' Craig stopped and waved his hands helplessly in front of his sister. He looked lost, reminding her of a time when he was very young and had come off his bike and hurt himself badly. She remembered him staggering towards her, blubbering incoherently for help.

'Look, Craig,' she began, 'if you promise there won't be any lovers' tiffs...'

It took a moment to sink in, then Craig's eyes gleamed with sudden brightness. 'If she gets out of hand,' he laughed, and jerked a thumb in the direction of the street.

'As long as both of you don't bring your problems into the wine bar.'

Craig grinned at her and shook his head. 'Everything'll be hunky-dory. I promise.'

Maggie glanced at her watch. 'And you can do me a favour in return. There's a semi-final tonight. Germany versus Italy. So we'll be quiet I reckon. Would you mind if I take the night off?'

Smiling, Craig came around behind the bar. 'Sure. No problem, Maggs. Off out anywhere?

Maggie stared at her wine glass intently. 'Oh, a bit tired. Just thought I'd have a quiet night.'

Something about his sister's tone made Craig think that she was lying, but as he picked up the telephone behind the bar, he dismissed it.

'Who you phoning?' said Maggie. 'As if I couldn't guess.'

Craig grinned. 'Well, I don't want to keep her in suspense.' He finished dialling and threw his sister a look. 'Thanks, Maggs.'

Maggie nodded and took a large swallow of wine, then frowned thoughtfully. Must get Mandy to dress a bit better, she thought. She's got the worst dress sense of any girl I've ever seen.

***

The wad of money was stacked in a neat pile on the kitchen table in front of Mary, taunting her. Five hundred pounds! More money than she'd seen in years. It would make next week's Family Allowance look pathetic.

'Yes, but what are we going to do with it?' Thomas demanded for the umpteenth time.

Mary shook her head and blew on her tea. A cunning expression crept across Thomas's face.

'What's for tea, Mum?'

Mary shrugged and shook her head wistfully. 'Nothing very exciting. Just some cheese on toast and baked beans.'

A slight pause, allowing Thomas time to drive home his idea. 'I suppose we could always go out somewhere. That Chinese place where you can eat as much as you like. We could use some of that money.'

Simon glared at him and slammed down his can of Pepsi Max. 'I think we ought to give that money back.'

'Why?'

'Because it's our father's money. And he's a bastard.'

'Simon!' Mary cautioned.

'Well, it's true. So send it back to him.'

But Mary was already imagining the little luxuries the money could provide. All day the temptation to spend had been wearing, and avoiding the temptation seemed irritatingly priggish, as if she was some sort of religious fanatic, one of those goody-goodies who frown upon pleasure.

She looked Simon in the eyes and mustered up a rational reason to spend the errant father's money. 'Simon, I'd love to be able to send this money back, but how can I? I've no idea where he lives. None at all. Besides, when he left us and buggered off to America, we were entitled to some family maintenance payments. If he'd been in this country, the Child Support Agency would have chased him for money. Money to which we were entitled.'

Simon's eyes narrowed shrewdly. 'You've already made up your mind, haven't you?'

Mary rose with deliberation and her chair scraped back nosily. 'We can't send this money back, so that settles it.'

Simon scowled. 'What you gonna do?'

'We're going to have some fun for a change. We're going on a spending spree. We deserve it.'

Thomas stood up hurriedly, punched the air triumphantly, and gave a great whoop of joy.

***

Mike had spent much of the day pub crawling. He had telephoned most of his clients and postponed the appointments. He just couldn't face it after what had happened. In the late afternoon, he ventured home. It was a hot day and he needed to shower and change before going out to meet Maggie. And he needed a few alcohol free hours. He expected to find Claire home, and was prepared for sullen silences or raging arguments, but the house was empty. He was relieved. He needed to cheer himself up, put on a good mood to meet his old lover and rekindle their relationship.

He had arranged to meet her at seven-thirty in the Beau Nash, then he planned to take her to Thackeray's for a meal. It would be costly, but spending that much money on another woman was revenge, and he felt it was just what his wife deserved. Except she wouldn't know about it, which tended to take the edge off it.

He arrived at the Beau Nash fifteen minutes early, and was surprised to find Maggie had already arrived, and was halfway through a large white wine. Mike smiled and pointed at her glass.

'Another of those?'

She shook her head emphatically. 'I'd better not. I'll have a small one.'

But as Mike turned away to fetch the drinks, she called after him, 'Oh go on! You've twisted my arm. Make it a large one.'

When Mike returned with her wine, and a pint of lager for himself, they clinked glasses.

'So what's on the agenda?' she asked.

'I thought we'd have dinner at Thackeray's.'

She whistled. 'You're pushing the boat out.'

He grinned at her, then suddenly looked serious. 'When we were lovers, you ended our relationship because you didn't want to split up a marriage.'

She smiled. 'You believe in cutting the small talk and getting straight to the point, don't you?'

'I just want you to know, that I'm splitting up with Claire, and it has nothing to do with you. So now we're both free, and hopefully can start all over again. That's if you want to.'

She frowned. 'But why ...I mean, how come you're leaving your wife?'

'She's become a Scientologist. We had a screaming great row about it last night. She's taken a load of money from our account and given it to those wankers. And all she does is talk bullshit and gobbledegook. And it's ironic, isn't it: I thought I'd lose my wife by going with another woman. Instead, I've lost her because of a pseudo religious cult. I just don't know what to do. If I go back home, we'll just have another screaming row about it. I think I might have to move out and get a flat.'

Maggie leaned across the table and slipped her hand over his. 'And what about tonight?'

'Tonight?'

'Yes, you'll need a place to stay tonight. You can stay with me if you like.'

'What about your kids?'

She gave Mike a big smile. 'I think they need to meet you. Especially if you're going to be a fixture.'

He grinned back at her, and they clinked glasses again. As he looked into her eyes, he thought he saw them twinkle in a watery sort of way. It was either the love light or the wine. Or maybe a bit of both.

Forty-Five

The following day, while the children were at school, Mary went to the Royal Victoria Place and indulged in another shopping expedition. And it was a luxury to come back in a taxi instead of the bus. As soon as she got indoors, she unloaded the shopping, a new pair of shorts and T-shirt for herself, jeans, shorts, and t-shirts for the boys, and some luxury food items and wine from Marks and Spencer's. She had just managed to stack the food in the refrigerator when the telephone rang. She froze. Crashing back to reality.

What if it was Ronnie ringing? Payback time.

She went out into the hall, took a deep and tremulous breath, then picked the receiver up gingerly. It was Dave.

'Hello, sweetheart. It's me.'

Mary let her breath out slowly. 'Hello, Dave.' Her voice was flat, unemotional.

'Has he been in touch again?'

'Well, sort of.'

'What d'you mean: "Sort of"?'

She cleared her throat softly before telling him about the money, her voice full of guilt. He reacted in exactly the way she expected.

'You did what?!'

Her voice became thin. 'What else could I do?'

'You could have done what I told you to do in the first place. You could have gone to the police.'

'But what about the money?'

'You should have given it to them. Told them you didn't want it.'

She laughed dryly. 'Oh yes, and that would have ended up in the Police Benevolent Fund, I suppose.'

Dave exhaled loudly and disapprovingly. 'Don't you see what you've done, you little idiot. You've played into his hands. Done exactly what he wanted you to do. You've accepted his money. He wants to own you. And he's buying you.'

***

As soon as Maggie returned from dropping the children at school, she found Mike sitting on the patio outside the through lounge, sipping tea.

'You want some breakfast?' she asked.

'Never touch the stuff.'

Her voice rose in surprise. 'You never eat breakfast?'

'I can never face eating at this time of day.'

'How can you go to work... I mean, how d'you manage to get enough energy to get you through the morning?'

He pouted and shrugged. 'Cutting hair's not exactly energetic.'

'Even so,' she said, and slumped into a garden chair next to him. She took his hand and smiled. 'The kids seemed to just accept you. Which is a good start. So where do we go from here, Mike?'

'How d'you mean?'

'Have you made up your mind, about splitting up with your wife?'

Mike nodded gravely and thought about it. 'Definitely,' he said after a long pause.

'You know, you're welcome to move in with me, don't you?'

'I know. But I'm not looking forward to the scene that'll erupt when I tell Claire. I wish there was another way.'

Maggie shook her head forcefully. 'No. You're going to have to tell her. Trouble is, if you tell her about me, she's going to know that we had an affair in the past; that it's not just something to do with her crazy religious streak.'

'And that's what worries me. It would have been easier if I let her think that she was the one to blame, because of this Scientology crap.'

'If only life were that straightforward.'

Mike sighed and glanced at his watch. 'Much as I'd like to sit here with you, sunning myself, I've got a lot of work on this morning.'

Maggie smiled. 'You'd better get snipping then. Will I see you later?'

'Try and stop me.'

He kissed her lingeringly on the lips, gave her a cursory wave, then left via the side gate. She leaned back in her chair, enjoying the early warmth of the sun on her face as she heard his car start up. Everything felt sunny and fresh, and she could smell the faint trace of coffee from Mike's abandoned mug. After a while, she started thinking about the white wine they had opened the previous night when they returned from dinner at Thackeray's. There was still a quarter bottle left; and she'd been up a good couple of hours getting the kids ready for school; and it was such a glorious day; and she wasn't in the mood for another hot drink. So why shouldn't she pour herself just one glass of white wine?

To hell with it! Why not?

She went into the kitchen and poured herself a large glass, then returned to sit on the patio, closed her eyes peacefully, while she sipped her wine.

Two and a half hours later, across the other side of Tunbridge Wells, Mike felt hot and thirsty, and had a half hour to kill before his next client. So he dropped into the Cross Keys and had a pint of lager. He knew he'd have been better off eating something, but as it was such a glorious day, somehow a pint of lager seemed a harmless pleasure. Besides, he was still feeling the effects of the previous night's carousing with Maggie, followed by lovemaking which hadn't been exactly stunning. Maggie had had so much to drink, she climaxed in less than half a minute, then fell asleep, leaving him feeling uncomfortably affected. As he rolled off her and drifted to sleep, he couldn't resist smiling at the gender role reversal. It was men who were supposed to suffer from premature ejaculation.

Forty-Six

Craig Wanted Mandy to start work at the wine bar that same evening, but Mandy told him she'd had a word with her employer, Mario, who was insisting on a month's notice. Craig went round to see Mario.

'Hi!' the chip shop owner greeted Craig, feigning surprise. 'To what do I owe this visit?'

'You know bloody well why I'm here, Mario,' said Craig. 'It's about Mandy.'

Mario frowned and shrugged elaborately. 'What about her?'

'She ain't working for you no more. As and from today.'

Mario waved a stubby finger back and forth like a metronome. 'No way, Mr. Thomas. No way.'

'What d'you mean, "no way"?'

'Like I say to Mandy, the law's the law. There are regulations. You can't walk out. Not like that.'

'Mandy can. Just watch her.'

Mario glanced down into a fresh batch of batter he was preparing, and cleared his throat nosily and swallowed. Craig felt like smacking the chip shop owner but controlled himself, although he could feel the blood rise in his neck with every moment that passed.

'See,' began Mario, pursing his lips and shaking his head, 'Mandy's not part time.'

'So?' snapped Craig.

'She's a full-time employee. So she has to give proper notice. One month. Minimum.'

Craig shook his head. 'Not Mandy. I'm sure you'll make an exception in her case and bend the rules.'

Mario gave an explosive laugh. 'Make an exception? Why should I do that? Hmm?' He pointed threateningly at Craig. 'You can't go around stealing staff like that.'

'Oh come on, Mario. Stick a notice in the window and you'll fill her place in no time.'

'It's not convenient. She walks out of this job and – let me tell you – no wages for this week. No, sir.'

Craig smiled confidently as he thought about his trump card. 'You'd better pay her the money she's owed for this week. You don't want to make things difficult for yourself.'

'Me!' said Mario, thumping his chest with two fingers. 'Why should I make it difficult for myself? I have the law on my side. You can't just walk out of a job. And if she does, not only will she get no pay for this week, she'll get a solicitor's letter. I want recompense. Consequential loss. You see, I know about the law.'

'Good,' said Craig, his eyes glinting with anticipated triumph. 'So you'll know about sexual harassment in the workplace.'

Not a muscle moved in Mario's face. After a brief pause, Craig saw his Adam's-apple moving as he swallowed.

'I don't know what you're talking about.'

'Don't you? Then let me spell it out for you. Mandy's told me all about the way you try to touch her up in the back room. So if you wanna make a song and dance about her leaving...'

Mario smiled, almost a sneer, dropped his voice and leaned closer to Craig, trying to convey a worldly, lad-to-lad camaraderie, even though he was old enough to be Mandy's father. 'It was only a bit of friendly... you know.'

'Oh, I know,' said Craig, nodding seriously. 'In fact I know what your missus'd make of it. And these things can get blown up out of all proportion. Before you know it: wallop! It's hit the front pages and your life's in ruins.'

'You're bluffing.'

'Am I? Just try me.'

Mario stared into Craig's eyes for a moment, then looked away. He pursed his lips and shrugged, conceding defeat.

'Ok. Mandy won't be back no more. Fair enough.'

'And what about her wages for this week?'

Mario, seeing himself as the injured party, suddenly thumped the counter, making the salt and vinegar jump. 'Don't push it, Mr. Thomas. Don't push it.'

Craig moved closer to the counter and leaned menacingly towards Mario. 'I'll take her wages now. In cash.'

Mario stepped back nimbly, out of head butt reach.

'What makes you think...' he began.

Craig interrupted him. 'And if the sexual harassment charge makes headlines, think of your children. Their friends at school will have a laugh. You know what kids are like. They can be vicious. So what's it to be, Mario? After all, she's worked for that money. She's entitled to it.'

Mario thought it over for a moment, then opened the till and took out seven ten pound notes. He slammed them on the counter and sighed loudly..

'That's all there is in cash.'

Craig put on his hardest expression and put out the flat of his hand. 'There's another four tens missing.'

Mario fumbled in his back pocket. Craig noticed his hand was shaking. He brought out his wallet and handed over two twenties.

'That's it!' he said with finality.

Craig grinned as he picked up the money. On his way out, he turned at the door and pointed to the sad display of pies and wrinkled sausages.

'If you want my advice, Mario, change your cooking oil regularly. You're letting this business down.'

Forty-Seven

Pran was on his second cappuccino in Café Nero when Alan showed up. His ex partner gave him a cursory nod, deliberately keeping his expression blank, which gave him a severe look. Pran watched as Alan joined the queue to buy himself a coffee, and thought about the phone call he'd made two days ago. He'd told Alan he just wanted to be friends, meet up occasionally, maybe go to the pictures now and again. Which wasn't strictly true. He wanted more than just friendship, but that would have to do for now.

Alan got his coffee and came over to where Pran was sitting. There was a slightly awkward silence between them, until Pran cleared his throat before asking:

'So how've you been?'

'It's been hectic lately.'

'And what about the promotion?'

Alan smiled softly, looking deep into Pran's eyes. 'You are looking at middle management now.'

Pran felt a twinge of jealousy, which he managed to disguise with a weak smile. 'Congratulations! No more hands on nursing.'

Alan stared harshly at him, and his tone became defensive. 'Pran it isn't like that. I can't help being ambitious. Jesus! I hope this meeting isn't so you can have another go at me.'

Pran shook his head hastily. 'No, look! I didn't mean anything by it. I'm glad you got your promotion. I really am.'

Alan stared at him for a while, trying to ascertain whether or not he was being genuine. Eventually he nodded slowly, as if accepting Pran's word as the truth.

'So? Any work?'

Pran knew he had to lie about this, and lie about it convincingly. 'I start next week. At Morrisons. On the checkout. It'll be pretty boring, but at least it's a start.'

There was another awkward silence. They both sipped coffee. Pran was the first to break the silence, putting optimism into his tone. 'I've moved now.'

'Where to?'

'Next door to the old flat. Same landlord, but it's smaller and cheaper. Listen, if you fancy coming back...'

Alan shook his head. 'I'm sorry, Pran. I've met someone else.'

Pran slammed his coffee mug down, and frowned as he stared into Alan's eyes. 'Oh, right. But why...'

Impatiently, Alan interrupted him. 'Did I agree to meet you? From your phone call, I thought you wanted us to be friends. You said: no strings.'

Pran could feel himself on the edge of tears. His voice became small and remote. 'Yes, I know, but –'

'But you haven't moved on, Pran.'

'Look, I know I behaved stupidly...'

Alan glared at him across the table, dropping his voice to a whisper. 'It's in the past, Pran. We had great times, but it's history. Don't let's airbrush them with bitterness. Let's at least think of those times with love and affection.'

'So who's this... No, I don't want to know. Don't tell me anything about him. But I hope you'll both be very happy.'

Alan sighed. 'Don't be bitter.'

'I'm not.'

'It sounded that way.'

'I'm sorry. I didn't mean it that way. I just want you to be happy.' Pran smiled broadly, attempting to show that he meant it. He wanted to keep his ex partner sitting across from him as long as possible, but he could feel himself running out of conversation. 'Actually, I've been keeping up tradition. You know how we always went to the cinema – at least once a week. I've seen quite a few films lately. I saw a good French movie at Trinity. The Beat That My Heart Skipped. Have you seen it?'

'No, I went with Lance to see Superman Returns. It was good.'

Pran frowned. 'Lance?'

'He's American.'

Avoiding Alan's eyes, Pran stared into his coffee. His voice was tiny when he spoke. 'But you always used to say, America, and it's foreign policy, and its imperialistic...'

Impatiently and a touch angrily, Alan scraped his chair back from the table. 'Yeah, well that's got nothing to do with, Lance, has it? He's a lovely guy. I've got to be off.'

Pran looked up. 'Will I see you again?'

Alan shook his head. 'Maybe it's not such a good idea. 'Bye, Pran.'

Pran watched as Alan turned and walked away without looking back. He sighed and looked around the coffee bar. Two young girls, possibly in their late teens, were throwing him glances and giggling. He felt exposed and annoyed. Then he remembered that's what he and Alan used to do. Sit and observe other couples in pubs and restaurants, and make up stories about them.

He stared at the girls and they looked away, embarrassed. He checked the time. It was still quite early in the day, and he'd been trying to lay off alcohol at least until the evening. But what the hell! He felt he deserved a session on the booze after what he'd been through with Alan.

He left Café Nero and walked towards Wetherspoon's, where he intended getting inebriated. Yet again.

***

Mike knew he had to tell Andrew about leaving home and moving in with Maggie, but he was dreading it. He had debated with his conscience over who he should tell first: his wife or son. Not that it made that much difference, he decided. The end result was the same. And now that Claire had found her new religion, her alternative mumbo- jumbo lifestyle, he thought with bitterness, she was hardly ever around. So why shouldn't he tell his son first?

Andrew was sitting at the kitchen table, eating a bowl of cornflakes.

'Breakfast?' Mike asked, looking pointedly at his watch.

Andrew looked at him as if he was mad. 'It's four in the afternoon, Dad.'

'I know,' said Mike weakly, pointing at the bowl. 'But cornflakes.' He realised he was making small talk just to put off the dreadful moment. He was glad he'd had four pints of Stella. At least it would give him some Dutch courage.

'I just felt hungry and fancied a bowl of cornflakes. All right?'

Mike nodded. 'Actually, Andy, I wanted a word.'

'And I wanted a word with you, Dad.'

Mike was momentarily thrown. 'Er – with me? What about?'

'I'm leaving home for a while.'

'You what?'

'Me an' some mates are popping over to Ireland for a while.'

'Ireland!'

'Yeah, you know,' said Andrew, jerking a thumb over his shoulder. 'Big green country in the west.'

Mike let his Gladstone bag drop onto the floor, and sank into a kitchen chair opposite his son.

'I know where it is, Andy. So what's this in aid of?'

Andrew shrugged, pursing his lips. 'We just fancy trying our luck in Dublin.'

'Doing what?'

'It's a really wicked scene over there. It's the place to be.'

'Dublin. That's news to me.'

Mike stared at Andrew and shook his head disapprovingly.

Andrew pushed his bowl away with a clatter. 'I didn't think you'd understand.'

A key rattled in the front door, followed by several female voices, excited and breathless, all talking at once. Mike exchanged a look with Andrew, and they both waited for the women to arrive in the kitchen.

'In you go,' said Claire as she swung open the door, standing aside to usher in two women. The woman who entered was an attractive redhead. She beamed confidently at Mike, and also cast a glance at Andrew. She was dressed in white trousers and a tight white sleeveless shirt. She waved a circular open palm at Mike and Andrew and spoke in an American accent.

'Hi, guys. I'm, Lucy.'

Mike could feel anger welling inside him. 'Oh. You must be this other Ron Hubbard follower.'

Claire pushed forward a young blonde girl, probably in her late twenties, Mike decided. She wore a short skirt and had terrific legs, but her nose was hawk-like and her eyes were too close together. She moved timidly, and stepped daintily, as if she was frightened of walking on something fragile.

Mike deliberately let out a beery belch. 'And you must be Ron himself.'

Claire glared at him. 'This is Japonica.'

Mike laughed and put on a posh, twee voice. 'Japonica! A nice moniker for someone who believes all this new age mumbo-jumbo.'

Claire's voice was sharp and brittle. 'Mike! These are my friends. So try and behave with a little....'

Mike stood up, glaring at the two women, who had shrunk back into themselves.

'Well, I'm off out. So's Andy. He's leaving for pastures new. As am I. I've had it up to here. I shall just pack a few things tonight, and I'll be back for the rest of my things tomorrow.'

He swept out of the house, permitting himself a smile at the stunned silence he had created followed him all along the front path to the gate.

Forty-Eight

The line crackled when Mary answered the telephone and her own voice sounded peculiar, as if in an echo chamber.

'Hi, babe, I hope you bought yourself some sexy lingerie with that dosh.'

Mary shuddered. 'Ronnie, I...'

'You don't have to thank me, sweetheart. It's thanks enough to know you're grateful. Course, I admit I wouldn't mind you showing me a little gratitude, if you catch my drift.'

'Let's get one thing straight, Ronnie,' Mary yelled, 'you and I are no longer husband and wife. You have no rights to intrude into my life.'

'I'm still the father of your children.'

'You're not interested in the children, Ronnie, and we both know it. It's me you want, isn't it?'

Ronnie laughed. 'You said it. And I think I've just paid well over the going rate for a night with you, sweetheart.'

'I thought it was payment for the pictures you took without my permission. And also for all those past maintenance payments you'd have had to pay if you hadn't skipped the country.'

She heard a sound from the other end of the line, as if Ronnie was struggling with something, or having difficulty breathing.

'I look at those sexy pictures of you every night, sweetheart. You've still got great legs.'

Mary's voice became hard and brittle. 'You violated and abused me by taking those pictures. And breaking and entering into this house.'

She heard his breath quickening. Then he said: 'Know what I'd like to do to you?'

Mary screamed down the telephone, 'I'm not interested, Ronnie. Can't you get that through your thick skull?'

Ronnie laughed again. 'I'll bet that red-nosed clown don't know how to service you, girl. It used to be great sex with us. The best. You had to hand it to me, sweetheart, I had staying power. Does the clown have staying power? Does he satisfy my baby like Ronnie used to?'

Mary could hardly speak through the great heaving sobs which almost bent her double. 'Ronnie... I've had enough.' She felt herself gag. 'That's it. I'm calling the police. Right now. I'm definitely calling the police this time.'

As she slammed down the telephone, the last thing she heard was Ronnie's laugh. She ran upstairs to the bathroom and was violently sick in the basin.

***

Mandy arrived at the wine bar for her first evening twenty minutes early. Craig rushed forward and greeted her with a kiss on the cheek.

'None of that,' joked Maggie, though there was an underlying seriousness in her tone. 'This is a respectable joint.'

Mandy gave her a shy smile.

'It's fairly quiet at this time...' began Craig.

'So it's a good time to get to know the ropes,' Maggie added.

Mandy, noticing how Maggie ended Craig's sentence, smile inwardly, wondering if this was from sibling familiarity or because Maggie liked to boss her brother around. Mandy decided she would have to watch her step and not get involved in any family squabbles.

'An hour ago we were busy,' said Craig, 'but now we usually get a bit of a breather till around eight.'

Maggie glanced at her watch. 'Which doesn't give us much time to train Mandy. really think tomorrow morning would have been a better time for her to start.'

Craig gave an embarrassed laugh. 'My sister's forgotten you've had bar experience before.'

Maggie tutted impatiently. 'No I haven't. But this is a wine bar, not a pub. So Mandy needs to know something about wine.'

'Why?' Craig smirked. 'We never did.'

'Craig,' warned Maggie, her voice developing a hard edge, 'she needs to know the basic differences between the types of wine, for instance.'

She banged a bottle of rosé onto the bar. 'Now you may think this looks like red wine Mandy, but...'

Mandy, her lips drawn tight, interrupted her. 'I'm not that thick I can't tell the difference between red wine and rosé.'

Maggie reddened slightly. 'I'm sorry,' she began, becoming flustered and fidgeting with the wine bottle. 'I didn't mean to...'

'Yeah,' said Craig. 'Don't be so bloody patronising.'

'I said I was sorry. Why don't you introduce Mandy to the kitchen staff? And she can hang up her coat at the same time.'

***

An hour after Mary had telephoned the police to complain about being stalked by Ronnie, a female detective arrived.

'Who is it?' asked Simon, popping his head out of the living room door.

'Nothing to worry about,' Mary told him, stroking his hair and ushering him back into the living room. 'Go and watch the rest of the film.'

She took the detective through to the kitchen. 'I've just made a cup of tea,' she said. 'Would you like a cup?'

The detective shook her head. 'No thanks. It's coming out of my ears.'

She sat at the kitchen table and opened her notebook. 'Now then. Why did your ex husband give you five hundred pounds?'

Mary was stunned. She took a while to answer, while the detective watched her carefully. A sense of unreality intruded as she listened to the whine and crash of a car chase coming from the front room.

The detective coughed. 'Your ex husband has been in touch with us. He told us that you and he have an arrangement, and that you accepted the payment for certain favours.'

'That's not true. He only sent me the money after he...' Mary stopped and thought about this. How was the best way to explain about the pictures?

'Yes?' prompted the detective.

Mary hesitated. 'Doesn't it strike you as odd that Ronnie would contact you? Like it's all planned.'

The detective shook her head. 'The reason he gave us was that your current boyfriend is away from home – long term – and you want your ex husband to provide for your family and get back together again.'

Mary laughed bitterly. 'Ronnie, you bastard,' she said. 'You cunning, clever bastard. I've got to hand it to you.'

Forty-Nine

The Coal Hole was in the Strand, a short walk from Charing Cross Station. It was four in the afternoon and, apart from Pran and Tina, there were only half a dozen customers in the bar. Tina topped their wine glasses up, as Pran stared thoughtfully into the distance. He shook his head suddenly as a thought struck him.

'I really had no idea it would be as bad as that. How frustrating was that? I mean, is it deliberate, the way they go so slowly round in circles? Do they hope you'll get bored and drop the case?'

Tina shrugged and gave a helpless smile. 'It wouldn't surprise me.'

'I'm glad I told them about that comment Cruella de Ville made about me having a chip on my shoulder.'

Tina laughed. 'That name just about sums her up. What a bitch!'

'I think that Asian on the tribunal interpreted it as a racist comment she was about to make. I could tell by his expression.'

'What expression? None of them gave anything away. They were as inscrutable as rocks.'

Pran stabbed a finger down towards the table, highlighting his point. 'I could see it in his eyes. It may have been a faint glimmer, but it was there.'

Tina sighed, leaned back, and sipped her wine. 'And now it's back to the waiting game again. So much time out of my life. It's taking its toll.'

'You stick with it, girl. You've come this far. Don't give up now.'

'I've no intention of doing that. Especially with you helping me, which I really appreciate, because I know how hard it must be. It's very brave of you.'

Pran shrugged and drained his wine glass. 'I'd better make a move and catch my train.'

Tina leant forward and stared at him earnestly. 'Please don't feel insulted, Pran. I want to pay your fare up here.'

He frowned and shook his head, staring with embarrassment at his empty glass, which reminded him that he'd now got a taste for it, and might not be able to afford another bottle that evening. He began to make a token objection but made it sound deliberately weak.

'Well, I don't know if I can take money for this trip,,,'

He was relieved to see Tina was already getting her purse out of her handbag.

'You're not. This is your train fare. You wouldn't be coming up here if it wasn't for the tribunal.'

As she held out a twenty pound note, he said, 'It's not as much as that. And you also got the wine.'

She became mockingly firm. 'Do as you're told and take it.'

He gave her a small, regretful smile as he accepted the money. 'OK. But next time I'll get the wine.'

***

Jackie came into the kitchen and gasped. The mess was worse than she had ever known. Tears of frustration sprang into her eyes. Nicky, who had been watching a DVD in the living room, came scurrying guiltily into the kitchen.

'Hello, Mummy,' she mumbled lamely.

Jackie was staring goggle-eyed at the mountainous pile of washing-up stacked on the draining board. 'Look at it!' she moaned.

'We were going to do it. You should have telephoned to say you were coming.'

'I live here. I shouldn't have to do that. I ought to be able to come home whenever I want, without...' She gestured futilely at the mess.

Nicky wore a sullen expression. 'Since you came back from your honeymoon, you've been staying at Nigel's house. We thought you were staying round there permanently. If we'd known you were coming home, we'd have tidied up.'

Jackie shook her head vehemently. 'How can you live like this? You make work for yourselves. If you did it as you went along...'

Impatiently, Nicky interrupted. 'Most people these days have a dishwasher.'

Jackie gave a bark-like, humourless laugh. 'Ha! Even if we had a dishwasher, you would never bother to load it. I've never known such laziness. And where's Vanessa?'

'How should I know?'

Jackie glared at her daughter, as if she was finding it hard from physically attacking her. The telephone rang, and Jackie hurried out to the hall to answer it, relieved to break from the scene with Nicky. Jackie hated scenes.

Nicky sighed, and reluctantly began to tackle the washing up. She was about to turn the tap on but was distracted by her mother's telephone conversation. She stopped to listen.

'Oh God!' A pause. 'Oh, that's terrible.' Another slightly longer pause. 'How did he... Yes, I see. Who found him? That must have been terrible. Why not? His two girls have every right...'

A cold clammy feeling ran down Nicky's body as she suspected the worst. She knew now what it was. She was deathly still as she listened to the rest of her mother's telephone conversation, and waited for the inevitable bad news.

'Oh no. That's disgusting. Thank you for warning me. I'll try... I'll have a think about it and try to sort something out.'

When Jackie returned to the kitchen, Nicky saw the tears flooding down her cheeks, but they were almost on automatic pilot. There seemed to be no emotion behind them, other than a trace of anger perhaps.

'I'm sorry, Nicky. It's your father. He passed away.'

Nicky felt numb, but no tears came. Her mother saw the frightened, confused expression on her daughter's face, like a vulnerable animal being startled, and threw her arms around her and squeezed tight. After a while, Nicky drew back and calmly stared into her mother's eyes.

'Tell me about it.'

'That was one of your dad's drinking cronies in East Peckham. You know how he went to the pub every single night. Well, apparently he hadn't been for four or five days, so someone went round to look for him. They knew something was wrong and had to break in. That's when they found him. They think he'd had a heart attack. The chap from the pub wanted me to know before the police call. There's something...'

Frowning, Nicky waited for her mother to finish.

'It's too disgusting.' Jackie shuddered hugely. 'How could he? The filthy disgusting animal!'

***

Mary wiped the top of the cooker hurriedly. She didn't like letting the boys out on their own, but because Simon was older, and seemed very responsible for his age, she had agreed to them going off to the Grosvenor recreation ground, which was only a short walk from where they lived. She intended following them to the park after fifteen minutes had gone by. She wanted them to learn to be independent. It was a difficult balancing act to pull off these days, what with there being so many dangerous people around. Yet she knew she couldn't wrap them in cotton wool either.

So letting them go on their own, then following them a little later, seemed a perfect compromise. What could possibly go wrong in the space of ten or fifteen minutes?

But when the jarring sound of the knocker made her jump, followed by the muffled cries of Simon calling her from outside the front door, she immediately knew she was going to regret it.

She ran down the hall and threw open the door.

'Mum!' screamed Simon. 'He's got Thomas.'

Mary grabbed Simon by the shoulders as she felt waves of panic beating her. 'Who's got him? Who?'

'My dad, that's who. He stopped his car just as we were about to go into the park across the little footpath over the railway bridge. I told Thomas not to go with him, but he wouldn't listen. My dad offered to buy him an ice-cream and give him some pocket money. I told him! I told him not to go with him but he wouldn't listen.'

In the hallway, the telephone shrilled. Mary ran back and snatched at it.

'Hi, babe. Don't panic. Thomas's here with me. Ain't you, son.'

Mary screamed down the telephone, 'Ronnie! Bring him back now! You've no right to take him like that...'

Ronnie's voice was calm and businesslike when he interrupted her. There was a smooth coldness in his delivery, as if he'd rehearsed the speech. 'Listen, sweetheart: I can get at my son whenever I like, and there's nothing you nor anyone can do about it. So just listen up and I'll tell you how it's going to be. He'll be back with you in less than five minutes. We've only gone round the corner to buy an ice-cream. But bear this in mind, sweetheart: I can, and will do this again, and put the shits up you. You know, don't you, what I'm capable of. So here's the thing: I want you, baby. Just once. One night with you. Then, I promise, I'll leave you alone. I'll be out of your life for good.'

Mary's breathing was shallow and she felt as if she was hyperventilating.

Ronnie chuckled as he waited for her to speak.

'Ronnie,' she said, 'if I thought you would be out of our lives for good...'

Ronnie laughed louder. 'You'd agree. Look, sweetheart, I just want one night with you. Think of it as lust... a sort of magnificent obsession... with you preying on my mind, I need one night. Then it's closure, I promise you. I'll bugger off back to the old US of A again. So how about it?'

Mary drew in her breath before answering. Then was surprised at how calm she sounded 'OK. Come round tonight, after eleven-thirty, when the kids are sound asleep. I don't want them to know.'

'A wise decision, babe. I'll drop young Thomas off in less than five.'

Fifty

As soon as Vanessa arrived home and went into the living room, she knew it was bad news. A bad atmosphere hung in the air like a repugnant odour, and she could see her mother had been crying. She sank into the sofa, next to Nicky.

'What's happened?'

'It's your father. He's passed away.'

'In other words,' Nicky spat out bitterly, 'he's dead.'

Vanessa sat with her hands clutched tight, examining her feelings. Neither of them had been close to their father. They saw him occasionally, maybe three times a year, but he always remembered their birthdays, sent them cards, usually with a fifty pound note inside. The same at Christmas. But he had been a remote man, taciturn and cold. Vanessa couldn't ever remember a time when he had hugged her; or even pecked her on the cheek. He liked to keep a distance between himself and his family, as if he resented his own inadequacy as a parent.

After a long silence, Vanessa cleared her throat lightly before speaking. 'It's a shame, I know, but we were never close – any of us. We had no relationship with him at all.'

Nicky shuddered and began sobbing. Vanessa wondered why she was so upset.

'I feel...' Nicky began, between gulping and crying. 'I feel guilty. I don't even know what he did for a living.'

'He didn't like to talk about it,' said Jackie. 'He worked for British Aerospace, selling something. That's why he travelled abroad so much before he took early retirement.'

Vanessa frowned as she stared at her mother. 'You mean he was an arms dealer?'

'Components he said. Whatever he did, he was quite successful. When we split up he left us this house, and bought a small one for

218

himself – the one in East Pekham. About a year ago he telephoned me and told me he'd had a minor heart attack. So it prompted him into making a will. He's left everything to you two; whatever money he's saved, plus the proceeds of the house. That should brighten up the tragic news.'

This last statement, Vanessa noticed, was spoken with venom, and she wondered if her mother resented being excluded from the will.

Nicky wiped her eyes, blew her nose, and composed herself. She spoke to her sister, with a nod in her mother's direction.

'There's something she's not telling us.'

'What d'you mean?'

'About our father – the way he died.'

Vanessa stared at Jackie. 'Well, come on: we've a right to know.'

Jackie shuddered. 'He suffocated himself.'

'You mean he committed suicide?' asked Vanessa.

Jackie shook her head. 'I'd sooner not...'

'We're going to find out eventually,' yelled Nicky. 'There'll be an enquiry. So you might as well tell us what happened.'

'Well,' urged Vanessa, leaning forward on the sofa, 'did he commit suicide or not?'

Tears rolled down Jackie's face. 'It was an accident. It's too disgusting for words. Oh, all right – if you must know – you're going to find out sooner or later, anyway. He was watching a disgusting film on the video.'

'You mean pornography?' said Vanessa.

Jackie nodded. 'And he was... he was doing it to himself... while he watched it.'

Vanessa shrugged. 'I bet lots of men do. So what?'

'He was using a belt which he tied around his throat. Apparently it does something... I'm not sure what.'

'It's called something,' said Nicky. 'There's a name for it.'

Vanessa stared at the carpet, and held her hands level as she searched her memory. 'Auto erotic asphyxiation.'

'Whatever it is,' snapped Jackie. 'It's brought disgrace on the family. The disgusting bastard.'

Vanessa laughed, and Nicky and her mother stared at her, as if they couldn't quite believe they had heard right.

'Our father,' she laughed. 'A component salesman. Anyone'd think he was a rock singer.'

***

Ted still slept in the spare room. He was on an early shift and was finding difficulty in getting to sleep. After a long struggle, with many voices in his head, tugging and pulling and keeping him restless, he eventually managed to drift off into a deep, dreamless sleep. He had been asleep less than ten minutes when a hand on his shoulder shook him awake.

'Ted! Ted! Wake up!' Marjorie hissed.

He sat bolt upright, scared that something might be wrong with his daughter. 'What's happened?'

Marjorie's irritated voice came to him in the dark. 'Nothing's wrong. She just wants her feed. She's crying. Didn't you hear her?'

'No, I've only just got to sleep.'

'She wants feeding.'

'Can't you feed her?'

'No I can't. It's your turn.'

Ted's voice whined from a feelings of tiredness and injustice. 'But I'm on the early shift.'

'Are you going to feed her or not?'

Marjorie's voice sounded ominous in the dark, as if she were capable of committing a heinous act if crossed.

Ted sighed. 'Yes. All right. But what about my early shift?'

'What about it?'

'It's just that it's not fair.'

Marjorie snorted. 'Life's not fair. And I have to look after her all the time you're at work. I need a break. A rest.'

'She sleeps most of the time.'

'Yes, well, she's not sleeping now, is she?'

Ted listened to the urgent crying, louder now, starting to choke with hunger and a craving attention. He sighed again as he swung his legs out from under the duvet.

'OK. I'll go,' he relented.

'That's big of you,' snapped Marjorie as she swept out to return to her own room.

Ted struggled to find the sleeve of his dressing gown. 'Don't cry, poppet!' he called. 'Daddy's coming. Daddy's coming.'

***

Ronnie tapped the door knocker softly. He could hear soft music coming from the back of the house, probably the kitchen. He waited, but no one came. He checked his watch to make sure it was the right time. It was a little after eleven-thirty, just like she'd said. He banged the knocker again, this time slightly louder.

While he waited, he could feel anger growing inside him, rising to the surface. If the bitch had changed her mind...

He checked the street, making certain no one was passing by, then went to the side of the house and clicked the latch on the gate. He expected to find it bolted but she had either forgotten to lock it or one of the children had. He pushed open the creaking gate, felt his way along the side wall of the house, then turned the corner. There was a light on in the kitchen and he peered through the stippled glass of the back door and couldn't see any shadows or movement from within. Apart from the radio playing an old

Carpenter's number, the house was silent. Perhaps she had gone to bed, thinking he would give up and go away. Chance would be a fine thing! There was no way he was going to go away now, having come this far.

Not expecting to break in as he had before, he had neglected to bring any tools with him, so he searched around the garden until he found a large stone. His anger was mounting now, and he couldn't have cared less about the noise it would make. He hit the stone hard against the glass, smashing it over and over. It seemed to make a hell of a noise, but by now he was frantic and boiling with anger. He reached inside the door, found the large, old-fashioned key and turned it. Then he flung open the door and entered. He marched angrily through the kitchen and into the hall, then swung round and took the stairs two at a time. There was a suspicion growing inside him, feeding his anger and desperation. As soon as he flung open the bedroom doors he knew. The bitch had crossed him. She had taken the children and gone out for the night.

With no clear aim in mind, he ran downstairs and threw open the front door. He was confronted by two uniformed policemen.

'Hold it right there,' said one of them.

Instinctively, he turned round, knowing he could get out the back door, but a figure appeared at the kitchen doorway. Plain clothes and holding out his ID to Ronnie.

'You're not going anywhere, sir. I'm arresting you for breaking and entering. If you are asked questions about the offence, you do not have to say anything, but it may harm your defence if you do not mention when questioned something which you later rely on in court. Anything you do say may be given in evidence.'

Ronnie shrugged. He'd been caught bang to rights. She'd set him up and he'd walked into her trap. And for that the bitch would have to pay. Maybe not now, or tomorrow, or next year even. But eventually she would pay for it.

Fifty-One

Mandy lay on her side, a hand cupped under her chin, surveying Craig's bedroom now that daylight furnished it with stark reality. She stared at the salmon pink wallpaper with yellow roses, wondering if the pink had once been brighter. She frowned thoughtfully as her eyes followed the line of peeling paper down to the hideous, dark oak chest of drawers with its top drawer permanently jammed open . And she scowled at the miserable alcove that served as Craig's wardrobe, a curtain rail stretched across and a plastic shower curtain with an underwater theme.

Craig grinned as he came into the room, stark naked, carrying two mugs of coffee. Reading her mind, he said, 'I know it's not much but at least it's home.'

Mandy smiled weakly and caught sight of her dress, carefully draped across the wash basin, the only place she could find to put it last night.

'Does your tap drip?' she said.

Craig frowned uncomprehendingly. 'Sorry?'

She looked up at him, modestly trying to avoid staring at his eye-level nakedness.

'I said, does your tap drip?'

Craig looked down at himself. 'I... um... I'm not sure what you mean.'

Mandy snorted with laughter. 'The sink, you idiot!'

A broad grin spread across Craig's face as he realised. 'Oh! No, I don't think so. I'll hang the dress in the wardrobe, if you like.'

'Wardrobe!' she scorned. 'No, don't bother. Leave it where it is.'

'Well, if you're sure. There you go.'

He handed her the unchipped mug, then climbed back into bed on his own side.

223

'Craig,' she said thoughtfully, after blowing on her coffee. 'Mind if I ask you something?'

Craig nodded agreeably. 'I know what you're going to say. If the wine bar's doing so well, how come I'm still living in this tip?'

'I'll ask you that in a minute. This is about Maggie.'

'What about her?'

'Does she have a drink problem?'

Craig didn't answer immediately. He stared into his mug, his eyes distant. When he spoke, his voice was dry and rasping. 'I think she does. But she won't admit it.'

'No,' said Mandy, 'she doesn't strike me as the type to face up to being wrong about anything.' And, because she thought it sounded harsh, quickly added: 'I mean, she's got children, hasn't she? What about the kids?'

'I think Maggie's suffering from a delayed reaction.'

'From her husband's death, d'you mean?'

'Yeah. See, when he died, he was having a bit on the side. I mean literally when he died. She was with him in the car when it happened, giving him a blow-job as he was driving, which was when the accident happened. So naturally Maggie was bloody angry. She's hated Gary all this time. But now I think she might miss him.'

Mandy pursed her lips. 'Hmm,' she said, slowly and thoughtfully.

Craig, detecting slight disapproval in her tone, said, 'What's that supposed to mean?'

'Did Maggie drink when her husband was alive.'

Craig nodded slowly. 'Yeah, but nowhere near as much as she does now.'

Mandy slurped her coffee loudly before speaking, which somehow succeeded in irritating Craig.

'Maybe your sister's always had a drink problem, only now she's got an excuse.'

Craig stared at Mandy, the girl who had been so tender and loving a little while ago during their lovemaking, and who now sounded harsh and unsympathetic, and he was suddenly saddened. He had put her on a pedestal, wanting her to be the perfectly loving little girl at his side, agreeable and supportive. Not coldly analytical about his family.

He grabbed his wristwatch from the rickety, varnished bamboo table by the bedside, and glared at it pointedly before swinging his legs out from under the bedding.

'I'd better shower,' he said. 'We've got a delivery today, and I've got to be early.'

'Craig?' Mandy's voice quivered slightly. 'I'm sorry... I didn't mean to... Come back to bed. Just for a minute.'

Craig noticed the abrupt change, could almost hear the grinding of the gears, and wondered if this was manipulation on Mandy's part. But when he looked at her, she seemed so genuinely soft and vulnerable – and desirable – that he gave her a sensuous smile before climbing back into bed.

'OK, my sweetheart,' he whispered, 'but we can't be too long.'

***

Donald stood at the window, holding at arm's length a finely bound copy of King Lear. His lips moved silently, and every so often he would look out at the rhododendron bushes and sigh with contentment.

Bamber glowered and sulked on the sofa as he watched him. His mother was now in a hospice and her death was imminent, but he knew that if he stayed at her place in Lewes any longer he would go barking mad; but when he'd got back to Donald's house, he couldn't help but notice his partner had looked vexed.

'You're such a poseur, darling!' said Bamber, his voice oozing discontentment. 'Look at you! If that's not poncey, I don't know what is.'

Donald ignored it; continued reading in a deliberately relaxed fashion, knowing how much it would annoy Bamber.

'What are you reading, anyhow?'

'King Lear. Why?'

Bamber chuckled. This was the one Donald had been reading six months ago when they'd had that row because Bamber felt a need to go cottaging.

Bamber smiled craftily. 'What's it about?'

'Nothing that would interest you.'

'Oh, but it would. Especially that bit in Act Three when there's a storm.'

Donald frowned suspiciously and turned the pages quickly. Bamber watched him, elated by the prank.

'Swine!' Donald screamed, his face going purple with rage. 'You filthy disgusting swine!'

Bamber rocked back on the sofa, laughing loudly. 'Now there really is a storm,' he spluttered.

Donald stared coldly at him, his anger suddenly evaporating.

'Doesn't it turn you on?' Bamber said. 'Let's face it: it's much more exciting than Shakespeare. Surely even you must find it more exciting, Donald.'

Donald sighed wearily and threw the book onto the coffee table. 'In truth, no. I don't. And that sort of prank is far from original. Joe Orton and Ken Halliwell stuck pornographic pictures in library books while you were still in nappies.'

Bamber giggled proudly. 'I know. That's where I got the idea from.'

The doorbell rang. Bamber saw a glint come into Donald's eyes as he walked towards the door.

'Someone you're expecting?' said Bamber, undisguised jealousy creeping into his voice.

Donald turned and grinned at him. 'Yes, that'll be Ted. I'm expecting him.'

Bamber glowered. 'Come round for a Shakespeare night, has he?'

'As a matter of fact, we decided on a decidedly non-cultural evening for once. I told him you were back here, and managed to persuade him that three needn't be a crowd. It can be quite good fun.'

Bamber smiled. 'Well go and let him in, in case he changes his mind.'

Fifty-Two

Dark and painfully violent, shuddering sensations of shock pounded Maggie's head like sharp stones. Where was she? The sadistic pulsation continued and a loud noise brought her closer to the surface. She forced open her eyes and the light was painful, then Daryl's unsympathetic face loomed into focus. His voice ground her brains to mush like a hammer.

'Mum! Mum! Wake up! We're going to be late for school.'

She groaned, and her stomach lurched. The violent shaking of her shoulder continued.

'Daryl!' she managed. 'Stop doing that. There's a good boy.'

Daryl knew his mother was suffering from too much alcohol. He'd witnessed the same sort of thing on several other occasions, though never before on a weekday when she was supposed to drive them to school. And never as bad as this. Could this have something to do with the man who now occupied his father's bed?

'Mum!' he persisted, raising his voice. 'We have to go to school.'

Maggie felt Mike stir beside her. She moved her heel sharply backwards and it came into contact with his shin. 'Mike!' she moaned. 'Wake up! I feel terrible. I just want to die.'

Mike, determined not to let a little thing like a hangover get the better of him, shook his head to test the pain. It was bad, but nothing he couldn't overcome. He eased himself into a sitting position, and was about to swing his legs out of bad when he realised he was naked and didn't want to embarrass Daryl. He blinked hard several times and focused on the boy. His mouth felt parched and he desperately needed a long drink of cold water.

'Have you had breakfast' he asked Daryl.

The boy answered him as if he was a cretin. 'Of course we have. We're waiting to go to school.'

Maggie moaned. 'Please, Mike. Can you take them? I feel awful.'

'Okay,' said Mike. 'Daryl, my car keys are in my jacket pocket. The one on the floor. You and Hannah get in the car. I'll put some clothes on and I'll be down in just a minute.'

Daryl scowled at Mike, then rummaged around Mike's black leather bomber jacket which lay in a crumpled heap with the rest of his clothes. The boy could feel anger expanding inside him as he moved Mike's underpants which lay on top of the jacket pocket. He pulled out Mike's keys, gave his mother a withering look, then shot out of the door.

Mike hurried out of bed and hastily threw on his clothes. Maggie raised her eyelids an infinitesimal amount and saw the blurred outline of her lover.

'Sorry, Mike,' she groaned. 'I just can't. See you when you get back.'

Mike coughed and spluttered, then hurriedly left the room without saying anything. As soon as he had gone, Maggie felt a shroud of nausea enveloping her like bad breath. She swallowed saliva quickly, but her mouth was too dry and her stomach heaved agonizingly. She knew she was going to be sick but it was too painful to move.

Suddenly it came in a rush, and she vomited copiously in the bed.

***

Ted looked up at the darkening sky which had been so clear and bright up to a minute ago. He stopped pushing the pram and tucked the blanket tightly around Tracey. She gurgled and rocked her head from side to side.

'You'll be all right if it rains,' Ted told her. 'You'll be all tucked up nice and dry.'

She looked at her father quizzically. He tickled her under the chin and grinned at her. She rewarded him with a sudden and unexpected smile.

'Did you smile at me?' he said. 'Donald will be pleased.'

He continued walking along and pushing the pram on the periphery of the cricket pitch. An elderly man stood in the middle and threw a stick for his black Labrador. As Ted neared the corner of the pitch, Donald suddenly appeared, striding towards him, and grinning hugely. He rushed to look into the pram, pressing himself close to Ted.

'And how's my little Miranda?'

It was their secret name for her.

'I hope she's not going to get confused over her name,' said Ted.

Donald grinned at the baby. 'She can have two names, can't she? Most people have a second name.' Donald focused his attention on Ted. 'So how was it for you?'

Ted felt himself growing hot with embarrassment. 'I don't think...'

A pause. Ted stared at the black Labrador scampering across the cricket pitch.

'What?' Donald prompted.

'I suppose you mean last night... with Bamber.' Ted looked down at the ground, becoming flustered. 'To be honest, I don't think it's right.'

'Don't be so hypocritical,' said Donald, in a clipped tone. 'You seemed to enter into it with gusto.' Donald chuckled to himself. 'Your problem is you just don't like talking about things. Pretending they never happened.'

Ted sighed deeply and frowned. 'Oh, I don't know. Why does life have to be so complicated? Always.'

'What's up? This is not about last night, is it? Something's bothering you. I can tell.'

'It's Marjorie.'

'The wife from hell.' Donald giggled, then looked contrite when he saw the pained expression on his friend's face. 'Sorry. What's she done now?'

'Lately she's been getting loads of letters from estate agents. When I asked her about it, she told me it was none of my business.'

'Charming!'

'Only not in so many words. So I steamed open one of the letters.'

Donald laughed. 'You sneaky rat. Mind you, I think I'd have done the same myself. And?'

'She's been getting details of hotels for sale?'

'Hotels?'

'Yes. Small hotels. Bed and breakfast type places. I think she's considering opening a small hotel.'

***

Knowing he was still well over the limit, Mike had resisted the temptation to take any chances, even though the children had urged him to put his foot down because they were fifteen minutes late for school. He managed to drive exceedingly well, and dropped them off without any incidents. He began to relax on the return journey, knowing a cool glass of water, or one of the children's cold fizzy drinks, awaited him back at Maggie's.

As he approached the roundabout at the top of Major Yorke's Road, a Volvo estate car in front of him braked sharply. Although Mike felt he was in control, his reactions were slower than normal. He applied the brakes hurriedly, but wasn't quick enough and his car slammed into the back of the Volvo. It wasn't a huge impact, but Mike knew it was enough to have made a mess of the driver's rear lights, and probably his own. Suddenly, the previous night's alcohol binge manifested itself in a dangerous way. It gave Mike the effrontery to pass the buck. This was obviously not his fault.

Just the other day, he had been listening to one of Jeremy Vine's issues on Radio 2, following newspaper reports in the Daily Mirror, concerning an insurance scam when drivers deliberately slam on their brakes so that someone goes into the back of them, and then make a false claim for all kinds of damages to their person and other non-existent passengers.

So when Mike got out of the car to face the other driver, he was convinced it was part of a scam. 'What the bloody hell d'you brake like that for?' he yelled belligerently. 'You trying to put in a false insurance claim, is that it?'

The driver surveyed him calmly, taking in his unshaven appearance and the bloodshot eyes. Unfortunately, Mike was so angry, and convinced he was being conned, he staggered slightly, making matters worse.

The driver smiled humourlessly as he took out his mobile and pressed a redial button. As he waited for it to be answered, he stared coldly at Mike and said, 'I'm just going home off duty. I'm a policeman. And I know when someone's been drinking. There'll be a patrol car along here shortly. I'd stay put if I were you.'

A swarm of bees buzzed around in Mike's head. The scene was unreal. This morning was a bad dream. And things were about to get worse.

Fifty-Three

Holding up a 1989 Postman Pat Christmas Annual, Jackie said, 'You don't want to keep this, do you?'

Nicky looked as if she'd had boiling water thrown in her face. 'It's a shame to get rid of it.'

Jackie's lips tightened. 'I thought we were supposed to be having a clear out.'

'We are.'

'All you're doing is hanging on to all your old junk.'

Jackie was sitting on Nicky's bed, surrounded by cardboard boxes and black bin liners filled with rubbish. Vanessa came past the door and thought she'd make her presence felt. She leaned against the wall and said, 'Let her have it if she wants it. What difference can it make?'

'Yes,' added Nicky, glad her sister had decided to support her for a change. 'Why can't I keep my things if I want to?'

Jackie tapped the Postman Pat book with frustration. 'But this is a toddler's book, for heaven's sake. You're not a baby any more.'

Nicky suddenly screeched angrily: 'Throw it away then! Go on! Throw it away!'

'Well there's no need to...' Jackie began.

'You don't care about my memories. And I think Dad bought me that book.'

Jackie froze. The mere mention of his name was anathema to her since discovering the circumstances of his death. She put the book to one side and mumbled quietly: 'Oh...well...keep it if you must.'

Nicky, who had been standing with her back to the window, suddenly lunged forward, stepping over a pile of boxes in the middle of the room. 'I can't handle this.'

Jackie raised her voice. 'Where are you going?'

'I'm going to meet a friend for a drink.'

'You can't do that. What about all this mess?'

Nicky went past Vanessa, who had rather an amused expression on her face as she watched her mother trying to cope with Nicky's histrionics, and turned back in the doorway.

'I've got to get out for a few hours.'

'Just a minute!' yelled Jackie. 'It's not my fault the house went on the market and got a cash buyer wanting a quick sale.'

'Not my fault either,' shouted Nicky, and stormed off.

Vanessa stared at her mother and shook her head irritatingly. 'Great timing. A funeral and a house move the same week.'

Jackie clawed at the air with both her hands, her fingers forming talons of frustration. 'If only your father hadn't died when he did.'

'Yes. It was very inconvenient. Two of the most stressful things in one week. Funeral and house move. You should have gone for a hat trick and got a divorce from Nigel.'

Jackie looked up, taking in Vanessa's unsympathetic, almost cruel, smile. 'How can you make jokes about these things?'

'It's the only way to keep sane, Mummy. The funeral should be a laugh, knowing what we know.'

'It'll be a quiet affair,' said Jackie. 'Just a few of his friends from East Peckham. The sort of people I think of as his cronies. Probably ghastly people. And they'll all know the circumstances of his death. Oh, how could he?'

'And we've yet to go through his house, through all his possessions and belongings, as we're his next of kin. Who knows what we might find.'

Jackie shuddered. 'You won't catch me within five hundred miles of the place.'

Vanessa laughed. 'Well, seeing as East Peckham's less than twelve miles from here...'

Jackie bit her lip before speaking. 'You know very well what I mean.'

'D'you mean to say, you're just going to let Nicky and me do all the donkey work, clearing out all his old clothes, and taking stuff to charity shops?'

'Try to understand: in the circumstances, I can't. I just can't.'

Vanessa turned to go. 'Oh, I understand all right. You really are a selfish bitch sometimes.'

'Vanessa!'

But Vanessa had already left the room. Jackie leaned forward and put her face in her hands. If only Nigel were here, but he'd made it abundantly clear that he had an important meeting to attend with the directors of his telecommunications suppliers.

***

Mike got back to Maggie's just after lunchtime. He found her lying out on a sun lounger on the patio, wearing dark glasses. Her face was ashen, and stood out like a mask against the tan of her body.

'D'you want the bad news or the bad news?' Mike announced.

She twitched slightly. 'I didn't hear you come in. You made me jump. I was asleep. I still feel terrible.'

'So you've just been lying there recovering – sunning yourself – while I've been in the local nick.'

'What?'

'On the way back from dropping the kids at school, I was breathalysed and I was over the limit. My driving days are over for at least a year.'

She took her dark glasses off, and blinked in the sunlight. 'Oh, Mike! 'm sorry. Christ! That was my fault. What the hell will you do – about work?'

He gave her a lopsided grin. 'I think you might need another part time barman.'

***

On Saturday Dave finished his season at Blackpool. He thought about driving back home on the Saturday night, had second thoughts. At least Mary's ex was now banged up out of harm's way, and he hoped he would get a decent sentence once he was put on trial.

Arriving home late Sunday morning, Dave pushed open the front door awkwardly, burdened by the carrier bags and boxes of presents he had bought for Mary and the kids.

'I'm home!' he sang out.

The refrigerator hummed, and the house creaked and clicked. Apart from that, silence.

He sighed disappointedly as he kicked the door shut. Then he went into the living room and dumped the parcels on the sofa. He stood staring at them for a minute, feeling tired and hungry. What had kept him going during the long motorway drive was the imagined scene of his homecoming; Mary rushing into his arms, and the children's excited glowing faces as they tore open the parcels.

Now he felt numb with disappointment. Where were they? Mary had known of his plans to drive back, leaving early in the morning, so where was she?

He made a disgruntled growling noise with the back of his throat, then went into the kitchen.

'Oh! Thanks a bundle!' he cried when he saw the dirty breakfast crockery on the table. She hadn't even bothered to clear the table, let alone do the washing up!

A note had been left for him on the work surface, stained and greasy from a spilt pool of cooking oil. He snatched it up and read it.

'We've gone to Mum's for Sunday dinner. Hope you had a good journey. Why don't you come over and join us? See you later. Love, Mary.'

Dave sighed, screwed the note into a ball and threw it into the sink.

'Oh, that's all I need – dinner with your mother!'

Fifty-Four

Dave smacked his lips contentedly and put his knife and fork together with a clatter.

'That were the business, that were,' he said, exaggerating his Yorkshire dialect. 'There's nowt like a traditional Sunday roast. Ta very much, Mrs Fernhill.'

Mary's mother shook a finger admonishingly. 'Please! Janet!'

'Janet.'

Mary, noticing Simon and Thomas's bored expressions, said, 'You've both done very well. And Nanny gave you enormous portions too.'

Mary's mother smirked. 'Clean plates. Jolly good, you two.'

'Is it all right if they get down from the table?' Mary asked her mother. 'They can watch some cartoon DVDs they've brought with them, as long as they don't have the volume too loud.'

The children were confined to staying indoors, as their grandmother lived in a sheltered accommodation flat. Nanny tugged delicately at her recently permed hair and sat upright, giving herself a regal air.

'You watch the television if you want to. Nanny'll have a between courses puff. You can switch it off when I serve dessert.'

Dave, who had always called it pudding, suppressed the urge to laugh, especially as Mary's mother said certain things with pursed lips which reminded him of the wide mouth frog joke.

'Thanks, Nanny,' said Thomas, staring at the blue in his grandmother's hair, which always fascinated him.

'Good boy,' she replied.

Simon mumbled his thanks and they both went and sat on the floor near to the television set and switched it on. Mary started to clear the plates away.

'Just leave them in the kitchen,' said her mother. 'It'll give me something to do later.' She turned to Dave. 'You get bored on your own.'

Dave nodded and grunted non-committally. Mary's mother fetched a roll-your-own cigarette kit and a tin of Old Holborn tobacco from the sideboard, then returned to the table.

'You've never smoked, have you?' she said.

Dave, who thought this sounded like a criticism, replied, 'It's not one of my vices.'

'No, I'm sure it isn't. How long have you known Mary now?'

Dave frowned, trying to follow her train of thought.

'Er, must be almost a year now.'

'You're much better for her than that filthy beast she was married to.'

Dave nodded seriously, his frown deepening. He wondered just how much Mary had told her mother about the recent events and being stalked by her ex husband. Not much, he decided, by the way she spoke about him. Perhaps Mary didn't want to worry her.

'Can't you get Mary a job in your pantomime this year? She's a very good actress.'

Dave shifted uncomfortably in his seat. 'I thought,' he said, clearing his throat, 'she was a dancer.'

'Oh, no. She's been to drama school, you know.'

'Where?'

'Hayward's Heath. Not one of the top London establishments, I know. But very good and highly thought of in Sussex. And Mary's played fairy in panto. She's worked with Bernie Clifton.'

Dave took a swig of Leibfraumilch.

'The one I'm doing at Blackpool's already cast, a long time ago, Janet.'

Janet produced an incredibly thin cigarette from her roller and lit up. Mary came back into the room.

'I was telling Dave,' said her mother, 'about you career as an actress.'

Mary sighed deeply. 'Some career. Mostly kicking my legs up in the back row of the chorus.'

Her mother tapped the table with her index finger. 'And a few bits and pieces. If only you'd stuck at it like Yolande Brewer.'

Dave saw Mary's jaw tighten.

'Yolande,' Janet went on, 'lived next door to us in Hayward's Heath. She went to Bright Lights, too. That's the drama school. Yolande did awfully well for herself. Awfully well. Did a Rowntrees Fruit Gum advert, then there was no looking back. She never stopped. She was always on the box in something or other. I wonder what ever became of her?'

***

As soon as Mike walked into the kitchen, Claire fixed him with a frosty glare. She was sitting at the table reading the Mail on Sunday. He tried to think of something to say, some sort of greeting. Anything would be better than the silence, which was widening the distance between them. He turned away from her unnerving stare and stood, hands in pockets, looking out at the garden which was deteriorating rapidly. The grass was overgrown and weeds were taking over in the flower beds. When Claire eventually spoke, her voice was a blistering triumph of the self righteous.

'At least I was here to say goodbye to Andy.'

'He's gone to Ireland then.'

'You knew he was going?'

'He told me.'

'At least I was here for when he was leaving. So where have you been?'

Knowing he had to face up to this discussion, he came and sat opposite her at the table. 'We need to talk.'

She didn't say anything. Just stared at him, waiting for him to continue. Deliberately making him feel uncomfortable.

'I've come back to fetch more of my things. I'm moving out.'

She laughed humourlessly. 'I don't believe I'm hearing this. We're actually splitting up, breaking apart, and for what?'

Something snapped in Mike. 'I'll tell you for what,' he shouted. 'Your depression I could tolerate. It was something that couldn't be helped. But this ridiculous Ron Hubbard religion, and giving them money, that was the last straw as far as I was concerned.'

Claire remained infuriatingly calm, raising her eyebrows at him. 'Really? And where is it you're living now?'

'Does it matter?'

'Are you staying somewhere on your own?'

Mike avoided her stare and shook his head slowly. 'I've moved in with someone.'

'Anyone I might know?' Claire enquired sarcastically.

'A client of mine who died some time ago. His wife. I've moved in with her.'

Claire frowned as she worked it out, then her lips became taut and her nostrils flared. 'Not that woman who now runs a wine bar.'

Mike nodded slowly.

'I knew as soon as we walked into that wine bar that night that something was going on between you two.'

Mike stared into Claire's eyes as he spoke. 'There was nothing going on then. I promise you. OK, I admit, I always fancied her, even when Gary was alive. But nothing happened between us. Not until you started giving our money away to those lunatics. That's when I asked her out to dinner. And that's when I realised I'd fallen for her.'

He held her look, inwardly congratulating himself on the brilliant performance he was giving. She seemed to back down suddenly, looked at the newspaper and turned over a page. When she eventually spoke, the sudden gear change took him by surprise.

'We're a one car family. How on earth am I going to manage without a car?'

'That's OK. You can have it. It's all yours.'

She looked up from the paper. 'And what about your work?'

He shrugged. Then her mouth opened as the truth dawned on her.

'You've been done, haven't you? After all these years of drinking and driving, finally you've been caught.'

He noticed the slight expression of triumph flitting across her face. He decided it was time to make a move, slid his chair back from the table and stood up.

'I'll go and get my things. And I'll need to order a taxi.'

'Oh, Mike,' she said, sighing deeply. 'What are you going to do for work?'

He shrugged again and sidled out of the kitchen.

***

Following an awkward silence, Dave asked, 'Since when have you rolled your own cigarettes, Janet?'

She hesitated before answering. 'Well, I've always enjoyed a roll-up at home, but when Mary's father was alive, he liked me to smoke ready made cigarettes. He thought it was more feminine.'

'Was he a smoker?'

'Oh yes. Sometimes as a special treat he'd bring home Black Russian cigarettes. Or coloured cocktail ones. He thought they were elegant. You don't see them anymore.'

Janet gazed wistfully at a cloud of blue smoke drifting towards the ceiling.

'How long is it since your husband passed away, Janet?'

As soon as he had said it, Dave felt the frozen silence, like a coffin lid closing. Mary deliberately avoided catching his eye.

'It's nearly twenty years to the day,' Janet muttered hastily.

Ignoring the warning signs – perhaps it was perversity on his part – Dave decided he wouldn't let the subject drop.

'He must have died quite young. What did he die of?'

Janet rose quickly. 'Now then,' she said with forced brightness, 'I've got some lovely treacle tart in the oven. Who's ready for dessert?'

Fifty-Five

Numb with shock, Pran sat on his sofa, staring into space. He remained immobile for a good hour, his thoughts swirling like garbage in a gale. His radio was playing the Pop Master quiz, hosted by Ken Bruce, but Pran was unaware of anything other than his own suffering. The doorbell rang. Wondering who it might be, but also relieved that it was a diversion from his depression, he struggled to stand up, switched off the radio, then went out into the hall and opened the front door.

Her smile greeted him, and her hand came out from behind her back, waving a bottle of champagne in his face.

'Celebration time, kiddo! We made it. And it was all down to your appearance at the tribunal. I think your evidence swung it in my favour, Pran.'

'Hi, Tina,' said Pran, his voice heavy with gloom.

Tina looked concerned. 'What's wrong?'

Pran shook his head, unable to answer her immediately. 'You'd better come in.'

She followed him into his cramped living room, sank into an easy chair, and watched as he dropped back onto the sofa, her brow furrowed with concern for her new-found friend. She waited, knowing he would tell her as soon as he was ready. His eyes were glassy and he stared at the floor. Eventually, he looked up, his expression lost, like a small boy appealing for help.

'I don't expect you've seen the Daily Mail.'

Tina shook her head.

'They did a full page on the tribunal. A big splash. I suppose that's because it was such a big payout. A record payout, they said.'

Tina stretched forward in her chair. 'And you can go down the same route, Pran. It's not too late. I'll back you up. You said so

244

yourself. You can take them to the cleaners. It'll give you a fresh start.'

Shaking his head gravely, Pran said, 'No money's worth what I've had to go through. My father buys the Daily Mail. He read about me being gay. He doesn't want to see me again. Ever. I'm no longer his son, he said.'

Tears suddenly ran down Tina's cheeks. 'Oh, Pran.'

'He telephoned,' Pran went on. 'He was ranting and shouting. I can't believe the terrible things he said to me. I hung up. I couldn't take it.'

'Oh, Pran,' Tina sobbed. 'I'm sorry. So sorry. If I'd known, I... Oh, God! I feel terrible. I should never have dragged you into this. Never.'

'It's not your fault, Tina. I had to do it. If my father has a problem with my sexuality, then... well, it's time I stopped blaming myself.'

Tina rummaged through her handbag, blew her nose in a tissue and wiped her eyes, smearing her eye make-up. 'I can't believe it. Your own father. Perhaps if he's given enough time, he might eventually come to accept it. Maybe it's just the initial shock of finding out the way he did. I mean, in this day and age, surely...'

Pran broke in. 'Maybe. Who knows? But my father's living in another, more traditional age.'

Tina tried to stop further tears bursting to the surface but failed. 'I'm so sorry, Pran. So very, very sorry.'

***

As soon as Ted came home from work he heard Tracey bawling. He dashed upstairs and into her room. Marjorie was leaning over the cot.

'What's wrong?'

'She's got colic.'

'Oh my God! What's that?'

'Griping stomach pains. According to Freda, her Kevin had it really bad when he was a baby.'

Marjorie picked up the screaming, red-faced bundle from the cot and thrust her at Ted. 'Here! See what you can do. I've tried everything. She's driven me mad.'

Ted held the baby against his shoulder and rubbed her back but she continued to scream in his ear. 'It's all right,' he crooned softly. 'Daddy's here, Miranda.'

Marjorie's sharp ears picked up on the name. 'What was that?'

Ted winced. It had slipped out without him thinking. He put on a dense expression, something at which he was quite accomplished. 'What?'

'What you called her?'

'I've no idea. I must have been thinking of someone else.'

Marjorie scratched her chin thoughtfully and suspiciously. 'Miranda you said. Who do you know who's called Miranda?'

'Nobody!' Ted yelled above the baby's cries. 'I don't know anyone called Miranda.'

'You must do. Else you wouldn't have called her it.'

Becoming thoroughly exasperated, Ted bounced the baby up and down. 'Oh, can't you do anything to stop her?' he pleaded to his wife, who was stony faced.

'I want to know who this Miranda is.'

'Oh, she's just a character in a Shakespeare play. The Tempest.'

Marjorie over-reacted, as if Ted had just told her that Miranda was someone with whom he was having a wild affair.

'Stupid bloody name!' she screamed. 'I won't have you calling her after some little tart in a Shakespeare play.'

Ted was nonplussed. 'I only...' he began.

'Her name's Tracey!' Marjorie shouted. 'Tracey!'

'Yes! All right! I just thought she might like a middle name, so that she can choose for herself when she's older.'

'Oh, for God's sake take her out for a walk. I can't stand that screaming no more.'

Ted looked confused. 'A walk?'

'Yes! A bloody long walk. The movement of the pram'll soothe her. Calm her down.'

'How d'you know?'

'Freda told me.'

'Oh,' said Ted, taking the screaming bundle towards the door. 'Freda. If that's not a stupid bloody name, I don't know what is.'

'What was that?' snapped Marjorie.

'Nothing. I'll see you later.'

***

When the doorbell rang again, Pran looked across at Tina and frowned. 'I've no idea who that could be.' He gave her a weak smile. 'Maybe it's one of my father's Muslim hit-men. He's probably got a gay-bashing contract out on me.'

Tina shuddered. 'Oh, don't joke about a thing like that. Answer the door.'

She waited while he went out to the hall, holding her breath as she listened to the door being opened.

'Alan! What are you doing here?'

Tina registered the way Pran's voice had leapt energetically.

'I thought I'd look you up. I was just passing in the old neighbourhood.'

'You'd better come in.'

Alan entered the living room. Tina smiled and nodded at him, especially as he looked so taken aback at finding Pran with a girl.

'Sorry, I didn't realise you had company,' he began.

Pran gestured towards her. 'This is Tina. Alan.'

As they shook hands, Pran added, 'Alan's my old flatmate.' Then laughed foolishly. 'Er – partner, actually.'

Sensing that Pran wanted to be alone with his ex-partner, she stood up. 'Well, I must be off. Good to meet you, Alan.'

'You don't have to dash off on my account,' he said.

'No, I've got to get back to London. I said I'd meet my boyfriend.'

'Congratulations on winning the case.'

'Yeah, it's been a long hard struggle. But thanks to Pran here.' She looked at her friend and leaned forward to kiss his cheek. 'Thanks again, Pran.'

As soon as Pran had seen her out, and returned to the living room, they both stared at each other in silence for a while.

'So how've you been?' Pran asked, after inwardly analysing the silence, and realising they were both comfortable with it.

'Oh – not so bad. I read about the tribunal. I thought you might need some moral support.'

'You're right, as it happens. My father knows about it. And he confirmed my worst fears. Goodbye family.'

'Sorry, Pran. It was brave of you. To do what you did. It really was.'

'Either that, or foolhardy. So how's life with...?'

'Vance?'

'Vance!'

Alan grinned. 'He was American. And he wanted me to go back and live with him in the States. But I couldn't. So we decided to split up.'

Pran frowned thoughtfully. 'When was this?'

'About two months ago.'

'You mean you've been on your own that long? Why didn't you get in touch?'

'Kept meaning to. Then, when I read about the tribunal, I guessed you'd need someone who once meant as much to you as family.'

Pran felt a warm shower washing away his depression. He grinned hugely at Alan. 'You guessed right.'

'So how about coming out with me for dinner tonight?'

'Try and stop me,' Pran said, his eyes suddenly alive and optimistic. 'And I promise I'll watch the intake of wine.' He giggled. 'A gay Muslim who drinks alcohol. I must remember to do the lottery this week.'

Alan laughed. He had been dreading this meeting. But now he was confronting his old partner, and saw how he had missed his sense of humour, he suddenly wept tears of relief.

Pran threw his arms around his ex partner, saying, 'It's OK, Alan. It's going to be OK. I know it is.'

Fifty-Six

Thomas frowned and chewed his bottom lip, a sure sign that he was about to ask for something. 'Thanks for the presents, Uncle Dave. Can me an' Simon, um, have a bit of money to get some sweets?'

Mary pretended to look shocked. 'Thomas! After all the presents you've had.'

Dave smiled and waved her objection aside. 'Course you can.' He fumbled in his pocket and brought out two fifty pence pieces. 'Here we are, Thomas. There you go, Simon.

'Thanks, Dave,' said Simon as he accepted the coin and swaggered to the door.

'Race you to the shop,' Thomas said, pushing in front of his brother.

'Nah. Don't feel like it.'

'It's starting to get dark early,' yelled Mary. 'Come straight home after. No loitering.'

The front door slammed. Mary tutted and shook her head. Dave smiled tolerantly. He leaned forward and picked up the vanishing egg trick from the Penn and Teller conjuring set he'd bought Thomas.

'I used to have one of these when I was a boy. Different magician but exactly the same tricks. Things don't change that much.'

Mary watched him. She could feel a certain tension, knowing he was dying to ask her something. He stared at the plastic conjuring trick, giving it more interest than it deserved. Then he cleared his throat, sat back in the chair and looked directly at her.

'I'm afraid I put my foot in it at your mother's on Sunday.'

'What d'you mean?'

'When I asked about your father.'

Mary smiled thinly. 'You're dying to know, aren't you?'

Dave coughed awkwardly. 'Well, it's just that you've never talked about him.'

'Are you being sympathetic or nosy?'

'Bit of both, I suppose.'

She took a deep breath then let out a long drawn-out sigh before telling him, picking nervously at her nail cuticles as she did. 'I was only fourteen when he died. Darren was nearly sixteen and a bit of a tearaway.'

'You never talk about your brother much.'

Mary shrugged. 'What's there to talk about? We were close once but now he's 12,000 miles away. He hardly ever writes. I think he's cut himself off. Trying to escape from the past.'

'So what happened? With your father?'

'He committed suicide. Just went out for a walk early one Sunday and never came back. They found him in a corner of the park, a plastic bag over his head.'

She stopped speaking, waiting for his reaction.

'God!' he whispered. 'What a terrible thing to...Why did he do it?'

Mary shook her head angrily. 'No one knows. He seemed to be perfectly normal. There didn't seem to be any rhyme or reason. I've thought about it – why, why, why a million times and I still can't come up with anything close to an answer.'

'Was he depressed?'

'Not really. It was hard to tell. Dad didn't have a sense of humour. He was a very reserved man. It was always difficult to tell what he was thinking.'

Mary's eyes blazed with anger.

'D'you know, he never once got down on the floor and played with us as children. He wasn't like a normal father. Me and Darren could never remember him having played with us. Not once.

'I feel more angry about it now. After he died I cried so much. I seemed to have cried myself dry. I've got no more tears left for him anymore.'

'And what about your mother?'

'She avoids talking about it. I suppose, in a way, she's doing the same as Darren.'

After a slight pause, Dave went and sat on the arm of Mary's chair and slipped a hand across her shoulders. 'I'm sorry,' he whispered. 'I'm so sorry. It must have been terrible.'

She looked round at him and gave him a forced smile. 'Got a lot in common, haven't we? We both had weird fathers.'

'There's nowt so queer as folk.' He felt her shiver. 'What's wrong?'

'I was thinking of Ronnie. His burglary of this house will be a first offence. He might not get a jail sentence. Then what?'

'Well the trial's set for two weeks' time. Let's hope they put him away.'

'And if they don't?'

'Let's cross that bridge when we come to it. Whatever happens, they're not going to let him stalk you again.'

'But if they don't put him away, what can they do to stop him?'

'Well, they can...' Dave began, desperately trying to think of something reassuring to tell her. But he knew as much as she did that it was useless.

'I know that bastard,' Mary said bitterly. 'He'll already be plotting his next move.'

***

'I'm in the lounge,' Marjorie called out.

Fearing the worst Ted entered, and Marjorie pointed at the best Draylon chair in the room.

'Sit down!' she said. Then, to soften the command, added, 'Now we've got a quiet moment, I want to have a word.'

Ted sank reluctantly into the chair, sneaked a glance at his watch, then pulled himself into a more upright position, perched on the edge of the chair. 'Will this take long? Only I've got to be at work...'

Marjorie waved it aside with a regal gesture. 'Oh, it doesn't matter if you're late for once.'

Ted looked shocked. He was always conscientious, and could never remember a time when he'd turned up late. He felt he was partly responsible for keeping the trains running to time.

'But the fast Cannon Street train...' he began to protest.

'Might be late!' Marjorie finished with a chuckle. 'This is our future I want to talk about. Let's have a glass of Bristol Cream.'

That was when Ted noticed the small schooner on the coffee table and realised his wife had already had a tipple or two.

'I never drink before I go on duty.'

This wasn't strictly accurate. He occasionally allowed himself a half of bitter. But just the one, followed by an extra strong mint, in case alcohol was detected on his breath and people thought he'd had more than a half.

But Marjorie, refusing to take no for an answer, poured out two glasses of sherry and handed one to Ted.

'It's not as though you're the driver,' Marjorie said in a belittling sort of way.

'Even so,' replied Ted, regarding the miniscule glass as if it contained poison. 'It's still a responsible job. And if they smell alcohol on my breath...'

'Buy some chewing gum,' Marjorie said, closing the subject. 'Now then, I expect you've noticed all the letters I've been getting from estate agents.'

Ted nodded fearfully, dreading the outcome of the conversation.

'Well, I've decided,' continued Marjorie, in between a quick slurp of Bristol Cream, 'that this house is too big for us. And I shan't be sorry to get rid of it. Have you seen the way them next door look down their noses at us?'

'They seem all right.'

Marjorie snorted derisively. 'Bloody snobs. They always look at you as if they was laughing at you. Be glad to see the back of 'em, I will.'

'So where are you thinking of moving to?'

'A hotel. In Tunbridge Wells.

Ted formed his mouth into a silent 'O'. Marjorie regarded him suspiciously through narrowed eyes.

'You don't seem very surprised.'

'Well, yes, I am. It's come as a shock. I mean… a hotel. Who's going to run it?'

'We are. You and me.'

'But what about my job? And my pension?'

Marjorie waved it aside, and downed the rest of her sherry before speaking. Her eyes were glassy.

'Oh, stuff your job, Ted. This is a lot more exciting. This is something I've always wanted to do; run a small commercial hotel. Think of all those reps in the bar, telling jokes and stories. There'll never be a dull moment.'

Ted downed his drink. His legs wobbled as he rose. He glanced at his watch.

'I'd better…' he croaked and cleared his throat.

'Ted! Are you all right? You've gone very pale suddenly.'

Fifty-Seven

Two days after the funeral of her first husband, Jackie refused to make the journey to East Peckham to sort out his house contents. Vanessa and Nicky hadn't learnt to drive, so Nigel reluctantly agreed to take them over and lend a hand.

The house was a nondescript, early sixties built semi-detached, in a rather characterless street of similar houses. The girls, expecting to find the house a mess inside, were surprised at how neat and tidy everything was. It was almost too pristine, as if someone had been round to put everything in order before they began the house clearance, although they didn't think anyone else had a key.

The house had one through lounge downstairs, a spacious kitchen and dining room, and upstairs there was one bathroom and two reasonable size bedrooms. Nothing in the house reflected the personality of its occupant and it remained as characterless as the building itself. There was not a single framed picture or photograph on the bare walls. It was as if their father had deliberately wanted to remain an enigma, even after death. Except that the circumstances of his accident had a neon presence imprinted on their imaginations as they let their eyes wander from the sofa across the carpet to the wide screen television set.

Nigel's curiosity burned with excitement as he tried to tug open two doors of a large teak sideboard and discovered it was locked.

'I wonder if there's a key to this hideous piece of furniture,' he said.

Knowing the sideboard would probably contain items of a more personal nature, such as holiday photographs, possibly official documents like insurance policies and hopefully a last will and testament, they began a search for the key. Nicky found it in the cutlery drawer in the kitchen. Vanessa grabbed it from her and pushed it into the lock.

'Well, let's hope he put his house in order,' she said with a small nervous laugh as she pulled the sideboard door open.

Nicky gasped. 'Oh my God!' she exclaimed.

Nigel tried to suppress a smile, knowing how it would upset the girls if they saw how amused he was.

'I've never seen so much filth,' he said. 'It's disgusting.'

The sideboard was filled with stacks of hard-porn videos and DVDs, with titles such as Suburban Gang Bang, Close Cum Shots and Teenage Slags Get Punished. And, as if the pornography wasn't bad enough, there were sex toys and contraptions of every description. Some were still unpacked in their polythene wrappers. Vanessa took hold of a peculiar looking object and held it at arm's length.

'What the hell is this?' she said. She turned it over and read on the underside of the package: 'Treat yourself with this blow-job simulator.'

Nicky began crying. 'Get the bin liners,' she wept. 'Let's get rid of this stuff.'

'Are they still in the car?' Vanessa asked Nigel. But he was miles away, his head buried in a pornographic magazine.

'Hmm?' he murmured without looking up.

'Men!' snapped Vanessa. 'They're all the bloody same.'

***

'Let me top you up.' Donald poured red wine into Ted's glass. 'I'll open another bottle. You look as if you need a sedative.

Ted mumbled his thanks, gazing forlornly into the distance. Donald left the room, returning a few minutes later with another bottle of Rioja.

'Hey! Stop feeling sorry for yourself.'

'Ted looked up. 'I'm sorry.' His voice was tremulous. 'I've been depressed lately. I don't want to give up my job on the railway and run a commercial hotel.'

Donald came and sat next to him on the sofa. 'Well, just refuse.'

'That's easy for you to say.'

Donald patted his friend's knee. 'Yes, I know. It's always easy to dish out advice. But if you want my advice.'

Donald took a sip of wine, waiting for Ted to respond.

'I suppose,' said Ted with a trace of bitterness, 'that you're wondering why I want to keep my job as a guard.'

Donald nodded fervently. 'I must admit running a hotel would seem to offer more of a challenge. I mean, to-ing and fro-ing to Charing Cross every day's a bit of a dead end job I would have thought.'

'But you don't understand, Donald. I need to keep the job because of you.'

'Me?'

Ted took a large gulp of wine before continuing. 'Yes, I have a certain amount of independence at the moment. Marjorie doesn't show much interest in my rota, overtime and all that. So I get to see you whenever I like.'

Donald frowned thoughtfully. 'Yes, I know what you mean. Once she's got you in her sights all day long.'

Out in the kitchen something clicked loudly, making Ted start. 'What was that?'

Donald laughed. 'The dishwasher tablet coming out of its little box as it starts its cycle. You thought it might be Bamber, didn't you? No need to worry about that any more, now that we've broken the ice between us.' He caught Ted glancing at his watch. 'How long have we got before you have to dash back to the wife from hell?'

Ted leaned back on the sofa, feeling relaxed as the wine went to his head. He giggled. 'Yes, to hell with her.'

'That's my boy,' Donald encouraged.

'You know, there was a time, Donald – recently – when I thought things would be better between Marjorie and me. If only...'

'What?'

'I don't want to share you. If only you could get shot of Bamber, and I could get rid of Marjorie, we could both live together and look after Miranda. Life would be perfect.'

A mischievous glint came into Donald's eye. 'Well, we'll just have to get the poison bottle out, won't we?'

***

Nigel reversed the car into a space by the household waste area at Tunbridge Wells rubbish tip. Vanessa threw open her door hurriedly, dashed round to the back and opened the boot. She grabbed one of the offending black bin liner bags and was about to lift it to hurl it into the pit of rubbish and waste below, when an officious voice chilled her.

'One moment. This is household waste.'

Vanessa gave him a sharp look. 'This is household waste.'

The council official moved towards her black bundle. He was a short, stocky man with a ragged moustache, and Vanessa would have liked to pull it off his face, causing him a great deal of pain. He looked at her bin liner suspiciously.

'That looks like books and magazines. That's for recycling.'

Vanessa raised her voice. 'Look, you idiot, this is household waste. So mind your own business.'

She lifted the bag and was about to hurl it into the mess below.

'But it is my business. We've got a good record for recycling. And we're looking to improve it.'

He grabbed the bag. Vanessa tried to pull it from his grasp and it split, spilling its contents on the ground. Eyes widening, the council man stared in fascination at the bundle of hard pornography, and especially a picture of a peroxide blonde in the full-throated act of fellatio.

'What the hell's this?' he demanded.

But Vanessa had already turned and got back into Nigel's car. 'Quick!' she yelled. 'Let's get out of here. The bag split, and the council man saw what was inside.'

Nigel laughed uproariously as he drove away.

'That's not funny,' said Nicky, cringing in the passenger seat next to him. 'And there's another bag of the stuff. Now what are we going to do?'

'Let's drive to some woods and dump it,' said Vanessa.

Nigel stopped laughing. 'But that's fly-tipping. It's illegal.'

'I don't care,' said Vanessa.

Nigel snorted, couldn't contain himself and began laughing again. In spite of her recent shock, Vanessa suddenly saw the funny side of the incident, and she too began laughing. Before long, all three of them were sharing the joke, and Nicky's tears were tears of laughter now.

Fifty-Eight

Mandy snuggled close to Craig under his umbrella and giggled. 'This is crazy,' she said. 'Whose idea was it to go for a walk across Tunbridge Wells common?'

He smiled, stopped walking and kissed the top of her head, her hair damp but with a slight scent of something floral. 'I think,' he replied, 'it was someone not a million miles from here.'

Mandy shrugged and pursed her lips. 'Well, I thought it would get us out of your grotty flat. If I have to stay there too long I get depressed. Couldn't you afford somewhere better? I mean, it ain't as if you was working for a pittance, Craig. You an' Maggie own the wine bar.'

Craig sighed and irritation crept into his voice. 'I haven't got around to thinking about moving yet. We seem to spend so much time at work. Maybe after Christmas.'

'But that's a couple of months away.'

Craig forced a grin. 'It's not long. The supermarket shelves are loaded with Christmas gifts.'

She stared probingly into his eyes and he guessed where this conversation was leading.

'I spend most of the time at your place,' she said. 'My parents are convinced I've already moved out.'

Craig looked away, his eyes focused on the green dome of the Opera House in the town below. He frowned and shook his head before speaking. 'I'm worried about the future. It's just that it doesn't feel all that stable.'

'Because of Maggie?'

'Partly. And now there's Mike working for us.'

'Only part time.'

'Don't get me wrong. I like him, and I thought at first he was going to be good for Maggie. But now I'm not so sure. It's like they're both on some sort of self destruct partnership, like a suicide pact.'

Mandy's voice became disapprovingly harsh. 'We have to face it, Craig, they're both alcoholics.'

Craig nodded slowly and thoughtfully. 'And that's what worries me. How can we continue to run the wine bar? It's like leaving children in charge of a sweet shop.'

Mandy squeezed his hand. 'Look, whatever happens, Craig, I want to be with you. We're both capable of working, and with two salaries coming in...'

She stopped speaking deliberately and gazed into his eyes.

'It'll get dead quiet in the new year,' he said. 'I promise that whatever happens we'll definitely find a flat where we can live together. That's if you fancy moving in with me. I mean permanent, like.'

Mandy grinned hugely then kissed him full on the lips.

***

Dave stretched across the kitchen table and reached for the sugar. 'I can't do without at least one teaspoon of the stuff.'

Opposite him, Mary pushed the bowl towards him. 'Stop worrying. It's not as if you're fat.'

He spooned a guilty half teaspoon of sugar into his mug and stirred, then tapped his stomach. 'I'm getting a bit of a paunch.'

Mary made an impatient clicking noise with her mouth. 'For God's sake! You think you've got worries. I've got to appear in court the week after next for Ronnie's trial.'

Dave sighed exasperatedly and shook his head. 'I told you, for stalking and burglary they'll put him away. It won't be a problem.'

'Until he gets out.'

'One bridge at a time.'

'And what if he gets off?'

'He won't.'

'How can you be so sure?'

Dave sighed again. 'The police caught him in the act of breaking in. Bang to rights. With all the other evidence of him stalking you, and how you complained about it to them...'

'That's just it,' Mary cut in. 'Ronnie's such a bullshitter. He can be so convincing. He's one of those liars who remembers everything he's said, and he never seems to get caught out.'

Dave leaned across the table and squeezed her hand. She found the gesture irritating and withdrew her hand impatiently and picked up her coffee mug.

'I know what I'm going to say in court. I've got to fight fire with fire.'

Dave frowned. 'How d'you mean?'

'I'm going to lie about some of the things he said. Tell them about his threats to kill you, me and the kids.'

'I wouldn't do that, if I were you.'

'Why not? No one can prove differently. It'll be my word against his.'

'Yes but...' Dave stopped, unable to think of a convincing argument why she shouldn't make up lies about Ronnie.

'But what?' Mary snapped.

'I just don't want you to get caught out. Supposing he has a good lawyer who finds out you're lying?'

Mary pushed her chair away from the table and stood up. 'You must think I'm really stupid.'

Dave looked up at her, a hurt look in his eyes. 'I didn't think that for one minute.'

Mary's lips pursed stubbornly. 'Well then.'

'It's just that these lawyers are professionals used to leading people into saying things they don't want to.'

'You've been watching too much television.'

Dave opened his mouth to speak but she broke in hurriedly. 'OK. I'll only tell them the truth, exactly as it happened, and everything Ronnie said. The truth. I'm going to pick up the kids from school.'

Dave watched her as she left the room, sceptical of the way she had changed her mind about telling the truth.

***

At the wine bar that night Craig and Mandy found time to sit down and have a spot of supper together, leaving Maggie behind the bar and Mike serving at the tables. They both noticed Mike's eyes were glassy with drink and kept eyeing him warily. And Maggie's voice was becoming strident and her laugh irritatingly loud. They hurriedly finished their meal so they could get back to work again and had secretly agreed that what Maggie and Mike needed was food inside them.

'Your turn,' Craig told his sister as he went behind the bar. 'Why don't you and Mike have a leisurely meal together? It's not as if we're that busy.'

'Not that quiet either,' Maggie replied, waving her wine glass in the direction of the bar in general, and spilling wine onto the counter. She wiped it with a bar cloth and grinned challengingly at Craig, as if he had criticised the accident, but his eyes were frosty. Maggie shrugged, feeling some discomfort from his accusing stare.

'OK, I'll get Mike, and we'll sit at that table over there.'

She went and sat at a corner table, taking with her a bottle of Chardonnay for herself and a bottle of Australian Shiraz for Mike. After Mike had sat next to her at the table, Mandy got their food orders and went out to the kitchen to ask the chef if he could please prioritise their steak and fries.

Craig stood behind the bar, moodily scowling as he watched Mike running his hands up Maggie's thighs. They whispered and giggled and fondled each other in between large gulps of wine, and Craig prayed that the food would arrive soon.

The chef managed to produce their meal in under ten minutes, and at first they both attacked their food with relish, but when Maggie was halfway through her steak she pushed the plate to one side and came behind the bar to get another bottle of Shiraz for them both.

'Don't you think you've had enough?' Craig said.

Maggie gave him a withering look before returning to her table. She filled their glasses and they drank deeply. Then Mike began kissing her in earnest, as if he had forgotten they were in a public place, running his hands over her breasts. Most of the customers were by now casting curious glances in their direction. Especially as Maggie was responding to Mike's advances by squealing and moaning with pleasure, now having totally forgotten where they were.

Craig and Mandy stood transfixed, looking on in horror as the couple noisily dropped to the floor under the table, pawing at each other's clothes, attempting to undress each other, oblivious that their drunken lovemaking was being watched by a dozen customers.

Fifty-Nine

Following the funeral of their father and the house clearance trauma, both Nicky and Vanessa became immune to any further stress and accepted the move from their house in Tunbridge Wells to Crowborough with resigned indifference. But two days after the move, as they enjoyed a leisurely Saturday morning breakfast with their mother, Nigel came storming into the kitchen.

'I can't concentrate,' he yelled. 'That radio's so loud it's distorted. Can't you hear it?'

They looked up at him expressionlessly and he seethed because he thought this was passive aggression and all three were ganging up on him.

'I don't believe it!' he ranted. 'Am I the only one who can hear how distorted this racket is?'

Vanessa caught her sister's eye and they sniggered. Nigel glowered at them and his face burned.

'Well, I'm glad you think it's funny. Some of us have got some work to do.'

'I'm sorry,' said Nicky. 'We weren't laughing at you. It's just that you sounded like that old bloke on TV, the one who's always complaining.'

'I'm not always complaining.'

'Nicky didn't say you were, darling,' said Jackie in her most reasonable tone, which Nigel found so irritating.

He fiddled with the tuning dial of the radio. 'Look at that! It's not even tuned in properly. Couldn't you hear it was out of tune?'

'No, I couldn't!' snapped Jackie.

'Well I don't know,' Nigel muttered to himself and turned the volume down so that it was barely audible.

'Oh, for heaven's sake!' said Jackie. 'It's Saturday. You must learn to relax more. You'll have a nervous breakdown if you carry on like this.'

'I must get these quotations written. The deadline's at noon on Monday.'

'And how long will that take?'

'Most of the weekend, I should think.'

'What!'

'I'm sorry. I can't help it. It's what I do for a living.'

'You won't remain living for very long if you carry on like this. You're overdoing it. At fifty six you need to slow down a bit.'

Vanessa and Nicky watched this exchange with mild interest. Nigel suddenly ran out of steam.

'It's all right for you,' he mumbled lamely.

Jackie's lips tightened. 'Do I take that to mean because I'm not working at the moment?'

'Of course not. I like having you at home. You know I do.'

With the edge of her knife Jackie pushed the crust of her toast to the side of her plate with a positive clatter. 'I think we ought to get one thing straight...' she began.

Nigel waved his hands about with frustration. 'Please! I'd like to have a lengthy discussion about your duties, but I don't have time.'

Jackie looked horrified. 'Duties!'

'Yes, duties. After all, if I'm to be the provider, working all hours God sends, then I hope it's not too much to expect you to fulfil certain housewifely obligations.'

Jackie stared at him, her face set in an expression of numbed disbelief.

'And another thing,' Nigel continued, 'I'm not having you dictate to me who cuts my hair. Mike cuts it the way I like it and I'm going to give him a ring.'

Nigel felt this was a good exit line and marched out of the kitchen. Jackie started as he slammed his office door closed. She looked helplessly at Vanessa and Nicky, hoping for sympathy, but they both stared at her accusingly, as if to say: "We told you so."

Nicky suddenly laughed nervously and said, 'Shall I turn the radio up a bit?'

Jackie sighed and shook her head. 'No. Better not.'

***

As Ted hurried along Church Road past Trinity Theatre, where he always looked longingly at the posters, hoping one day they might present a decent Shakespeare play, he went over the lottery numbers in his head. He had been doing them independently of Marjorie for several months now, and had chosen the numbers from his favourite works of the bard of Avon in the chronological order of when they were supposedly written.

He had ten minutes to spare until he was due to arrive at the station for his shift and he hurried into the newsagent's in Mount Pleasant to place his bet. He knew the odds were stacked against him but keeping it a secret from Marjorie gave him a vicarious thrill, and if he won just ten pounds one day, the sweetness of the deception would make him feel empowered. Just three of his numbers. That was all he craved. A modest little win. But it would be a major triumph.

***

Craig dreaded visiting his sister but it had to be done. He went around the side of the house and was relieved to find his niece and nephew were playing quietly in the garden, building some sort of toy village in one of the flowerbeds. He called out to them in passing but for once they were so engrossed that they just gave him a cursory wave.

He crossed the patio, rapped his knuckle on the sliding glass door, and went into the house. Maggie was in the kitchen drinking coffee, her face blotchy and her eyes watery and bloodshot. As Craig entered, her eyes flitted, darting to and fro, lost and unnerved by his sudden entrance, as if she needed time to prepare herself. He could see the panic in her disposition, the fear of being confronted by the hard-hitting truth of her behaviour. Her voice was sombre when she spoke, knowing why he was here.

'Hi, Craig!'

On the way over, Craig had thought about the ice-breaking way of saying what he wanted to say, but now he was confronted by the devastating sight of his sister, suffering from yet another hangover and amnesia from her terrible behaviour in the wine bar, he went straight to the point.

'Maggie, this has got to stop. Right now!.'

Her eyes blazed as she swung round to face him. 'What the hell are you talking about, little brother.'

'Your behaviour. You and Mike. Having it off under the table in the wine bar.'

She frowned and her eyes looked distant.

'You don't remember, do you? You were both so pissed, you were at each other under the table. Don't you remember?'

She turned and glared at him. 'We were just having a bit of fun. Deliberately having a laugh with the customers. Pub games, that's all it was.'

'Oh, come on, Maggie. You were both out of it.'

Maggie picked up her coffee mug angrily, then slammed it down again onto the work surface. 'Now look, Craig, keep out of it. It's none of your bloody business.'

Craig's mouth opened and closed several times before he was able to speak. 'It is my business. You're forgetting I'm a partner in the wine bar. I sold the chippie to come into this venture with you.'

Maggie's eyes bulged as she stared at her brother, the veins standing out on her neck. 'And who gave you the chippie? You were nothing. One of our employees. If it hadn't been for me, you'd be back in prison by now. Where you'll probably end up.'

Craig was astounded, his mouth wide open as he stared out his sister, unable to speak. She was still very much under the influence of alcohol, he realised, and was not behaving rationally.

'Where's Mike?' he said after a long and uncomfortable silence. 'Still in bed?'

'He's gone on the bus to Crowborough – to do some hair cutting.'

Craig decided it was time to leave. He walked to the door and fed her his parting shot. 'I pity the poor sod who has Mike to cut his hair today. Unless he's going for the punk style.'

***

When Ted got home that evening, Marjorie was in the lounge sipping cream sherry. She shushed him as he sank into an easy chair and started to speak. The lotto balls were about to be released. The crowd in the BBC studio applauded and brayed as they tumbled and fell. Then, as a ball rolled into the hole and down the ramp, the crowd whistled and cheered as though they all had the same number and everyone in the studio was a winner.

Marjorie glared at the TV set. 'The worst week ever,' she said. 'Not a single number. Not one.'

She cast a glance in Ted's direction, then her eyes became glued to his face. He had a strange look in his eyes and a slight smile tugging at the corners of his mouth.

'Ted! What's wrong?'

'Nothing,' he said. 'Nothing at all.'

Five of his beloved Shakespeare plays had turned up trumps, and the sixth was a bonus ball. He was a winner at last. But he was not about to tell Marjorie. This little nest egg was his insurance policy. His lifeline.

Sixty

Dave walked Mary away from the court, his arms about her. She was numb with shock. Ronnie had been given an 18 month prison sentence, which meant he would probably be out in a year.

As they past a pub, Mary stopped suddenly. 'I think I could do with a large drink,' she said.

Dave nodded gravely. This one looks seedy enough. Probably be the usual late afternoon winos. Sure you wouldn't prefer to look for somewhere more salubrious?'

Mary shook her head emphatically. 'I don't care where we go. Let's just have a drink.'

Dave was right. The pub had an air of neglect about it, and a stale smell of beer, sweat and smoke. And the few customers drinking had obviously been there most of the day and their voices were over loud.

Dave bought Mary a large brandy and Coke, himself a pint of bitter, and they found a corner well away from the noisiest customers. Mary took a large swallow of her drink, then shook her head as if she couldn't quite believe what she had been through.

'He'll be out in a year, Dave. What the hell am I going to do?'

Dave shrugged. 'It was a light sentence. But then, it was a first offence. And it didn't go down too well when they discovered you'd deliberately set him up like that.'

She slammed her glass onto the table. 'What was I supposed to do?'

'I know, I know. I'm just saying that they seemed a bit – how shall I put it? – a bit angry that you seemed to be taking the law into your own hands.'

'But the police were useless, you know that.'

Dave bit his lip before speaking. 'I'm sorry, sweetheart, I'm going to have to say this. It didn't help, you lying like that about him threatening to kill us all. His lawyer really jumped on that.'

'But the point is,' Mary said, her voice rising in anger, 'he's quite capable of doing that. He scares me. He really does. I saw the evil smile he gave me in court, and he knew it was freaking me out. As soon as he gets out of jail it'll be ten times worse because now he'll want revenge. What the hell are we going to do?'

There was a long pause while Dave thought about this. He pursed his lips and his brow furrowed into a thoughtful frown.

'I've been thinking,' he announced, waiting for her to prompt him into continuing.

'What about?'

'I get most of my work up north. It's where I'm from. Why don't we disappear to somewhere in Yorkshire, the outskirts of Leeds, say. For what I can sell the house in Tunbridge Wells, we can probably get much better up there.'

'You don't think Ronnie'll find us?'

'Why should he? I mean, let's face it, because you were still living in the same town when he came back from America, you were probably quite easy to find. But if we move away completely, how's he going to find us? We could be anywhere in the British Isles. He'd have no way of knowing.'

Suddenly there was a spark in Mary as the gloom lifted In spite of her doubt, there was now the excitement of a fresh start, a new horizon for which to aim. She knew she had to investigate her feelings slowly, work out all the pros and cons.

'What about my mother?' was her first concern. 'And it'll be an upheaval for Simon and Thomas.'

'It's not as if we're going to the ends of the earth. She can come and visit, and vice versa. And as for an upheaval for the lads, you know what kids are like: some of them love a great big change in their lives. To them it'll be an adventure.'

Mary placed a hand on his leg and squeezed, snuggling close to him on the bench seat. 'Oh, Dave,' she said, 'you'd really do that, sell the house and everything? Move away – just for me.'

He grinned at her. 'No. Not for you. For us.'

***

'Can I help you, sir?' the young woman with red hair asked Ted as he slid into the seat by the desk opposite her. A pristine desk, smooth and paper free, hygienic and dust free, but characterless.

'I wish to open an account.'

She smiled at him reassuringly. 'Do you have an account anywhere else?' she asked.

Ted hesitated. 'Well, yes, I have a joint account with my wife. But now I'd like to open one of my own.'

The young woman stared at him, keeping her expression deliberately impassive, waiting for him to continue. Ted shifted in his seat and it made a creaking noise.

'There's nothing wrong with me having my own account is there?'

The young woman shook her head slowly and frowned. 'Of course not. But...'

Ted leaned forward and fixed her with a desperate look. 'But?' he questioned.

'Nothing wrong at all,' she said hurriedly.

Ted felt it was time to be impressive. 'I'd like to open an account and deposit this cheque.'

He took the folded cheque out of his pocket and pushed it across the desk towards her. It was his moment of triumph. He'd had the cheque sent to Donald's address and they had celebrated with champagne when it arrived. Even now, two days later, he was still on a high.

He watched carefully as the young woman's eyes widened slightly as she saw the amount, although she was doing her best not to show anything in her expression. She eased her chair away from the desk and stood up.

'I'll just go and see if the manager's free. I won't keep you a minute if you don't mind waiting.'

Ted smiled confidently. It was amazing how such a sum of money could boost your confidence.

'Of course not,' he said, relaxing back into his chair. His smile widened as he began to fantasise about the life that lay in store for him. His own secret, and a very healthy, bank account. That was one in the eye for Marjorie. Except she would never know about it.

Sixty-One

Considering the units of alcohol he normally consumed, for several days now Mike had managed to keep his consumption to a tolerable level, so that physically he felt the glow of something intangible, giving him sensations of inhabiting someone else's body. What had made him cut down drastically was the disastrous visit to cut a client's hair. He had been so drunk he had made a terrible hash of it, and the client had refused to pay, leading to a violent argument. Then, on the bus back from Crowborough, he saw a man get on that he recognised from a pub in which he used to drink years ago. Mike knew something of the man's history. A successful antique furniture restorer, with plenty of wealthy clients, a large house on the edge of Southborough Common, and married with a young family. Then he lost everything through alcoholism. As Mike watched the man shakily hand the driver his fare, he observed the skeletal frame, the skinny legs and the bloodshot eyes, and this, coupled with his experience in ruining his client's hair, had been a slight turning point for Mike. He knew he was still very dependent on alcohol, couldn't get through the day completely teetotal, but at least he'd reduced his intake, so that now he felt able to cope with the visit to meet Claire; a visit he anticipated with a sense of righteous malice. And, a few days ago, something had happened indicating his luck was about to change for the better. Killing time to cut a client's hair in Warwick Park, instead of going to a pub as he usually did when he had time to spare, he browsed in Hall's famous second-hand bookshop, and was rewarded by finding a book called Bare-Faced Messiah, an exposé of L Ron Hubbard and Scientology. Now he could go home and confront Claire, armed with some interesting facts about her ridiculous beliefs.

***

Jackie had insisted they all four should sit down to a family dinner together, and she had gone to the trouble of making a lasagne with fresh ingredients, served with an Italian style salad. They sat at the dining table waiting for Nigel to join them.

'This lasagne will get cold,' said Vanessa, staring challengingly at her mother.

Jackie sighed and said, 'Oh well, why don't you start? I'll wait for Nigel.'

Vanessa shrugged, pursed her lips, and grabbed her knife and fork, her attitude suggesting that her mother was being wimpish. Nigel bounded into the room.

'Sorry about that. I just had to finish off in the office.'

Vanessa and Nicky looked up at him, caught each other's eye, and spluttered with laughter. His face flushed with annoyance and embarrassment.

'Yes, I know, I know! It's a bloody awful haircut, and I've been too busy to get it rectified, but there's no need to make me feel worse than I do.'

Jackie concentrated on dousing her salad, deliberately avoiding eye contact with Nigel, as she spoke. 'Well, I'm sorry to have to say this, but I did warn you about using that hairdresser again. I never liked him.'

Nigel ignored it, sank into his chair. His hand brushed the sprouts of hair sticking up from the back of his head and he sighed impatiently before licking his fingers, then tried to smooth down the offending hair. The family ate in disgruntled silence, and the sound of eating and scrape of cutlery highlighted the awkwardness of their attempts at a harmonious dinner.

After what seemed an overbearingly long silence, Jackie cleared her throat gently. 'Anyone got any news?' she asked with false brightness.

It was the cue Vanessa had been waiting for. 'Yes, I have.' She waited for them all to look in her direction, enjoying her moment.

'We've found a flat in Tunbridge Wells. I'll be moving there the week after next.'

Jackie frowned and put down her cutlery with a clatter. 'This is all very sudden. Who's we? And how can you afford it?'

'I'm moving to a new flat with Tom. He's my boyfriend.'

'And how long have you known this Tom?'

'Nearly three weeks.'

Jackie's eyes widened with alarm. 'What! Just three weeks, and you're going to be living together.'

Vanessa smiled confidently, deliberately goading her mother. 'Well, at least we didn't meet through a dating agency, like you and lover boy here.'

Nigel scowled at her. 'But at least we dated for quite a long time before...'

He stopped as the thought and the sentence left him high and dry.

Vanessa pounced. 'Before you had it off, you mean.'

Nigel pointed at her with his knife. 'Steady on!' he warned. 'Let's not get personal. I respect your mother. Which is more than I can say for you two.'

Jackie silenced him with a wave of her hand, her attention focused on Vanessa. 'So you're in a relationship with this boy...'

Vanessa grinned as she interrupted her mother. 'Hardly a boy. He's thirty six.'

Jackie pushed her plate to one side and leaned forward. 'I can't believe I'm hearing this. You're sharing a flat with an older man. And if that's not bad enough – I mean, you're still a student – how on earth will you find your share of the rent?'

'Oh, Tom's not worried about that. He's loaded.'

Jackie's mouth opened almost in a parody of alarm. Then she became aware of a snuffling sound. She and Nigel directed their focus to Nicky, whose hands were clasped tightly on her lap while tears trickled down her cheeks.

'Nicky! What is it? What's wrong?' said her mother.

Nicky turned to her sister, appealing through her tears. 'How could you leave me alone like this? Alone in Crowborough with these two. Now what am I going to do?'

Vanessa shook her head impatiently. 'You're such a baby. You've got a job. Why not go out and get your own flat?'

Nigel, who couldn't wait to get rid of the daughters, was unable to suppress his joy. He scooped up great portions of lasagne, as if the food was a great source of comfort and brought him a sense of well being.

'Mmm,' he said through a mouthful. 'This is a lovely dinner, darling. The best you've cooked for ages. I'm really enjoying this.'

Jackie stared at him with a mixture of confusion and loathing, unable to decide whether she loved or hated him at that moment.

***

Mike still had his key and let himself in the front door. He heard voices coming from the living room. Female voices, giggling and speaking enthusiastically. They hadn't heard him come in, and were surprised when he pushed open the living room door.

Claire gestured in her other two friends' direction. 'Mike. I think you've met Lucy and Japonica.'

Mike smiled charmingly. 'Of course, how lovely to see you ladies again.' He managed to say it without a trace of sarcasm. He cast a look towards the redheaded American. 'Lucy, you're from America, I believe.'

She flashed a set of perfect teeth at him. 'The big apple.'

He nodded and smiled. 'Of course. Chicago.'

A small frown of confusion tugged at the American's brow. 'No, I think you'll find it's New York City.'

Mike grinned at her. 'Sorry, I get confused. My engrams get in the way. But then I haven't had to pay a small fortune for an auditing.'

Claire reddened angrily. 'If you've come here just to ridicule our beliefs...'

Japonica, the young woman who looked to Mike like a bird of prey, focused him in her sights, as if she might swoop.

He widened his arms in a gesture of reasonableness. 'How can I possibly ridicule someone who may eventually make it up the ladder to attain the status of Operating Thetan Three – the level in which you learn the secrets of the universe?

You'll be surprised to hear, my darling wife, that these people believe that 75 million years ago a galactic warlord controlled some over populated planets – Xenu he was called, straight out of the comic books. And Xenu got these trillions of people and brought them to earth, where they were vaporised and became radioactive souls.'

He stared challengingly at the American woman. 'Well, am I right so far?'

The American shrank into her chair, as if Mike was the devil himself. Her eyes were fearful, and she looked towards Claire as if she had just suffered a beating. 'I'm afraid,' she said, 'that your husband is a Suppressive Person. I think we all ought to leave. Now!'

They all three rose in tandem, picked up their bags and ring binders and prepared to leave. Mike's anger rose in his chest and throat. He felt helpless now. Unsatisfied. He was looking forward to destroying them with the ridiculous things he had discovered about their movement, but if they were just going to ignore him and walk away, there was nothing he could do about it.

As Claire walked out of the door, Mike spoke quickly, wanting her to hear everything he had to say. 'I don't suppose they've told you yet the science fiction story they want you to believe in. Don't let them get you, Claire. It's silly. Childish. You might just as well believe in Batman and Robin, or Ming the Magnificent.'

He followed them to the front door. Without even glancing back at him, Claire left with the other two women, closing the door quietly behind her.

Dazed and confused, Mike stared helplessly at the closed door. Then, like a dog coming out of the sea, he shook himself, went into the kitchen and grabbed a bottle of Merlot from the wine rack. He sighed deeply as he searched for the corkscrew.

'Just one glass,' he muttered. 'Just one. I promise.'

Sixty-Two

After a busy lunchtime at the wine bar, Craig helped himself to a bottle of Beck's. As Mandy past him, on the way to the kitchen with a tray of dirty plates and glasses, he asked her if she wanted a drink. She shook her head and frowned.

'I'll just have a soft drink. An orange J2O.'

Craig nodded thoughtfully. Had he detected a tone of disapproval in her voice, trying to make him feel guilty about having a beer? There was something self-righteous about the way she'd given 'soft drink' an undeserved emphasis.

When she returned to the bar, he poured out her drink and said, 'We've had a hectic lunchtime, so I think I deserve this beer.'

Mandy shrugged. 'I never said you didn't.'

'You didn't have to.'

'What's that supposed to mean?'

Craig sighed. 'It's just... it's just the way you looked at me when I poured myself a beer. It doesn't run in the family, you know. Just because my sister's got a problem...'

Mandy broke in: 'Problem! That's a bloody understatement, Craig. That's another day she hasn't managed to come in – to her own bloody wine bar – and we know why, don't we? It's cos she's too drunk or hungover.'

'And it's getting worse,' said Craig. 'She really ought to do something about it. I was hoping her having a boyfriend would help, but...'

Mandy snorted disapprovingly. 'They're bad for each other. A couple of piss artists, leading each other on.'

I know, Mandy, but the last couple of nights Mike has come in to help out, and he's been comparatively sober.'

Mandy laughed humourlessly. 'That was big of him. Doing us a favour like that. You mean he doesn't get paid for working here.'

'That's not the point,' Craig snapped unintentionally. 'I think he's trying to make an effort. And I had a word with him about my sister's drinking.'

'When was this?'

'While you were out in the kitchen. He agreed that her drinking's way out of line. He's going to see if he can get her to overcome it.'

'Meanwhile, we're having to run this place by ourselves.'

Craig gave her a helpless, defeated smile and shrugged. 'The alternative's a lot worse. The more time she spends in this place, the less customers we'll have.'

A cough from behind alerted Mandy that a customer needed the bill that had been asked for at least five minutes ago.

***

Ted was smiling to himself as he pushed his key into the front door. 'I'm home,' he sang with renewed energy. His voice, usually so lacklustre, now positively beamed with delight at his deception.

'I'm in the kitchen,' Marjorie called out.

Marjorie was in her usual place at the table, drinking tea and devouring a plate of Jaffa Cakes. Ted would normally have kept his disapproval suitably blank of expression, but today he found the image of Marjorie, indolently tucking into her biscuits, funny. He chuckled.

'What's so funny?' Marjorie demanded.

'You are, dear,' he said, daringly and with a satirical edge.

Marjorie gave him a look that would have frozen hell. He beamed at her and brought the gift-wrapped parcel from behind his back. He congratulated himself on his timing, which he thought was perfect.

'It's a surprise present,' he said, as his grin grew wider.

Marjorie frowned, bemused by this unexpected behaviour from her normally unimaginative spouse. She accepted the gift cautiously and began to unwrap it carefully, as if she worked for the bomb squad.

Ted watched her, a glint in his eye. 'Where's Miranda?' he asked.

'I told you, her name's Tracey. She's having a nap.'

Marjorie tugged the bright oblong box from the wrapping paper. She frowned as she saw what it was. 'A mobile phone! What on earth do I want with a mobile phone?'

'It's a present. I thought it would come in useful as you start looking around for hotel properties. Then, when you do eventually find a place, you're going to need one. Keep up with the times, and all that.'

'Well, I suppose...' Marjorie accepted grudgingly.

Ted sat down next to her and started to open the box, unable to keep the excitement out of his tone. 'I'll see if I can sort out how it works. I'll show you how to send a text, then when you need to contact me at work – like when you've got some news about the hotel business – I'll always be contactable.'

Marjorie nodded approvingly. 'This is the best idea you've ever had, Ted. I have to admit.'

Ted smiled craftily. All that lovely money in his very own bank account. And now the most devilish, cunning plan he'd devised. Admittedly it wasn't original – he'd read about it in a discarded tabloid on the train – but it was going to be the sweetest revenge of all time. It was almost a shame he wouldn't be around to see Marjorie's face when she got his text.

***

Music pounded loudly as Mike walked up the front path. He wondered if it was Maggie's children, then realised it was only three o'clock and they would still be at school. As he opened the door, the blast of sound hit him like a battering ram, and he realised the stereo was probably turned up to maximum. He went into the living room, hurriedly crossed to the stereo and switched it off. The contrasting silence was a relief and he let his breath out.

'Maggie!' he yelled. 'Where are you?'

He went into the kitchen, where he discovered an empty Gin bottle and a shattered glass on the floor. He dashed back into the hall and took the stairs three at a time. But where was Maggie? He checked the upstairs bedrooms and bathrooms and she was nowhere to be seen.

Then a thought struck him that filled him with fear. Her car. He didn't remember seeing her car outside. Then again it might be in the garage. He rushed outside and opened the garage door. No car.

The fearful thought struck Mike that Maggie had probably got pissed, realised she had to get to the school to pick up the children, and had driven in an inebriated state. The worst that could happen was being stopped by the police on her way there and being done for drinking and driving. But what if she killed someone? Or managed to get to the school to pick up the children, then drove home in a terrible state.

Panic gripped him as he fumbled for his mobile. If only he could get a taxi to get to the school to pick up the kids before Maggie did, he might be in with a chance.

He found the taxi firm in his phone's address book and clicked the send button.

As soon as they answered, Mike broke in hurriedly. 'Look, I need a taxi in the next ten minutes. Urgently.'

'Sorry, sir, we've got nothing for half an hour, at least.'

'But this is a matter if life and death.'

There was a pause. 'Hang on a minute. I'll see what I can do.' He heard the man speaking to someone else, then he came back on, speaking sincerely and apologetically. 'I'm so sorry, everyone's out. It's the school run. I just haven't got anyone. If, as you say, it's urgent, why not try the emergency services?'

Mike swore and clicked off the phone. Now what could he do? The school was two miles away and he was out of condition. He glanced at his watch. It was just possible for him to get there before she met the children.

He set off down the road, jogging at a steady pace.

Sixty-Three

Mike was choking and spluttering as he arrived at the school gates. The punishing run had taken him longer than he thought. He was so out of condition, and he promised himself that he would do something about it.

He edged his way through the throng of children leaving the school and found Daryl and Hannah waiting on the front steps of the entrance. There was no sign of Maggie. Daryl's frown, the one which was almost permanent, grew more pronounced.

'Where's Mum?' he demanded.

Mike shrugged and tried to speak, but he was too out of breath.

'Have you been running?' said Hannah.

Mike nodded. Daryl turned to his sister and spoke to her matter-of-factly.

'He's been done for drinking and driving.' He stared up at Mike, his eyes hostile and challenging. 'So where's Mum, and how are we getting home?'

'I've no idea. I thought she was picking you up, seeing as the car wasn't at home.'

'Have you tried her mobile?'

Mike shook his head as Daryl turned to Hannah and muttered something he didn't catch. Precocious little bastard, thought Mike. He had tried to make the effort and like the boy, but it was difficult. He was hoping to avoid the old cliché about stepfathers and resentful stepchildren but somehow the boy wound him up the wrong way, especially when he stared at him in that infuriatingly knowing way.

He took his mobile out of his pocket, scrolled down to Maggie's number and dialled. It was on voice mail. Gritting his teeth, he clicked it off impatiently. Daryl stared at him accusingly.

'If you got her voice mail, why didn't you leave a message?'

Mike was about to answer when the mobile rang. When he answered it was Craig, breathless and speaking hurriedly.'

'Mike! We have a major problem – at the wine bar. My sister's here and she's out of it. Christ! I've never seen her so drunk. She's collapsed and we've managed to get her out into the kitchen, but not before she insulted a party of some of our regular customers. Hello? You still there?'

Mike answered gravely, 'Yes, I'm still here.

'You'd better get over here, Mike, and see if you can get her home.'

'That might be a bit tricky. I've just picked up Hannah and Daryl at their school. So I'm going to have to take them home on the bus.'

'Can you take them to my mum and dad's house in Rusthall? Then maybe get back here. I don't think it would be good for the kids to see their mother like this.'

'Yeah, OK. And I'll get down to the wine bar as soon as I can. I'd get a cab up to Rusthall, only it's the school run, so the bus might be quicker.'

He glanced at Daryl and Hannah who were staring at him intensely, trying to work out what was going on. He said a brief goodbye to Craig and hung up.

'We going to Nanny and Grandpa's?' asked Hannah.

'What's happened to Mum?' said Daryl.

'She was working at the wine bar and she's not feeling too well. Come on, we've got at least a ten minute walk to catch the bus. We'd better get going.'

As they walked out of the school gates, Mike noticed how sullenly quiet both the children were, probably both suspicious about their mother's illness and the cause of it. He started to feel sorry for them.

'Sorry about having to go on the bus. Maybe we can grab a bar of chocolate on the way.'

Both children visibly brightened, Mike thinking it was at the prospect of chocolate. But he was mistaken as they both had an excited conversation about a bus journey, a journey that was probably a novel experience for them.

'Have you ever been on a bus before?' Hannah asked her brother.

Daryl frowned thoughtfully. 'Once... I think. But I can't really remember it. I wish it was longer bus ride than just to Rusthall though.'

'Yeah, me too,' said Hannah.

'Hey!' said Mike, with false cheerfulness. 'Maybe we could go on the bus to Brighton one day. That's quite a long journey.'

They both looked at him so gratefully, that he warmed to them for the first time.

***

When Ted arrived at Donald's house, Donald took him by the hand, led him into the living room and sat him down on the sofa.

'Have you thought about it yet?' Donald asked, with a tremor of excitement.

Ted nodded. 'I have. And I'd like to take you up on your offer.'

Donald laughed. 'Dear boy, I'm delighted!' He bent forward and kissed Ted on the lips briefly. 'But don't make it sound so formal. Your offer makes it seem like a job offer, like I've just asked you to become an employee. Not someone I want to spend the rest of my life with.'

Ted smiled sheepishly. 'What about Bamber?'

Donald tapped the side of his nose. 'I can handle Bamber, who I think will be living at his mother's house in Lewes from now on. But the hard part is dealing with the wife from hell.'

'I think I've sorted it out,' said Ted. 'I bought her a mobile phone. I had to spend an hour teaching her how to receive text messages.'

Donald frowned. 'What about sending them?'

'No need for that. I saw this story in a newspaper I found on the train. Some pop singer gave her husband his marching orders by sending him a text.'

Donald giggled excitedly. 'And you're planning to give your wife the heave-hoh in the same way?'

Ted smiled, preening himself at his devilish plan. Sweet revenge.

Donald clapped his hands together. 'This calls for a celebration. I'll go and open the bubbly.'

'While I write the text,' Ted said, grinning hugely.

While Donald was in the kitchen, Ted composed a brief message in his Messages mode.

Marjorie Am leaving U. I want a divorce. Goodbye and good riddance. Ted.

Ted stared at the message for several minutes. And then he thought about Donald and their trips to the theatre. And the money he had in his own bank account. Money that had given him so much confidence. He felt like a new man. It was a new beginning. Discovering the person he had always wanted to be, but couldn't because of her.

He pressed the send button, and imagined his message travelling like a magic carpet across the air waves, bleeping its way into Marjorie's phone.

'I've done it!' Ted yelled triumphantly. 'Donald, I've done it!'

Sixty-Four

Mike stared worriedly at Maggie as she lay supine on the sofa in the living room. He slurped noisily from a steaming mug of coffee, hoping it was loud enough to bring her out of her inebriated slumber.

Two hours ago he had dropped the children off at her parents' house, and felt obliged to tell them the reason. Her father had frowned worriedly but didn't seem surprised, and Mike promised he would try to at least get her to cut down drastically on her alcohol intake. Her parents said they would look after the children and run them to school the following morning. Then Mike had taken a taxi to the wine bar to collect Maggie. She had sworn loudly and obscenely as he dragged her in full view of the customers across the wine bar. At first the taxi driver refused to take her, and then Mike told him she had already thrown up, was over the worst of it, and clinched it with the promise of a double fare.

Now, as he sat and stared at her, he pondered their future. He was having serious doubts about what he had got himself into. Now the view looking back was suddenly so much sweeter. He began to think the better option might have been to talk Claire out of her devotion to Scientology, an easier bet than trying to convert a serious alcoholic.

Suddenly Maggie turned her head, and her eyes opened and focused on Mike.

'Maggie,' he said, 'I'll make you a coffee, if you feel up to it.'

With a great effort, she pulled herself up to a sitting position, grabbed at a cushion, scowled at it and hurled it onto the floor.

'We need to talk,' Mike added.

She stared at Mike, as if he'd said something deeply insulting. 'What about?'

'About your drinking.'

She laughed humourlessly. 'My drinking! I like that. It's you who drinks too much. You're an alcoholic. I've never known such a...' She struggled to form a sentence and waved an arm loosely in his direction. 'You're the one who's banned from driving. I'm not. I've still got my licence. Because I just enjoy a quiet drink in the evening. It's you who goes out all the time and gets rat-arsed.'

'Listen, Maggie...' Mike began urgently.

'No, you listen,' she shouted. 'I can drive my car. You can't. And that's what it boils down to. Because you're a piss-artist and I've still got my licence.'

He realised it was useless to argue with her. She was projecting her own problems onto him. It was irrational behaviour and it was pointless arguing with an alcoholic who wasn't willing to accept there was a problem. Suddenly an idea struck him. It was cruel, but in the circumstances he didn't care as long as it got a result.

'Maggie,' he said, 'you went out in the car today.'

'So!' she sneered. 'I can drive. I've got a licence.'

'You went out in the car,' he continued. 'Do you remember where you parked it?'

'Of course I do.'

'OK then. Where is it?'

She waved an uncoordinated arm about. 'It's... it's... I don't bloody well know!'

'Do you remember picking the kids up from school?' Mike watched as doubt swept across her face like an eclipse. 'You almost killed them Maggie. They were so scared, they got out at the traffic lights to get away from you. Then they phoned me to come and get them. And I've taken them round to your parents'. You were driving so erratically Hannah was screaming and crying. You might have killed them. And you don't remember, do you? Don't remember almost killing your children? Well, do you? And if I asked you to take me to where you abandoned the car, could you do that, Maggie? Well, could you?'

She stared at him, fear in her eyes, and he almost regretted having lied to her. He saw tears trickle out of her eyes, as if a tap had been turned on, and she began shivering and shaking. He put down his mug and went and sat next to her on the sofa. She shook and sobbed in his arms as he comforted her.

'Maggie,' he said gently. 'Promise me it won't happen again. That you won't drink like this. We'll both do something about it. Together. We'll get help.'

He felt her head nodding on his chest.

'OK,' she said. 'We'll both get some help, Mike. But that's tomorrow. And at least the kids are safe and sound at Mum and Dad's. So why don't we just have one little night cap? Just one. The last one. I promise. Just for tonight.'

Sixty-Five

After a hastily eaten breakfast, Donald dashed off to open up the antique shop, leaving Ted alone in the house. Now Ted felt lost; unsettled. After having sent Marjorie the text message about leaving her, he had no option but to spend the night at Donald's. But, as Donald had insisted, Marjorie had to be faced at some point. Besides, Ted needed to make arrangements about collecting his things and moving out. And then he needed to come to some sort of agreement with Marjorie about taking joint responsibility over Miranda (he refused to call her Tracey).

It took Ted a teeth-gnashing hour to pluck up the courage to telephone Marjorie. She picked up the receiver as soon as it had rung, almost as if she had been waiting for the call.

'Is that you, Ted?'

He cleared his throat noisily before replying. 'Yes. Did you get my text message?'

'No! What text message?'

'On the new mobile phone I bought you.'

Marjorie's voice snapped impatiently. 'Oh, I can't be doing with those contraptions. I don't know how to switch it on.'

Ted's mind raced furiously. Last night it had seemed so easy, sending her the text saying he was leaving her. The fact that she hadn't received it was a major problem.

'And why didn't you come home last night?' she demanded.

'Um,' said Ted, as he tried to think. 'Leaves on the line.'

'What?'

'Last train couldn't leave Charing Cross because of leaves on the line. Remember it happened about five years ago, and they had to put us up at the Charing Cross Hotel...'

'Yes, yes, yes!' Marjorie said, impatiently. 'So when are you coming home?'

Ted's voice sank into a bottomless well. 'I'll be back shortly.'

'As soon as you possibly can.'

Hugely depressed now, Ted was unable to construct a reply.

'Because I need to have a very long talk with you, Ted,' Marjorie added, ominously.

***

Nigel was on his way to a meeting in Croydon and had offered Vanessa and Nicky a lift to Tunbridge Wells Station, which was on his way. Nicky sat in the front passenger seat and Vanessa sat in the back, next to Nigel's laptop and bundle of telecommunications brochures and leaflets. As they drove towards Eridge, Nigel whistled tunelessly, which irritated Vanessa.

'Do you have to?' she said.

Nigel chortled. 'Someone got out on the wrong side of bed.'

'Not at all. I'm fine. It's just that your tuneless whistling is getting on my nerves.'

'I might drop you off at the bus stop,' Nigel teased. 'And you can make your own way there .'

'Anything would be better than your whistling.'

'I can't help it if I'm happy. Life is good at the moment. Full of problems. But then problems create challenges, hopefully leading to solutions.'

Nicky, who wasn't interested in joining in the conversation, nevertheless felt as if she ought to say something. 'So if life is good,' she said, 'what problems d'you have?'

Nigel glanced round at her and grinned. 'Who said anything about my having problems? It's secondary schools that are having problems. And your mother and I intend doing something about it?'

Intrigued and puzzled, Vanessa stretched forward. 'But we've long ago left school, and so has your son. So why are you getting involved with schools?'

'We want to persuade them to offer pupils the option of being taught Intelligent Design as well as all that Darwin poppycock.'

Vanessa laughed harshly. 'You've got to be joking.'

'No, I'm perfectly serious.'

Vanessa made an impatient clicking noise with her tongue. 'There is not a single shred of evidence that something intelligent created the universe. Not a thing. You creationists are a bunch of morons and no one's going to take you seriously.'

As Nigel neared the bottom of the hill near Eridge Station, he spotted the number 29 Brighton bus. He put his foot down and overtook it going up the hill on the other side of the valley. As soon as he reached the next bus stop, he screeched to a halt.

'What are you doing?' Nicky asked, nervously.

'Letting you catch the bus,' said Nigel. 'There's one just a few seconds behind. I've decided to cut through High Rocks and Rusthall and miss the Tunbridge Wells traffic.' He turned and stared at Nicky. 'Sorry about that. But you know how it is?'

They both scrambled hurriedly out of his car, and watched as he zoomed off, seconds before the bus pulled up. As they boarded the bus, Vanessa said:

'What a bastard that man is. I'm so glad I'm moving out.'

'You and me both,' said Nicky. 'I've made up my mind. I'm going to start looking for a flat in Tunbridge Wells. I don't care if I never see him again. I hate him.'

***

While Maggie was still in bed, still in a deep inebriated sleep, Mike caught a bus to Crowborough and visited her parents. As soon as they opened the door, they saw the concerned expression on his face and were immediately alarmed.

'It's OK,' he assured them. 'Maggie's asleep. She's hungover – again – but she'll be all right.'

Gordon, Maggie's father, nodded gravely and invited Mike into the kitchen. Once they had all settled round the kitchen table with a cup of tea, Gordon glanced at his wife and said:

'We've known all along that Maggs had a problem. Haven't we, Gloria?'

Gloria nodded sombrely and sighed. 'We want to help. But we don't know what we can do?'

'It's got really serious,' Mike said. 'She can't even remember where she parked the car yesterday. But I've got an idea what you can do to help. It means involving the children. But it's the only thing I can think of.'

Gordon looked at Mike with a sad, dog-like expression. 'We'll try anything to help our daughter. Won't we, Gloria?'

Again, he looked towards his wife for encouragement, and she gave him a nod of approval. Mike began to outline his plan and they listened carefully.

***

As soon as Ted arrived home, he called out, 'I'm back.'

Silence, as if the house was empty. He went into the kitchen where he expected to find Marjorie. He found piles of crockery on the draining board, and the kitchen table was strewn with mail that had been torn open and abandoned. Ted frowned. This was uncharacteristic. Marjorie was usually so fastidious.

'Marjorie!' he called out, nervously.

He crept out into the hall and pushed open the living room door. He started as he caught sight of his wife, sitting in an easy chair, half facing the door, as if she was waiting for him. Her face was hard, like a block of ice, and her eyes were red from crying.

'Sit down!' she commanded him.

Nervously, he swished across the carpet and sank onto the sofa. Her wrathful voice came at him like a battering ram.

'So you thought you'd send me a text, you cowardly little worm. You couldn't even tell me to my face.'

Ted gasped and tried to find his voice. 'I – I didn't think you'd got my text.'

'Oh, I got it all right,' she yelled. Suddenly she was on her feet and hurtling towards him. 'Fuckin' little worm. You shitty little bastard.'

Fists clenched, she hit him hard in the face. He felt his nose crack as her fist came into contact and the blood spurted. A knuckle caught him in the eye. He tried to shield his face with his hands but she seemed to have the strength of an ox as she beat him about the head. He sank onto the floor, trying to protect himself with his arms about his head, but now she began kicking him in the stomach and ribs. The pain was unbelievable and he begged for her to stop as he choked on the blood from his nose. But still she went on unrelentingly.

Eventually, after what seemed like minutes, but was probably only seconds, Ted heard crying from the nursery upstairs. Marjorie stopped beating him and hurried away to attend to Miranda. As injured as he was, Ted still couldn't think of her as Tracey.

Sixty-Six

When Donald arrived at Pembury Hospital, Ted was sitting in the waiting area, staring zombie-like, his face covered in bruises and traces of the beating he'd suffered. Donald slid into the seat next to him.

'I'd have brought flowers,' he said, but people might talk.'

In spite of the shock he'd suffered, Ted responded with a watery smile. 'I couldn't care less. That's the least of my worries.'

Donald patted his knee and summoned up a hearty brightness. 'You don't have any worries any more. You've now got every reason to get shot of the old cow.'

Ted shook his head in a mystified manner. 'I don't understand. The police came to the hospital, asking me questions about what happened. How on earth did they know?'

'Because I told them.'

Ted's head swivelled around to face Donald, causing him to wince slightly from the pain he was still feeling. Marjorie had done a thorough job in her husband battering.

'Why did you call the police, Donald? What was the point of that?'

Donald grinned and tapped the side of his nose. 'Because, my dear boy, it puts you in a strong position with regards to our little Miranda.'

Ted frowned uncomprehendingly.

'Don't you see, if a custody battle ensues, this will give you grounds. A few stories about her neglect of your daughter, and perhaps some little embellishments about other times she physically abused you – which they'll have to believe now they've got police evidence of tonight's events – and I reckon you'll be home and dry in any custody battle.'

Ted sighed deeply. 'Yes, but what happens for now?'

'How d'you mean?'

'Where am I going to go?'

Donald laughed pleasantly. 'Home, of course.'

Ted's eyes wavered uncertainly. 'Home?'

'Yes. Your place and mine. You live with me now. Remember? That decision was already made.'

From the row of seats in front of them, a drunken man with a bloody face and hair matted with blood seeping from a deep gash on his head, turned round and said, 'If you ask me: wanker had it coming to him.' He glared aggressively at Donald. 'You agree, pal?'

Donald nodded effusively. 'Oh, absolutely. I'm sure the bastard deserved it.'

He grabbed Ted's arm and pulled him to his feet. 'Come on, Ted. We are off home.'

'Home!' Ted said, in a dreamlike voice, as if he couldn't quite believe what was happening to him. Recent events had swamped his otherwise safe emotional barrier, and he was feeling a wondrous shift in the discovery of a new life available to him, like a young child experiencing snow for the first time.

As he shuffled out of A & E, supported by Donald, he grinned hugely, and in an intoxicated-sounding voice said, 'We're going home!'

***

After Daryl and Hannah had sat at the kitchen table and finished a packet of crisps and a can of Coke each, Maggie's father, Gordon, asked them if they wouldn't mind having a serious talk about 'Mummy' in the living room. Both children frowned, looking concerned, and he reassured them.

'We just want to help her. And I know we can do it. So why don't we go and talk it over with Nanny in the lounge?'

Both children nodded silently, got down from the table and went dutifully into the living room. They discovered their grandmother was sitting on the three-seater sofa, and patted either side, indicating that they should sit one either side of her. Once they were seated, Gordon pulled up a light easy chair and sat opposite them. He cleared his throat before speaking, like someone about to launch into a long speech.

'It's your mother...' he began, exchanging an awkward look with his wife.

Impatiently, Daryl broke in. 'If you mean her drinking, yes we know.'

Gloria patted his knee. 'Daryl, we've come up with a plan to help her. Tell them, Gordon.'

Hannah and Daryl watched their grandfather struggling with what he was about to say. He stared at the floor, shifted uncomfortably, and spoke in a tremulous voice when he looked at them.

'I know it's wrong to tell lies, but sometimes we have to if it means helping someone. It was Mike's idea. Your mother went out yesterday in her car. She was too drunk to drive and she can't remember where she parked it. Mike told her she came to pick you up at school, started to drive you home and almost crashed. You both got out of the car and ran off.'

Hannah frowned thoughtfully. 'Wouldn't she remember if she'd done that?'

Gordon shook his head gravely. 'Unfortunately, your mother was so drunk, everything's hazy. You could tell her anything and she'd have to believe it. She needs treatment. It's not going to be easy, but she needs to feel responsible for something terrible that might have happened.'

'Before it does happen,' said Gloria. 'We need to prevent her from getting any worse. It's a sickness, you see. And we need to help her.' She sat forward on the sofa and turned to each of them.

'I hope you don't think it's wrong to tell lies like this. But we're desperate. And the only way we can get her to seek help is if she thinks she nearly hurt her children. And I know she loves you both so much, she wouldn't want that to happen?'

Gloria fell silent, waiting for the enormity of what was expected of her grandchildren to sink in. Hannah seemed to shrink back into the upholstery, her face a mask. After a pause, Gordon cleared his throat lightly, and said, 'Will you do it, both of you? It might be the only way.'

Daryl stared into the distance as if he was weighing everything up. Suddenly he smacked a palm into his hand, as if this was an adventurous challenge, something to be enjoyed rather than endured.

'Yeah, I will. We'll tell her she drove at ninety miles an hour down St. John's Road.'

Frowning worriedly, Gordon leant forward in his chair. 'No, Daryl, we must all stick to the same story. It has to be believable.'

Hannah recovering from her numb feeling of shock, glared at her brother across the sofa. 'Yeah, you couldn't go that fast down St. John's Road, you wally!'

Daryl sneered. 'You can go whatever speed you like, if the car's capable of it.'

'I think what Hannah means, Daryl,' said Gordon, 'is that there'd be too much traffic going along there during the school run. Perhaps if we say she was going too fast and went over a red light, that might be enough.'

'Whatever,' said Daryl sulkily.

'That's settled then,' said Gordon.

'I know,' said Gloria, brightly. 'Why don't we go out and get some fish and chips, come back and talk about exactly what we're going to say?'

'Cool,' said Daryl. 'But why can't we say seventy miles an hour? I mean, she's not going to know, is she?'

Sixty-Seven

When Mike, Daryl and Hannah arrived home, they found Maggie sitting on a stool at the breakfast bar watching *Pointless* on the portable television. Daryl rushed forward and said:

'You almost killed us when you gave us a lift from school.'

Hannah glared at her brother. She was worried that if he exaggerated their story about her drunken driving, then she wouldn't believe them.

Mike went over and laid a hand on her shoulder, and looked at her with concern. 'We need to have a serious talk, Maggs. All of us.'

Hannah screwed her face into a frown as she caught her mother's defensive expression, frightened as a cornered animal.

'Mum,' she began. 'Mummy...'

Daryl threw his sister a look that was both scathing and pitying. Hannah took a deep breath and continued.

'Can't you remember what happened? You were swerving and nearly hit one of those things in the middle of the road.'

'Bollard,' said Daryl. 'We were so frightened you were going to kill us, we jumped out at the lights. You must have been going along St. John's Road at...'

He paused as he caught the anxious look in Mike's eyes. 'You were doing over fifty miles an hour.'

Mike stared at the boy and gave him an almost imperceptible nod of approval. It was hard to believe anyone could do that speed during the school run, but at least it was an improvement on the boy's previous embellishment when they discussed it at his grandparents' house.

'You really don't remember, do you?' Mike said gently. 'Have you discovered what you did with the car yet?'

Maggie nodded slowly, her eyes watery and distant. 'I vaguely remembered going up to The Compasses for a drink. This must have been after...'

She stopped and stared at the children, and Mike was worried that she might realise she hadn't picked them up from school. She shook her head and frowned deeply, troubled by random thoughts of her movements that day.

'So where was the car?' Mike prompted.

'Just off Mount Sion.'

'That's nearly all double yellow lines round there. I expect you got a ticket.'

'I didn't. I know it's hard to believe, having left it on yellow lines for so long, but I just got lucky I guess.'

Mike gave a short sharp sigh. 'You were also lucky you didn't have a major accident in the car. And you're lucky Daryl and Hannah are still in one piece.'

Hannah, knowing it was time to pull out all the stops and deliver an Oscar-winning performance, stared at her mother with wide Bambi eyes, saying, 'Mum, please don't do it any more. Please. If something happened to you...'

She left the sentence unfinished, instinctively allowing it to do its work.

Maggie's eyes, Mike noticed, suddenly hardened with the irrational resolve of an alcoholic.

'I'll be careful,' she said, 'not to drink too much next time I drive. I really won't drink and drive. I promise.'

Mike felt anger rising inside him. 'It's not just the drinking and driving. It's taken you over. You're not the same any more. And you're a danger to your children. Next time it might be something you do in the home. For Christ's sake, Maggie, one morning you might wake up and you might have done something terrible – maybe not intentionally – but you won't remember what you did.

How could you live the rest of your life with the knowledge that you might have harmed your children.'

Maggie suddenly slumped forward on the breakfast bar, her head in her hands, choking and sobbing. 'I'm sorry. I'll try and get help. I really will. But I need...' She turned her tear-stained face up towards Mike. 'I can't do this on my own. I need you to help me, Mike. I'm frightened.'

Mike threw an arm across her shoulder and squeezed. 'It's OK. I'll organise something. We can start with your doctor's surgery. They'll be able to help.'

Maggie shook her head forcefully. 'But not one of those group therapies. I couldn't stand that. Alcoholics Anonymous.' She shivered hugely. 'Maybe some counselling. Just you and me.'

Mike let his breath out slowly, relieved that at least she had acknowledged she had a problem. It was a start.

'OK,' he said. 'We could both do with some help from a professional. We'll be fine, Maggie. We'll be fine.'

When Mike caught Daryl's eye, he noticed the boy was looking at him without his usual sullen expression. He could have been mistaken, but Mike almost thought he could interpret it as admiration.

***

Mary had spent most of the day tidying the house in preparation for the first visit from a potential buyer. Two days it had been on the market and already the estate agent had telephoned to make an appointment, telling them it was a single man and a cash buyer.

While they waited in the kitchen, staring across the table at each other, wondering what to say to kill the time, Dave and Mary recognised that neither of them wanted to move. It was fear that was driving them away.

As if she was hyperventilating nervously, Mary blew out a deep breath.

'What's wrong?' asked Dave.

'You know what's wrong. We're both running away. Neither of us want to live in Blackpool.'

'But I thought...'Dave began, frowning uncomprehendingly.

'Yes, yes!' said Mary, impatiently. 'They sentenced Ronnie to a year, and he could be out in nine months. Then what? It doesn't bear thinking about.'

Dave opened his mouth to speak, but there was a ring on the door.

'That'll be him,' said Mary. She glanced at her watch. 'Talk about punctual.'

When Dave opened the front door, he immediately realised he'd had preconceived ideas about what the prospective buyer would look like. He'd been expecting someone more professional looking. This man looked like the sort of bloke who always dresses in sports clothes but never exercises. He wore Addidas track suit bottoms, the elastic waistband being stretched to an optimistic level of support by an enormous beer belly, and a purple polo shirt. His arms displayed a plethora of tattoos, and a shaved head dominated an otherwise insipid red face.

'Mr. Whitby?' he said.

Dave nodded, trying not to look too taken aback. 'You must be – er – Mr Caven?'

'Please. Call me Terry.'

Dave smiled and stepped aside for the man to enter. 'I'm Dave. Come in.'

As he entered the man put out his hand. 'Good to meet you, Dave.'

Dave tried not to let the agony of the bone-crushing handshake show. Recovering, he shut the front door. Mary emerged from the kitchen.

'This is Terry,' said Dave. 'This is my other half – Mary.'

The man grinned and looked Mary up and down. 'Good to meet you, sweetheart.'

Dave gestured towards the living room. 'Shall we start with the lounge?'

As the three of them stood in the living room, and Dave and Mary took it in turns to explain what everything was, the man seemed remote and disinterested. Dave was explaining about why the electricity meter was housed in a cupboard next to the fireplace when the man interrupted him.

'So why are you selling the place?'

Dave looked towards Mary before replying. 'We've – er – decided we're going to settle up north.'

The man smiled and looked Dave in the eye. 'Don't I know you from somewhere?'

Dave blushed slightly. 'Well, years ago I used to be on the telly. I'm a stand-up comedian. But I'm sure you're too young to remember.'

The man's grin got wider. 'That's the great thing about DVDs and all these other channels now. You can catch up on the oldies.'

Dave laughed uncomfortably, and was about to commence with his explanation about the meter, when the man leapt in again, almost as though the house was incidental to his interest.

'So you're going back up home, are you?'

Dave frowned. 'Sorry?'

'Well, you're from up north. I detect the accent.'

Dave tittered foolishly. 'Well, I'm from Yorkshire, but actually we're going to settle in Lancashire.'

'Oh? Whereabouts?'

'We're looking to settle in Blackpool. Or somewhere near there.'

The man nodded thoughtfully. Dave gestured towards the door. 'Shall we take a look at the rest of the house?'

'I don't think so.'

'I'm sorry.'

'I only came round to give you a message from Ronnie. See, him and me's great mates, and he guessed you might move out the district. So he sent me round to find out where. Job done. He says one way or the other he can find out where you bugger off to. So it's no good trying to avoid him. And he told me to tell you, nine Or ten months'll go by just like that.'

The man clicked his fingers and walked to the door. He turned back and stared at Mary, whose face was drawn.

'Ronnie said you was a looker. He was right. No wonder he don't want to let you go. Some things are meant to be, eh?'

The man walked into the hall and let himself out as Mary clutched Dave's arm and tears sprang into her eyes.

'Oh my God, Dave! I'm scared. I've never been so scared. Even from prison he's got a hold on me.'

Sixty-Eight

Donald chuckled softly as he stared at Ted across the breakfast table. 'That bruise is amazing.'

Ted pursed his lips before replying. 'I'm glad you think so. It bloody well hurts, I can tell you.'

Irritatingly, Donald laughed again. 'I don't think I've seen so many colours in a bruise before. There must be at least seven. That's it! It's the spectrum! You've got a rainbow shiner.'

Ted sighed deeply. 'Seriously, Donald, what am I going to do about my things?'

'Buy a new wardrobe of clothes. You can afford it with your winnings. I'll take you out shopping. Make a new man of you. A new, trendier-looking Ted.'

Ted shook his head unbelievably. 'Oh my God! That's what I was afraid of.'

'Come on, Ted – cheer up. You're free of her at last.'

'But it's Miranda I'm worried about.'

Donald eased his chair back from the table and stood up. 'We're seeing the solicitor this afternoon. Wheels will be set in motion.'

Ted frowned. 'Yes, but what worries me is what Marjorie will say about you and me.'

Donald walked over to the window and stared out at the garden, talking to Ted with his back to him. 'She's bound to say we're living together as a gay couple. So we just deny it. Who can prove otherwise?'

'I'm not very good at lying.'

Donald spun round and grinned at his partner. 'Now that is a lie. I think you're better at lying than you think you are. And look at the lie you've been living all these years – with her.' He glanced round at the garden again. 'Oh this dull, depressing, damp weather. It would get me down but for one thing.'

'What's that?' said Ted.

'Even though the weather's been like it for weeks now, the same old everyday drizzle, I still feel brand new. And you must too, Ted. Changes are taking place. Changes for the better. Come on, let's get ready and go out shopping.'

***

In spite of the never-ending tedium of the overcast sky, hanging over the country like a shroud, and the mild unnatural temperature for the time of year, changes were taking place. Not only with Donald and Ted, but also with Maggie, who, along with Mike's support and help, recognised she had a major problem and made a start by going to see her GP and speaking openly about her condition.

Because of her behaviour over the last few weeks, Craig and Mandy had been left to run the wine bar on their own. Neither of them minded. In fact, they were glad they no longer had to contend with Maggie's behaviour, which they suspected had lost them customers.

Late one midweek night, Mike arrived at the wine bar. Craig greeted him hesitantly. He was reticent in committing himself to being to over friendly with his sister's boyfriend, as he saw Mike as a bad influence; but when Mike outlined his plans to attend counselling with Maggie to help her through the bad times, Craig became slightly more affable, telling Mike a few topical jokes he had received by text on his mobile.

Mike laughed diplomatically, not wanting to spoil the developing relationship, as they were now practically brothers-in-law, by admitting he had already received the same jokes on his mobile.

'Look, Craig,' he said, 'I know we've been absent from the wine bar recently. But I think Maggie should still have some time off, spend a little time away from temptation for a while.' He waved a hand towards the alcohol stacked behind the bar. 'I know you can't go on working seven days a week. So I'll be quite happy to work on the quieter nights, then you can have some time off.'

Mandy, who was stacking glasses in the dishwasher behind the bar, said, 'That would be great, Mike. Because Craig needs time off to look for a new flat.'

Craig's mouth dropped open as he looked at Mandy. Her eyes twinkled mischievously as she stared back at him.

'You're right, Mandy. But I'm only going to move into a new flat if you move in with me.'

Her expression was impassive, and Mike could see the wheels turning in her mind. Suddenly she beamed at Craig, and said, 'I thought you'd never ask.'

***

Change too was taking place at Dave and Mary's, where they'd had an offer for his house, this time from a genuine buyer. They had accepted the offer, and Dave hatched a plan to put Mary's ex-husband off the scent when he came out of prison.

'I don't really want to leave the district,' he said. 'I've got used to it here down south. And now we know it's pointless trying to run away. Ronnie can always find us.'

'So what do we do, now that we've sold the house?'

'I think we make it official... you become my other half, and change your name to Whitby.'

Mary's intake of breath was an excited gust as her eyes lit up. She threw her arms around him. 'D'you mean it?'

'I wouldn't joke about a thing like that. Once we're married, you go and see Ronnie in prison and give him the news. Then you can tell him the newlyweds are going to settle in Blackpool. He'll have no reason to disbelieve you, especially as he'll already have heard from his mate how we planned to escape up north. With any luck, he might just consider you a lost cause.'

Mary snuggled closer to Dave. 'I don't know about that. Ronnie's hell-bent on revenge.'

'Well, we go and see that detective who gave us his card. And we tell him about what happened; about that bloke coming round to see the house and threatening us. Then, when Ronnie's released, if we have any more problems, we get straight in touch with the police again. Any more nonsense, and they'll bang him up again. But for a while, he's going to think we really did go to Blackpool.'

Mary looked into her lover's eyes and frowned. 'So what do we do about this house, now you've accepted the offer?'

'Oh, we go through with the sale – hopefully. And I've been looking in The Courier. There's a nice house in Rusthall I want to look at.'

Mary giggled. 'I feel really safe now. I mean, Ronnie'll never be able to work out how we escaped from High Brooms, and made it to the wilds of Rusthall.

One mile the other side of Tunbridge Wells.'

***

Most changes that were taking place in the new year were positive, but if Ted could have been the proverbial fly on the wall and seen his wife after she returned from the meeting with a solicitor, he would have been shocked. The solicitor had explained to her how, even though she had inherited the house from her grandmother, Ted might be entitled to half. As soon as she got home, her face white with the deadly heat of suppressed rage, she suddenly exploded. Everything Ted owned she dragged out of drawers and cupboards, took out into the garden and set alight. Then she got every photograph, memento of their lives together – weddings, anniversaries, birthdays – tore them into shreds and added them to the pyre. She began to feel cleansed as she air-brushed him out of her life completely. And then she remembered Tracey, whom she had left with her friend Freda while she visited the solicitor. Tracey would be the perpetual reminder that she would never be able to expunge all traces of the man she had grown to hate.

***

Vanessa moved in with her boyfriend. Not long after, unable to bear living in the same house as Nigel, Nicky found herself a small flat in Tunbridge Wells. A week later, Jackie arranged to meet up with them and took them out to lunch at Pizza Express.

After they had ordered, Jackie sniffed, brought out a small lace-bordered handkerchief, and dabbed delicately at her nose and eyes, as if she was appearing in a television costume drama. Vanessa could see her mother was upset, and was both annoyed and amused by this over-genteel display.

Nicky asked: 'Is everything all right, Mummy?'

Jackie sighed and shook her head. 'It's just such a wrench. My babies leaving home for good. I know you both used to irritate me, but I do love you. And I loved having you around. Now you're no longer there... well, it'll take some getting used to.'

'I'm sure you'll manage,' said Vanessa. 'Now you've got lover boy all to yourself.'

'I do wish you wouldn't call him that.'

Vanessa smiled cruelly. 'And how is our... er... stepfather?'

Jackie blew her cheeks out, showing how difficult life was. 'He's hard work sometimes. I bought him some socks for Christmas...'

'Socks!' exclaimed Nicky, and startled herself.

Jackie glanced around the restaurant nervously. 'Keep your voice down. I did buy him other things as well. The socks were an extra present. Pretty dull I know. Especially as he only wears black socks. The day after boxing day, he came into the kitchen, dropped the socks onto the kitchen table and went on about his sock stock rotation. And I had to sit down there and then and sow in little pieces of different coloured wool into the ankle of each pair so that he can tell them apart.'

'But you don't have to do that anymore,' Vanessa said. 'You can buy plain socks with different colours on the toes and heels, so you never get them muddled up.'

'I wish I'd known that.'

'Oh, Mummy!'

Vanessa caught Nicky's eye and they both spluttered and laughed.

'I think Nigel's a sandwich short of a picnic,' said Nicky.

Jackie surveyed them both and smiled. 'At least he's reliable. I didn't think I could cope with all the changes. Especially you two leaving home. But at least Nigel with his stick-in-the-mud ways will always be solid and dependably dull.'

Vanessa grinned hugely at her mother's forthright confession of how she really felt about Nigel. 'No change there then,' she said.

'No, thank God!' said her mother.

Although Jackie acknowledged and accepted change was taking place, with her daughters leaving home for the for the first time, at least she felt comforted by the knowledge of her husband's unwavering beliefs and rituals.

It seemed to be a time of change. Jackie felt that change was all around. Not just her and her family, but she almost felt a sixth sense, a supernatural feeling about the people all around her, the hundreds of people she didn't know, who were all searching for something knew, yet still clinging to the calming protection of day-to-day routine.

Also Available

From Andrews UK

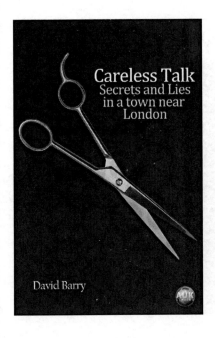

Careless Talk

by David Barry

Mike, an itinerant hairdresser living in Tunbridge Wells, learns all the gossip of the town. He cuts the hair of holy hypocrite Nigel, who is seeking a new relationship, but disapproves of his new lover's daughters. And as Mike cuts deeper and deeper into this superficially respectable town, he soon learns it is a hotbed of vice, intrigue and gossip, and even his own family life, he realizes is not so very secure. By the end of a tempestuous year, many of his customers will become involved in revenge, rape, murder and suicide.

Also Available

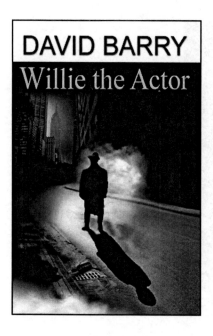

Willie the Actor

by David Barry

Glancing quickly over the bar, he saw the bartender lying face down in a pool of blood, senselessly gunned down simply because he was in the wrong place at the wrong time... New York City in the prohibition era, and Bill Sutton's wife thinks he earns an honest crust as a rent collector. Instead, he leads an extraordinary double-life as 'Willie the Actor', a notorious bank robber. Based on a true story, the novel's protagonist is a gentle gunman who never once fires a shot. However it was believed he was jinxed and almost everyone he works with comes to a violent end.

Lightning Source UK Ltd.
Milton Keynes UK
UKOW031215171212

203682UK00006B/22/P